Best Stories
of
2018

<u>*Best Stories of 2018*</u>

No portion of this book may be reproduced or used in any manner whatsoever without the express written consent of the author, except for brief quotations used in book reviews.

This is a work of fiction. All events, people, businesses and events mentioned in this book are fictitious. Any resemblance to actual events, businesses or people, living or dead, is purely coincidental

ISBN:
ISBN-

ACKNOWLEDGMENTS

Any writing of substantial length is the product of contributions from multiple individuals. First, I'd like to thank the observations and suggestions of the members of the Portland Writers Workshop. Their collective talents and experience, as well as their generosity and conscientiousness, have improved the quality of both the material and its arrangement within this book. Also, recognition is owed to Mary Slocum and Joe Schrader for contributing their time, knowledge and skills to the process of editing.

Best Stories of 2018

Contents

The Sea and the Old Man

The dot on the watery horizon continued to grow, and soon was large enough to know with certainty.

"There he is again," Chris said.

"Yep. Right on time," Skinny Sam replied. "Dang, he's predictable."

Roger was kinder. "Ya gotta admire his doggedness. Never gives up."

"You mean, never learns," Chris said.

"Well, let's get going. He's still coming out. We better move out, leave him be." Benny as usual was all business.

They swam north, away from their home waters. They had learned to eat hearty as early as possible before the boatman arrived. And it wasn't only survival that motivated them, though that would have been sufficient. They enjoyed teasing him. Every few minutes, one of them would break the surface, then laugh as the old man pulled in his line and cast in a new direction.

They swam outbound for another 10-minutes. "Any of you guys see other boats?" asked Skinny Sam. The rest reported in the negative.

"Then how come he's still sailing on?" Chris asked.

"Something's up," Skinny Sam said. "We better steer clear."

Randolph spoke up. "Listen guys, just to be safe, let's get the heck north a safe distance. No point in taking chances."

Everyone agreed and they all swam northwest, considerably beyond most fishing boats' habits. "We should be safe here," Chris said. They spent the rest of the morning relaxing, playing catch with a few clams, and soaking up the warmth of the surface waters under the sunny sky, only occasionally interrupted by one of the few tall cumulus clouds. In the afternoon, they played pin-the-seaweed-on-the-fin. At one point, when Randolph was "it", their attention was entirely engaged with the game. None of them noticed the boat.

As Randolph turned left and dove, Benny spotted it and shouted a warning. But Randolph, the largest and fastest of the group, had pulled too far ahead of him. On his way down, he spotted a morsel, and figured he might as well have a snack. Because of his speed, the hook went deep. He tried swimming away, but could barely move.

Benny looked on in horror as the rest of the group arrived. Nobody knew what to do. They had learned long ago that chewing on the line was futile; their teeth could not sever it. All they could do was encourage Randolph to keep fighting.

"Don't let him pull the rope in!"

"Keep swimming away from the boat!"

"That's it! You're doin' fine. Just keep it up."

"Randolph's tiring," Benny remarked to the others. But they continued to encourage him. "Keep pulling. He'll give up."

But the old man did not give up. After two days, Randolph began to tire. "Guys, I can't keep this up. I think I'm done for."

"No, don't. I've got an idea," Chris said. "Swim east – with the current."

"How's that going to help?" Randolph asked.

"You'll pull the boat so far from his harbor, he'll have to let go or not be able to get back."

"Great idea!" Roger said. "Gonna make his life hard. Teach him good. Make him trade his life for yours!"

"And to return home, he'll have to sail against the wind and the current," Benny pointed out. "It'll take him forever to get back."

And so, Randolph, infused with the energy of hope, began swimming eastward. He swam for a whole day, but the old man never cut the line. All were disappointed.

"Holy starfish," Chris said, "I said he never learns, but I never thought he was this dumb."

Eventually, Randolph ran out of strength. "I'm sorry guys. I gave it all I got. But this is it for me."

Everyone was sad, but helpless. All they could do was whimper. Eventually, Randolph was pulled to the boat and raised from the water, where he expired within 10 minutes.

"Are we going to let him get away with this?" Skinny Sam asked.

"What can we do?" asked Benny.

Chris had an answer. "Guys, this is going to sound crazy, but I think maybe we need to talk with the sharks."

Roger answered first. "You're pointy nose is dead center, dude: You *do* sound crazy."

Skinny Sam agreed, but Benny was more thoughtful. "Wait. Let's hear Chris' plan."

"Look, Randolph is dead. There's nothing to be done about that. But we can have our vengeance. We can deny the old man at least the crux of his victory. If we make a deal with the sharks, they can eat Randolph's body before…"

"What!" the others shouted, followed by a few choice words that should only be repeated underwater. Horrified, they inquired about Chris' sanity, his morals, and even his loyalty to the group. After all, any one of them might be a future victim, and the target of a similar suggestion from him.

"Just listen," Chris implored. "Then if you don't agree, I'll drop the subject and never mention it again." As they quieted down, Chris explained, "If the old man makes it home, Randolph's corpse will be eaten by humans. As much as we dislike the sharks, they're better than land grubs. At least they swim and worship Fish God. Who knows what kind of god humans worship?"

Everyone else nodded, taking care not to stab each other with the points of their noses.

Chris continued. "And here's the thing: if the old man makes it back with the whole corpse, others of his kind will be encouraged. Pretty soon, we won't have any safe place."

Everyone had to agree: Chris' logic was as secure as Davy Jones' treasure chest. It was decided that Roger would be the emissary. He swam under a flag of truce (two kelp ribbons stuck to his pointed nose) to the sharks' favorite spot, just off Diamond Island.

"Well look who just dropped in," Axel said.

"Yeah, dinner," Zach said. All the other sharks chuckled.

"OK, watcha wanna talk about?" Rajon asked him.

Roger waited until he was sure he had their attention. "We've lost one of our own. Randolph."

Everyone became quiet. Then Guzman spoke for the group. "Randolph was a big guy, even for a Marlin. I had a lot of respect for him. How old was he?"

"Not that old," Roger replied. "He didn't die a natural death. He was caught."

At this, all of the sharks were surprised. They closed their gills in sadness.

Robby spoke for all the other sharks. "Caught by land grubs, I suppose."

Roger nodded.

Guzman said, "As you know, we've had our own problems with them. It is sad that a marlin as mighty as Randolph should become their victim."

Axel reminisced. "I tried to keep up with him once — not to catch him, but just to see if I could. Not a chance."

"We grieve with you," Rajon offered.

"Listen, we'd like you to do him an honor," Roger said.

"Sure. Anything," Zach said. "Just name it."

"We'd like you to eat his corpse."

"WHAT?!" All five spoke in unison, shocked at Roger's request.

"Besides, if he's been caught, how would we get into their boat?" Guzman asked.

Roger explained. "You know the single sailboat with the old man? Well, he can't seem to get Randolph into the boat. He's hanging on the outside."

"You want us to eat him?" Robby asked with an expression of disgust.

"Come on. You've eaten a lot worse. Hell, one of you even ended up with some land grub's leg."

"That was me," Zach said. "I was extra hungry, but let me tell you, it was gross."

Guzman spoke for all of them. "We won't eat Randolph."

"If you don't, the land grubs will, and that would not only dishonor him, it would defile his corpse." Roger paused. He could see his arguments were having an effect. "They are not worthy of Randolph's prowess. You are. I know it would be what Randolph would prefer."

For several seconds, no one spoke. Then the sharks moved off a short distance to confer among themselves. Finally, they returned and Guzman said, "Give us an hour to round up the 'hood. Then you can take us to the boat."

The sun rose in a nearly clear sky. The sharks circled the boat in large numbers, rattling the boatman. On Guzman's signal, they began coming in from different directions – first from the east, then from the west and the north. The boatman seemed to fight, stabbing at one, then another, but hitting only water. But after a quarter-hour, his harpoon struck home. The sharks gasped as Billy twisted and grunted for a few seconds, then went limp.

"Bastard!" shouted Axel.

"Puto!" said Rajon, as he went straight for Randolph's corpse – the only way he could punish the boatman. His bravery rallied everyone else, especially when they saw the harpoon rope get pulled into the water. They sped toward Randolph's corpse.

The marlins had watched the scene with great sadness as they saw bits of Randolph's corpse repeatedly torn away. But when Billy died, vengeance displaced dejection. They too joined in the anger, wanting only to see the boatman punished. They were not disappointed.

But then Guzman shouted, "Careful! He's got another harpoon!"

The sharks began swimming along more erratic paths to dodge the weapon, until Zach shouted, "No, it's only a knife."

"It can still do ya, dude," shouted Rajon.

Robby scoffed. "That little thing? Don't be...arg!" He writhed in pain.

"Robby!" shouted Axel.

"I'm OK," Robby said. "It's only a flesh wound."

The attack continued for an hour more before Guzman noticed a change. "Look out, he's got something else."

"Crazy old man," Ramon shouted. "He's tearing his boat apart to hit us."

"You mean the two sticks?" someone asked.

"No," Ramon replied, "the big thing at the back of the boat. It's a lot bigger and could do some serious damage."

They all tried to dodge the weapon as they came in for bite after bite, but eventually a few of them got hit. Two paid with their lives, but over time, as they saw the boatman's efforts become progressively weaker, they all became more daring. Randolph's corpse was being reduced ever faster. Eventually, his bones were uncovered. On seeing this, the marlins wailed

"I never thought success could bring such sadness," Benny said.

Eventually, the work was done. The sharks gathered around the Marlins.

Guzman spoke for them all. "We're very sorry for your loss. Before we depart for our home, we'd like you to lead us in a prayer for Randolph's soul."

After a few seconds, Roger said, "Chris, why don' ya speak for us all."

Chris looked at the others, who nodded in agreement. "Dear Fish Lord, our cousins of the sea, usually our adversaries, have joined us on this sad day to honor our brother Randolph. They are worthy of Randolph's majesty; the land grubs are not. Let this remind us all of what we hold in common. We are all of the sea – the sea which Fish God provides us in his loving wisdom and grace. Many have asked why, if Fish God exists, he would have created the land with its awful creatures. We can never know this, anymore than we can know why he chose, in his infinite grace, to make us. The ways of Fish God are mysterious. But this I do know: Randolph is in a better place now, in that Paradise that lies beneath the ocean floor. Even now, he is surrounded by the music of whales and dolphins. We praise Fish God for his infinite goodness. Amen.

After several more amens, the sharks departed for the waters off Diamond Island. But the marlins were not through. Out of pure vengeance, they swam around the old man's boat, ridiculing and laughing at him, flippering him off. Eventually, the boatman approached the bay, and the marlins returned to their home waters to fast for three days of mourning.

Unknown to them, that was a lucky choice, for on seeing the size of Randolph's skeleton, the other land grubs wanted to know the location where it had been caught. Every island fisherman went to the same area, but after catching nothing but bait for three days, they got discouraged and returned home. They spoke among themselves about the old boatman's deception, his desire to hide the actual location of the large marlins. And so it was that two reputations were damaged: The old man was considered selfish; and the marlin gathering spot was said to be barren of game fish, not worth the time or effort.

Both of these waterlogged tales were passed down through the decades in their oft-repeated folk tale called, *The Old Man and the Skeleton.*

The Man Who Couldn't Cheat

*"I cried because I had no shoes, until I saw the
man who had no feet," admonished the man to
the beggar.   "Ah, yes," replied the beggar, "but
you would still need shoes."*

Josh Carruthers couldn't grasp the situation. He had
never been fired before, even during his teen years.

"I'm sorry, Josh, but you brought this on yourself."

Josh remained silent as he tried to recover.

Sigstrom spoke again, this time with irritation. "Come
on Josh. You were warned. Don't tell me you weren't
expecting it."

"Look, Ted knew and…"

"Ted Knowland did things his way. Now I'm in charge.
Apparently he was willing to indulge your so-called ethics.
When I took over two months ago, I told you you'd have to
become a team player."

"Steven, KSP has plenty of clients with honest
quarterly reports. Ted assigned me their audits. And I'm
perfectly willing to continue working on sections where
someone else signs them." Josh had modulated his speech,
but he couldn't completely cover the traces of begging.

"I hate to say it, Josh. I really do. But the only clients
with totally honest quarterly reports are the smaller
companies. Kolnika, Sousset and Portman has decided to
chuck them. There's a lot more fat on whales than
minnows." He leaned forward and spoke more deliberately.
"Look, Josh, I can find competent auditors any day of the
week – maybe not as good as you, but good enough to get
the job done on small accounts. What I needed from you
was loyalty – loyalty to the whole team. As far as I'm

concerned, your end of the arrangement with Ted is no longer of value to the company."

Josh was silent. Obviously, nothing he might say would save his job.

Sigstrom sat back and tried to soften his voice, but his saurian nature seeped through. "You've got a pretty good 401k, I'm sure, and KSP has a good severance policy for its associates. In addition, we're willing to offer a bonus. I'm certain you'll find it fair." He slid the paper across the table.

On the way home, Josh turned on the news to tune out the noise in his head.

> "And in Iraq, government forces retook the town of Mosul. Their victory was muted by the sight of a mass grave of 200 executed civilians. This proved to be only half the horror. It appears that the enemy had not had time to bury the evidence of their crime, as they had nearby, where neighbors and relatives had to excavate another 300 bodies to provide them a proper burial."

He turned off the radio. He preferred the noise in his head.

***

"You're taking a second glass?" Emily Carruthers asked.

"It's a good wine," Josh said.

She stared at him for several moments. "Jesus!" She sat back from the dinner table, crossed her arms and shook her head slowly. She stared directly at him. "You got canned."

He nodded.

She slapped the table. "I told you this would happen. Why couldn't you just go along with it?"

"You know why. I just can't lie like that. Sign my name to corporate audits that I know are bullshit? I'm afraid that's not the man you married."

"I hate your father." She said it with an air of resignation.

"You're lucky you didn't know him. You'd hate him more."

"I doubt that – unless I had been his wife. I hate him for what he did to you."

He raised his eyebrows. "What, for making me an honest man?"

"For making you unable to fudge the line a little bit. In human relations, that's what you do."

He didn't bother answering. They had had this conversation before.

"Remember right after we started dating?" She said. "The time the stylist botched my hair? And you said my hair looked just fine? Wasn't that a teeny lie?"

"It was. But there's a difference between lying and cheating. Now if I had been after your money, that would have been a whole different thing."

"Yeah. As poor as we were, it would have been a sad case of insanity." It was the first time she smiled in this conversation, and it didn't last long. "So how does lying on an audit cheat anyone?"

"People buy and sell stock based largely on the companies' quarterly reports. If a fake audit encourages people to buy instead of sell, someone's going to lose money. And if it's my signature at the bottom, I'm responsible for it."

Later, they watched the news on television.

> "Yesterday in Pakistan, an American drone mistakenly bombed a wedding party. The building was often used by Al Qaeda leader Rachim Habbani, but at the time of the attack, he was elsewhere. The exact death toll is unknown, but is believed to be between one and two dozen people. And now, this."

As the commercial began, Emily turned to Josh. "I've been thinking. I don't make enough for the two of us, even if we skimp, and Larry has seven more college years. At 45K a year, that's over $300,000. You know the numbers. You might not have thought about it, but this affects all of us."

"For gosh sales, Emily!"

She took a breath, then looked back at him. "I'm sorry, but I'm worried."

"The money will be Okay. They'll cut me a severance check next week, and there's a bonus of 150-thou."

She was delighted at first, then puzzled. "A bonus for what? Not doing your job the way they wanted?"

"For keeping my mouth shut, "he blurted out. "Hush money."

She considered having him explain the ethical difference between signing a false quarterly report and helping KSP keep it a secret. On the other hand, she might convince him, and he'd reject the bonus. Instead, she said, "Then I guess we're OK for now, except for one thing. At the next job, they're going to expect you to sign off on *their* audits. What are you going to do then?"

"Hopefully they'll be more honest...Don't roll your eyes! You know I hate that."

"It's just that you're good at what you do. All you had to do was play along. Not only would you still have a job, you would have gotten raises along the way, maybe a promotion. Instead..." Her voice trailed off.

Over the next two weeks, Josh sent out several applications, but during the remainder of each day transitioned into the role of househusband.

One evening, Emily remarked, "This veggie casserole is great. The pepperoni adds a nice contrast. You're getting the hang of cooking."

"Thanks. How did it go today?" The words were barely out of his mouth when he realized his mistake.

"Not too bad, except one of the shipments is late. We're looking for a second source. Any luck with your résumés?"

The question he dreaded. The question he tried to fend off night after night with talk about politics, the garden...anything except employment. "No," he said, "still waiting."

"Look, I know you don't like going through headhunters, but there's no reason not to. If you find a position before they get you one, you've lost nothing. And a lot of companies hire only through headhunters."

"Twenty-five percent of the first year's salary is a hell of a hit."

"Seventy-five percent is better than 100% of nothing. And if it takes you three months to find a job on your own, you're already out the 25%. Look, Josh, all I'm saying is work both roads. If you land something before they do, you still win."

He was silent for a while, but his accountant's mind couldn't argue with her logic. "OK," he finally said.

"You'll talk to a headhunter? I mean, like tomorrow?"

"Yes. I promise. And they're called *recruiters*."

"If they land you a position, I'll call them *angels*."

***

Ten weeks later, as he sat in the waiting room of Lanton Placement Services, he looked at the television. It displayed a barren landscape filled with tents as far as the eye could see.

> "These ten-thousand refugees are only a fraction of those who have fled the fighting in Kolaboko. They were caught between two rebel forces fighting each other as well as the government. In combat areas, these civilians faced bullets and starvation. Here, the United Nations provides them all a ration of food, but there is barely enough water to drink, and none to waste on bathing or cleaning. A dozen die here of disease every day as the small and overworked medical staff do their best to save lives despite a shortage of antibiotics and other medical supplies."

"Josh?"

"Oh, hi Carrie." He followed her into her office. It was small, with modular walls, but at least it was enclosed, and included a door – a bit of privacy that reduced the stress of the process.

"Josh, I want you to understand that I have not been lounging on your résumé. With your experience and your work for prestigious companies, I figured this would be a slam dunk. I'm wondering if you've been totally open with me."

"Carrie, I certainly would not lie to you. Why would you think such a thing?"

"Did you piss off anyone at KSP? I mean specifically, in management?"

Josh weighed his answer. "There was some friction there. Yes."

"So it wasn't just..." she read from his résumé, "*...the nature of their clientele changed, making my specialty irrelevant to their revised business model*?"

"Carrie, what is it you're getting at?"

"I've seen this a couple of times before. I have no proof. In cases like these, we never have proof, but I suspect KSP might have put the word out on you."

"Steven Sigstrom!" Josh exclaimed. He recovered, and continued quietly. "The bastard has it in for me. I knew he didn't like me, but why hurt me like this? I'm already out of his life."

"Like I said, I've seen it before. If you're in recruitment long enough, you get at least one of these."

"What do I do?"

"You're not going to like it."

He leaned forward. "I already don't...What do I do?"

"Reset your career downwards. Take a position with a smaller company, possibly doing a lower level of work. You'll take a cut in salary, Josh, but after a couple of years, you'll have an employment record that will allow you to stair-step your way back to better positions and the pay you deserve."

"How much of a cut in salary?"

"Let's see what we have..."

***

"How much?" Emily took a breath. She realized it must have been a blow to his ego, and he didn't need another. "Well, that's workable. Between that and my salary, we can get by."

"It's a step down, but like Carrie said, in a couple of years I can use it to leverage myself into another job. And by that time, Steven Sigstrom's hex will be forgotten by the bigger accounting firms."

"You think so? I mean, *will* they forget?"

"Management changes every couple of years."

She nodded. "I'm glad this is finally behind us."

Except it wasn't. A month later, as Emily sat watching TV, there was a shout from his office. She rushed in. "What happened?"

"Did you see this?" He was pointing to his computer monitor. "Sigstrom got nominated today for the president's Council of Economic Advisers. The piece of shit gets to go to Washington."

"Look – it says he's a longtime friend of the president." She shook her head. "What a world." She considered adding, 'I guess cheaters *do* prosper', but realized it would definitely worsen his mood. '*Besides,*' she figured, '*what's done is done.*'

Except it wasn't. Two days later he was sitting in attorney Rick Derrida's waiting room, watching JNN.

> "In Mexico today, a grisly
> discovery. The bodies of three families,
> were found in a culvert 12 miles from
> the city of Pavesco. The dead include
> women and children. Each had been
> shot in the head, execution style. It is
> believed that drug cartels are
> responsible. Murders such as these,
> involving whole families, are usually
> retribution for one family member
> cooperating with the police or military,
> and are meant to serve as a warning
> to..."

"Josh, good to see you. Come on in."

Once they were settled with their coffee, Josh got directly to the point. "Rick, I need some advice." He explained the entire situation, including his whole history of employment with KSP, and the difficulty he had finding new employment.

"Josh, the likelihood of proving this Sigstrom guy defamed you is extremely small. They would all have been private conversations on golf courses or in offices, and with his closest colleagues. None of them will verify it."

"I know that."

"Well then, how I can help you?"

"There is one area that doesn't require witnesses. I want to be a whistle-blower against KSP."

Derrida inhaled deeply. "Josh, if you want to commit professional suicide, I could not suggest a more effective way." He waited to let his words sink in. "Even in the federal government, which has an actual whistle-blower office, whistle-blowers usually end up unemployed, bankrupt, even divorced. And they never – repeat, never – succeed in getting the villain punished."

"Help me understand. You're telling me that if I have provable information that demonstrates the audits were falsified, KSP would still not be held accountable?"

"Josh, we've known each other for over a decade. If I thought there was any reasonable chance of attaining your goal, I would pursue it just to bring you a sense of peace. As your friend as well as your lawyer, I'm telling you not to do this." He realized Josh was only half-listening to him. "OK, let's just consider: Who would we have for a backup witness?"

Josh remained silent, trying to think who he could rely on.

Derida counted off on his fingers. "The other accountants who signed the false audits; the companies that cooked up the fake reports in the first place; and finally, KSP's upper-level managers. How many of those are going to testify to their malfeasance?"

"In other words, they can just lie on these reports for years, and there's nothing we can do? Even with publicly available quarterly reports whose numbers can be shown to be false? And Sigstrom gets a promotion out of it?"

"Pretty much, Josh. I'm afraid our parents lied to us. Cheaters *do* prosper."

The last three words floated out of Derrida's mouth easily, graceful as falling leaves, but to Josh they felt like knives piercing his viscera; and along their pathway, they cut through a leash wrapped around an unfamiliar something deep inside, something feral and cunning.

***

"What do you think? Is good?"

"You didn't exaggerate, Aleksei. They're delicious," Josh said

"I apologize for being late. An emergency. You probably heard about explosion in Azerbaijan."

"That was your company?"

"No, thank goodness. But they supply parts to one of my businesses. Unfortunately, they also supply parts to Russian military. Some people don't like Russian military."

"Are you saying it was terrorism?" Josh asked. "The news said…"

"The news, the news. Don't believe it. Especially when it comes from country like Azerbaijan, where freedom of press is only a theory, an idea more abstract than God."

"They said fifteen were killed."

"Employees. Regular workers."

"Jesus. They probably thought they'd have an ordinary day – go home at the end of the shift," Josh said.

Sokolov raised his eyebrows and nodded. "To be happy in this world, one needs a measure of blindness – or at least astigmatism. But let us not ruin fine meal with such talk."

"You're right, Aleksei. I apologize." He took another bite of beef. "I've never had genuine Russian cooking. When Elizabeth referred me to you, she said you had great taste in cuisine. Thanks for telling me about this place."

"My pleasure, Josh. It is least I could do to reciprocate for taking me to lunch."

"Oh, I think we can do a lot more than this in the way of reciprocation, Aleksei."

"My friends call me Alex." As he said this, his mouth smiled, but his eyes did not. Aleksei Sokolov was a serious player, one who often mixed business with pleasure, but never confused the two.

Josh spoke as casually as he could. "In my profession, one often learns a lot about business, and especially businesses. My time at KSP exposed me to a lot of companies' internal finances. I'm sure it won't surprise you that a number of large corporations lie about their financial condition."

Josh paused to take a drink, but Sokolov didn't take the bait. Josh continued with his script. "Some of those businesses are publicly traded, and four of them are in very bad shape. If the public were to learn of their actual conditions, their stock price would drop significantly. A sharp trader could benefit greatly from such a hypothetical situation."

Sokolov raised his head. "Hypothetical?"

Looking at him directly, Josh replied. "The condition of the corporations is not hypothetical. It's a certainty. But exploiting that knowledge – making the public aware of it – that would be hypothetical."

After several seconds, Sokolov asked, "And how could one do this exploiting? Hypothetically speaking, of course."

"The public is numb to rumors and small scandals, even reasonable accusations. It's the internal details that interest them. It's like a wife who is certain her husband is cheating on her. She might ignore it. She might even deny it, despite her intuition. But tell her the name of the other woman – even worse, the dates and times – and she'll be out for blood."

Sokolov nodded. "Is true. We humans love gossip. But the more details we have, the more we pay attention."

Josh continued, "If the condition of these corporations were released over a period of, say, two weeks, with increasing details exposed each day, the story would not be ignored. In fact, it would be a financial soap opera. And the stockholders would react. They would have to."

"And who are these corporations?"

Josh smiled. He needed Sokolov, but had no illusions about the flexibility of his scruples. "You surprise me, Alex. You have a reputation for patience."

Sokolov returned the smile, genuinely pleased with the banter. "I'm just worried your food will get cold. Then, can you tell me, what is stock value of these four corporations?"

"Collectively, their market value is around 60 billion."

On hearing this, even Sokolov could not maintain his poker face. His smile disappeared. He stopped chewing. "And what would you say is actual value?"

"Around 15 billion." Josh took another bite.

Sokolov remained silent. Finally, he resumed chewing his food. "And how much do you want?"

"From you? Why, nothing…at least no money. I can make money the same way as you…buy options on the four companies, then cash them in when the stock plummets. But in order for this to happen, the companies' conditions need to become public – and in detail. It's the actual details that are important. I don't have those. That would require hacking their computers. I don't happen to know any hackers, at least, not at that skill level." He let the implication hang in the air.

Sokolov finally smiled, then chuckled. "When you started talking about companies lying about finances, I thought you were talking about me. But, of course, my companies are not publicly traded."

"I never handled your account, but I did a lot of background checking on you." He looked Sokolov in the eye. "And the rumors I uncovered do not interest me in the least."

Sokolov paused as he raised his chin. "So, if somebody hacks into companies and releases details of actual financial condition, and happens to own options on companies, they could make a lot of money."

Josh nodded. "Provided they knew the week when the details would be exposed. In option trading, timing is everything."

"I see only one problem," Sokolov said. "In conditions like these, where stock suddenly drops on news, your government monitors market closely looking for insider trading."

"I'm certain you have a lot of friends. The trades could occur in pieces small enough to avoid red flags. You would be dealing in billions, but I would be quite satisfied with an extra million, and I could divide those trades among my own friends and relatives."

Sokolov shook his head. "Ah, my friend. You think too small. I've done some background checks on you too. With your ability, you could make big money like me." He raised his eyebrows and smiled. "Now, I suppose, the only question, is where would one find hacker with enough skill to get into large corporation?"

"I hear Russia has some of the best in the world."

"I think we're ready for dessert. Wait till you have their blini, Josh."

"Yes, I can hardly wait," he said with a smile.

***

A year later, Josh Carruthers was called to the stand on the second day of a trial known as *The State of Illinois and SEC v. Joskins International; Garristic Investments; Hivolm Petroleum; and Vorqualm Mining Corporation.* Daniel Franko stood directly in line with the bench, a technique he'd been taught a couple of decades earlier, when he argued his first case. Positioning oneself along that line, even eight feet away, conveyed an unconscious impression to the jury. Like a brush whose tip touches the surface of paint, Franko's position absorbed a tint of the judge's gravity and objectivity.

"Mr. Carruthers, when you were employed at KSP, were you ever asked to sign off on a quarterly report that you knew was false?"

"Yes." Josh had been well-coached: Answer the prosecutor's questions concisely; and those of the defendant's lawyer with long-winded, detailed responses.

"And did you sign them?"

"No, I did not."

"And why was that?"

"It would be dishonest, and could mislead investors."

"Then why did KSP management allow any of their auditors to sign them?"

"In the audit business, the larger clients are preferred, of course. Their audits are longer, more complex, and earn higher fees. Also, an accounting firm gains prestige by having larger corporations for clients. If the largest clients want their auditing firm to sign off on a quarterly report with bogus figures – ones that put them in a more favorable light – and the auditing firm refuses, the client will take their future business elsewhere. It would take little time for word to get around, and most large clients would avoid the honest firm. As a banker once put it, 'as long as the music is playing, you've got to dance to the tune.'"

The testimony continued for ten more minutes, with Franko demonstrating that Josh was a good guy, that his previous boss, Ted Knowland, allowed him to be the principle examiner only on honest audits, and that Knowland's replacement, Steven Sigstrom, had not.

Mark Pellman rose from the defense desk and walked toward the witness stand.

"Mr. Carruthers, would you say that you were well treated or badly treated at KSP?"

"Ted Knowland, my boss when I first went to work for Kolnika, Sousset and Portman, was very considerate of my moral and ethical qualms. But when he left, that consideration left with him. So my answer would have to be that in the beginning and for most of my tenure there, I was well treated, but after Steven Sigstrom replaced him, I was not."

"But you've also said that KSP knew their audits were false; which means Mr. Knowland knew they were false. How could he allow KSP to issue such audits if he were moral and ethical?"

Josh had hoped Pellman would take this route. "Actually, what I said was that Ted Knowland was considerate of *my* moral and ethical qualms. While I can criticize his choices, they were certainly understandable."

Pellman realized the word *understandable* was bait, and he was not going to bite. Instead, he pursued another tactic. If he couldn't depict Josh as merely a disgruntled employee, he could at least neutralize the morality aspect of his testimony. "Mr. Carruthers, did you ever work on the audits for Joskins International?"

"Yes, or to be more precise, I worked on part of the audits for some of the Joskins International quarterly reports."

Pellman made his next question more precise. "And did you 'work on *part* of the audits' for *any* of the Garristic Investment quarterly reports."

"Yes, I worked on parts of some of the Garristic Investment audits."

"And, am I correct in assuming you did the same for some for the audits for Hivolm Petroleum and Vorqualm Mining?"

Pellman waited as Josh answered verbosely in the affirmative. He then asked "Well, then I'm a bit confused, because I've looked over several quarterly reports for these companies, and your name doesn't appear on any of them. Could you explain why?"

"Audits for large companies are broken into sections, and different people work on each section. Some work on assets, some on income, some on expenses, depreciation, and so forth. Each auditor signs off on his section, with the principal auditor signing off for the whole project."

"But Mr. Carruthers, your signature doesn't appear on any of the sections either."

"My sections were always checked by another auditor, one assigned by the principal.

Pellman could smell victory. "Then, is it correct that while you didn't actually sign the supposedly 'false' audits for these companies, you did contribute to them?"

"Of course."

Pellman thought he was moving in for the kill. "Help me understand this, Mr. Carruthers. If you were part of the process in constructing these supposedly 'false' audits, how are you not at least partly culpable? I mean, it seems to me a bit like the, 'I-was-only-following-orders' defense."

Josh displayed as serious a demeanor as possible, acting almost offended. "To the contrary, it is nothing like, 'I-was-only-following-orders'. That defense was used by those who had committed the most immoral acts imaginable. But my work on those audits – on the sections I was assigned – was accurate. I never fudged a number. Whatever KSP auditors did with my work afterward – whether they changed some of the numbers or left them alone – was beyond my knowledge and beyond my control."

The testimony continued for another half hour, with Pellman vainly trying to dislodge Josh's moral stance. Emily had taken the day off to watch the proceedings, partly for moral support, partly out of curiosity. The trial was widely covered by the media, and she knew it could affect Josh's future. At the end of the day, as they left the courtroom, she said, "You did well. Really well."

He smiled and held her hand. "I know a great Russian restaurant."

The trial lasted two more days, with Josh called back to the stand a couple of times. The jury took another two days to find all four firms guilty.

***

It wasn't until the day after the final verdict was announced that Josh received the call from Sokolov, the first since their meal at the Russian restaurant. They met a few days later.

"Yes, is good, Sokolov declared. "You have good taste in restaurants. I never eat here before, but I will try again in future."

"Thanks for inviting me," Josh said.

"I would have invited you sooner, but I thought it safer to wait until the trial was finished."

"Yes, caution was wise," Josh agreed. "I assume you made out well in our venture?"

"You didn't lie. You didn't exaggerate." Then he chuckled. "Even the restaurant you chose is honest." He looked around, pointing with his fork. "No pretension, no copies of 16th-century paintings in heavy gold-painted frames, no white gloves on waiters. Just some pleasant prints on the walls, a few plants, and great French food."

"I'm glad you're enjoying it."

Sokolov continued without interrupting his meal. "You know, it occurs to me that we have paradox here. I trusted you because Elizabeth Nevsky vouched for your honesty. But really, we did break the law."

Josh nodded without looking up. "Insider trading. Definitely illegal," he said matter-of-factly.

"I hope you covered your tracks." Sokolov said it as much as a question as a statement.

"Of course. You are my tracks."

Sokolov paused. "What do you mean, *I* am your tracks?"

"I never bought the puts, Alex."

Sokolov's face changed expression instantly. His mind raced to calculate this new wrinkle, but nothing made sense. "Then how...why...why would you do this?"

Josh smiled, savoring the moment. "Well, not to make you rich, though that is nice icing for the cake. Perhaps now we can be partners in some future project."

Sokolov had an epiphany. Lifting his chin, he asked, "So, which of the four companies did you have it in for?"

"None of them." Josh paused, enjoying Sokolov's bewilderment – a rare event, he realized. "My target was Steven Sigstrom."

Sokolov instantly grasped the entire picture. He roared with laughter. "Good Lord! You knew the trial would reveal enough to destroy his reputation; that the president would have to fire him!"

"And no financial or accounting firm will ever want to be associated with him."

Sokolov smiled. "And people say Russians are devious!"

"They are," Josh replied cheerfully.

"You used me to reveal information on four companies to discredit another company, KSP, which would discredit your real target, Steven Sigstrom. Now *that* is devious." He took another bite of food. "You know, Elizabeth told me you were a...how do you say...straight-and-narrow guy. A follower of rules. Not devious, and your background certainly did not indicate a vengeful sort of person."

"I *was* a straight-and-narrow guy. And frankly, everyone treated me as naïve." He hesitated, then looked Sokolov in the eye. He quietly said, "My father was a cheat, Alex."

Sokolov stopped eating, surprised at the sudden change in Josh's demeanor.

Josh continued. "He cheated investors, he cheated his boss. He cheated on my mother. He hurt the whole family. If there were two roads to take, and the shortest, smoothest one was honest, he'd take the other. I believe he always had to prove he could outwit the rules. My whole life, I did everything to avoid being like him."

As Josh paused, Sokolov nodded, then spoke quietly and with sincerity. "You had allergic reaction. You let it haunt you to the point of paralysis." He raised his eyebrows, wondering if he had described it correctly.

"I did. Until I learned Sigstrom was going to Washington. Then something snapped."

At this, Sokolov smiled. "My friend – and from now on, we are friends – you were victim, until now. Welcome to fraternity of extremely dangerous people. But as veteran of that fraternity, I am going to recommend rule: Know your friends from everyone else. Never be dangerous to friends. Remember that, and I predict you will work your way into very rewarding situations."

"Funny you should say that, Alex. RZP Financial Services called me a few days ago, and another large accounting firm has expressed interest in me for upper management."

"You are popular guy now."

"Well, the trial was well-covered by the media, and the financial community truly admires a capable – and more important, a loyal – member of the team. The fact that I never divulged the shady workings of KSP, even after termination, impressed them."

"But at the trial…"

"No one expects you to perjure yourself on the stand. And of course, I didn't cause the trial to happen..."

Sokolov smiled. "No," he said with slightly exaggerated irony, "of course you didn't." He raised his glass. "To loyalty," he said.

Josh raised his glass. "To...whatever."

The Haunted Man

It was a casual incident, too insignificant a hint of the larger train of events it presaged. No, not an incident, exactly. More a fleeting observation. As I gassed up the car, I saw him sitting in the front passenger seat of a dark blue sedan at another pump. He was looking forward. Thinking back, I realize my gut was reacting, though my thoughts were elsewhere, unaware of the eerie feeling deep within me. Was it his absolute stillness? Perhaps he never blinked? I'm embarrassed to admit my lack of answers, but I was too busy thinking about my next destination. As I drove off, the driver emerged from the food mart to finish filling the sedan.

"Did you pick up my dress from the cleaners?" Sue asked.

"Got it right here," I said. During our 23 years of marriage, she had always been the nervous one, constantly checking and double-checking to make certain everything was in its proper place, every task completed. I joked a couple of times about her "obsessing" over such things – an unfortunate term to use on a psychologist. She snapped back at me, and I never made that mistake again.

"Oh, Tom called," she said.

"Everything okay with him?"

"Yes. Still struggling with his calculus. I think it's mostly a confidence issue with him."

"The senior year is usually a bear. I remember mine. Rachel will be facing hers in two years." I looked at her. "It's going to be an empty nest, soon."

"Yes. I've fully reconciled myself to that."

The following Sunday, I bought some garden supplies at the hardware store. As I was creeping my car toward the exit, I noticed a man entering the store. It took a few seconds to register. I looked back, and there he was – the same man I'd seen in the car at the gas station. The same thin hair, nearly white, the same stoop of the neck and shoulders, the same pale complexion. 'Coincidence,' I thought. 'Must live in the area.' Again, I have to admit a lack of attention to detail. I suppose Sue is right: I should be more observant, but then, her attentiveness is sufficient for both of us.

Four days later, I was sitting in the chair while Chet clipped and trimmed and combed as artfully as possible to obscure my gradually expanding bald spot. Across from the barber shop, the light-rail train arrived, then departed a few minutes later. And there he was. The pale, stooped man apparently had just gotten off the far side of the train. This time, I noticed he had a cream-colored shirt with thin vertical blue stripes. Recalling as best I could, I vaguely remembered that he had been wearing a similar shirt at the hardware store. '_Must like light-colored shirts,_' I figured. I had a whim to run outside and introduce myself, but of course, Chet was still valiantly working on my hair.

At first, I was convinced that seeing him for the third time verified a residency close to my neighborhood. '_But then, the barber shop is five miles from the hardware store._' Still, what other explanation was there? It was 4:00 in the afternoon, and he was probably returning from work – going home for the evening, just like me.

When I reached home, I changed clothes, and prepared the salad while Sue finished the sauce for the vegetables.

"How was work?" she asked.

"It was okay."

"You seem a little distracted."

"No, just a fairly busy day." I knew she saw through my smile, but I wasn't sure how to explain my thoughts. "How was your day?"

"The usual. Though I did have a small breakthrough. You remember I told you about the abused wife who left her husband behind in a carnival? Together, we evoked a memory from..."

I usually did not tune out her daily narratives. Her stories were real, meaning they involved human drama. And she did help people improve their lives. But this particular evening, I was upset, though at the time, I could not have told you the reason. Seeing a man three times in a little over a week? That probably happens now and then to everyone; I just wouldn't have noticed it. But that raised another question. '*Why* did *I notice him? In the gas station and barber shop, I had to wait; its natural to look around, pay attention. But leaving the parking lot?*' I decided I was probably making something of nothing. Besides, if I mentioned the incidents to Sue, I'd be inviting a full-scale psych analysis.

The following week I was selected to make a presentation to a group of Europeans who our company hoped to take in as partners in a Mongolian mining project. The startup costs would strain our financial capacity, so convincing the Europeans to join in the venture was important. And the unusual abundance of rare-earth minerals in the site would make the rewards high. Needless to say, the executives were nervous about the meeting. We did three dry runs before I had edited it to perfection.

Their consortium consisted of executives from French and German banks, plus a representative from a French refiner. Of course, I was nervous. Sue had instructed me in detail how to breathe to relax. It certainly made a difference. Once I had launched into the presentation, the words – even the gestures – became automatic. I was doing fine until I glanced out the second-story window. There he was. On the street below. '*What the hell?*' The same man, same shirt, even down to the thin blue stripes. In fact, I vaguely remembered the dark gray pants from the rail station. It took a few seconds before I realized I had interrupted my own presentation. I turned back to see everyone around the table staring.

I've got to say, I pulled off a pretty smooth recovery. "I'm sorry, ladies and gentlemen. I forgot to mention one important point." Actually, I had delivered the talk like a pro, but I then jumped forward to a point I was supposed to cover in the next section. Charles, our vice president, was staring darts at me, but relaxed as I smoothly transitioned forward , then back. At the end, the French lady asked me about the variations in ore densities at the outer ends of the proposed site. By chance, I had come across those figures and studied them out of curiosity. I answered her question with precise figures, which impressed the audience – even Charles.

After the guests had gone, he came over to my workspace. "Well done, Bob."

"Thanks."

"For a second there, I thought you'd lost it."

"Sorry about that. I was all butterflies inside."

"That's okay. You made one hell of a good recovery."

"My previous presentations were less...well, not as high of a level. I knew we had a lot riding on it."

"And you came through like a champ." His smile seemed sincere, but then, that was one of the reasons he was vice president. Then my thoughts drifted back to the man. *'He's got to be following me...but how could he know I'd be at that second-floor window?'* None of it made any sense.

During the following week, Charles called me into his office to let me know the Europeans had agreed to partner with us.

I called Sue. "Let's go out tonight."

"It's Tuesday."

"Of course it is."

"We should wait until Friday, so we can sleep in. And also, I have to go over some of my notes for tomorrow's patients. Besides..."

That's 23 years of marriage. Like clay, it's reshaped by daily kneading, until it gets too firm to change. Yet, I realized she was right. The high I was feeling would settle down eventually.

On Friday, I insisted on going to a new restaurant, upscale from our usual dining places.

"Did you get a raise?" she asked as she looked at the menu.

"A raise? No. Why?"

"I'm just wondering why you chose an expensive place."

"I just felt good – still feel good – over the success of my presentation. And why not try new places?"

"So, you exceeded your own expectations about yourself. That's good. Were you having trouble at work before?"

"Trouble? What kind of trouble?"

"I'm just wondering why you had such low expectations."

And so the conversation went, as too many did. Sue always had trouble coming down from her psych-analysis-self until Saturday afternoon, when I had my wife back for a day-and-a-half. We left the restaurant and I handed my ticket to the valet. As we waited in silence for the car to be brought around, I glanced at the diner across the street. There he was, sitting at the counter. It was difficult to discern details, but I was certain he was dressed in the same colors as before. This was too much. He was going to give me an explanation. I started toward him, but just as I reached the curb, the valet arrived with the car.

"Whoa, buddy. That was close. A good thing you hadn't stepped off the curb."

I looked around. Sue was staring at me. "It's probably the extra glass of wine," she explained to the valet.

I paid him and slid in on the passenger seat. I looked across the street again. He was still there. Something was wrong with the picture. As we drove home, I kept rerunning the tape in my head. Finally, I realized what was bugging me. We weren't anywhere near our neighborhood. This was downtown. *'Can't be a coincidence. He must be following me. But why?'*

The next time I filled up, I looked around the gas station – half expecting, half dreading to see him. But it was an ordinary fill-up. However, the next day, driving home, I was stopped at a light, the lead car in my lane. A bus facing the crosswise direction was picking up passengers. As it resumed its route, there was a man near the back of the bus, seated by the window.

'Is that him? Hard to tell...' And then, just before the bus reached the middle of the intersection, he turned toward me. His face held no expression. My blood ran cold,

though there was nothing about the scene to account for my fright. Nothing. Except, he seemed to be looking directly at me. Not casually outward. At me. After the bus had continued on its way, I thought, '*Was he actually staring at me, or was I imagining it? He doesn't actually know me. Jesus, Bob, what's with you?*' It was only then that I remembered: '*I've never seen him from the front.*' But why would that frighten me so?

By the time I reached home, I had argued with myself in 50 different directions. '*Positively not going to tell Sue about this,*' was my only certitude. '*Definitely not in the mood for psychoanalysis tonight.*'

Two nights later, I helped her wash the dishes. Afterward, as usual, we both retired to our evening activities – me reading some reports from work, she catching up with the news online.

"Gee," I heard her say from her office. "Can you believe this?"

I went into the room. "What's up?"

"I was going through the obits, and I found this."

I always thought it ironic that a shrink would be obsessed – no, I never actually said it – by obituaries. However, there on her screen was the picture of the man – the one I had seen repeatedly over the last month. He looked younger, and his hair was black.

"Who *is* that?" I exclaimed.

She looked at me. "Are you okay?"

"Yeah," I said in a more normal tone. "Yeah, I'm fine."

She turned back to the screen. "It's Leonard Sticks – Lennie."

"You know him…knew him?"

"Yes. We went to the same college. He proposed to me in my sophomore year. He was a senior. I liked him, but it wasn't practical. I wanted to finish my degree before getting married. I didn't think I could handle both at the same time."

"How old was he?" My voice carried more tension than I had intended.

She looked at me again. "Fifty-three."

"Really?" The man I had seen looked at least a decade older. "Well, what was the cause?"

"It says a brain tumor. That's sad."

"Yes, it is. I guess it was inoperable?"

"It doesn't say. All it says is he's been in a coma for a month."

"A month?" A chill engulfed me. That would have put it around the time I first saw him.

"Yeah. He died the day before yesterday."

Another chill – the day I saw him on the bus. "Any children?"

"No. Apparently, he never married."

***

I've never told her about the sightings I had. And I've never told her how sad I found Lennie's story. But since that evening, I've made it a point now and then to tell Sue that I love her.

The first time, she tried to analyze my motivation. Only the first time..

Nightly Bout

"Look, we agreed one show for each of us, and the only one I like on Tuesdays is at 7:00."

"But Joe, mine comes on at 7:00 too. You could watch Drug Pups at 8:00."

Joe Flinders furrowed his brow. "Damn it, Nancy, you know I don't like Drug Pups. I only watch it because you enjoy it and there's nothing else on."

"Look," Nancy said, "let's settle this like adults.

She went into the bedroom and returned with a coin. "Just promise me that if you win, you won't choose a so-called reality show."

"No, no, I wouldn't do that to you. I know how much you hate reality shows. I don't care for them either."

"Heads or tails?"

He chose, she tossed, and as the coin hit the floor, Joe smiled. "Like adults," he said triumphantly. As she plopped into the chair, Joe thought, '*Might not get any tonight, but it's worth it.*'

A few minutes later, the episode began with the usual lead-in followed by commercials, followed by the title screen: DEAD HEAT. At the second commercial, Nancy Flinders stared at her husband. "You actually like this?"

"Hell, yes. What's not to like? It's got mystery, action, and the good guy wins in the end."

"It's also got 'preposterous' written all over it."

And so began yet another night of two video aficionados debating and arguing over the merits of this movie or that television series. In fact, they had originally met as members of a movie club 11 years earlier. Their romance had grown slowly, like a very satisfying 10-part miniseries. However, the advent of streaming services and multiple production studios had made their nightly choices too numerous for them to agree on any movie or series. They had discussed the possibility of separate TV rooms, but that would have eliminated the after-show discussions they enjoyed even more than the actual movies. Besides, despite their arguments – often heated – they were still very fond of each other. So they settled on dividing the choices in half, each getting first pick on alternating nights.

This time, it was Joe's turn to object. "Preposterous? What's preposterous about it?"

"You really have to ask? First the prisoner has been framed. Is that cliché, or did you pull a Rip Van Winkle the last twenty years? Then he's recruited by a super-secret government organization. Wow! How original!"

"That's just to get the plot going. It's framing, not part of the action."

"You're right," Nancy conceded, "and if that were all, I probably wouldn't criticize it so harshly. But how does he kill terrorists? He steams them until they die, then continues steaming them until the body shrinks so it's easier to hide."

"Well, it's a little far-fetched, but..."

"A little? I guess they haven't heard of just burying them in a cement foundation, or dumping them at sea – you know, the good old-fashioned way they used to do when writers knew how to write."

Joe jumped at the opportunity. "Now that would definitely be a cliché. Dumping at sea – so overdone."

"Overdone? It's called *logical*. You ought to consider that when you're choosing a show. And what about the guy's name? Joe Flame – the guy who steams people to death. Flame? How is that imaginative?"

"Well, it's better than, say, Joe Steam would have been."

Nancy just looked at her husband.

He continued his connoisseur offensive. "And compare this to *Drug Pups*, with its ridiculous plots based on a ridiculous premise."

"What's ridiculous about drugs?" she said. "Drugs are big in this country, and I'd guess a lot of ordinary families are involved. I wouldn't be surprised if some of our neighbors were dealers. I mean, it's not like we would know. They don't hang signs on their front porches."

"It's not the drug-dealing," he said. "First, there's the names: The Kinks. Really?"

"It's comedy. That's what you do when you're writing comedy. You come up with a few funny elements. Billy Kink and Gini Kink. It's just to make it more humorous."

"Honey, humor I get, until it becomes so far-fetched that reality is too far away to see in the rear-view mirror. The daughter's name of Mimi Kink is okay, I guess, but a son named Link Kink? Come on. Who would name their son like that?"

"So you're going to reject a complex plot because of the character names?" she said.

"Complex plot? Their drug dealing bumps up against the Russian Mafia, who kill all sorts of people around them, but somehow, never manage to kill one of the Kinks."

"Of course not. How could the plot go on without the main characters? You're becoming awfully picky."

"For crissake, Nancy, they even killed a priest."

"But it was an accident. He was caught in the crossfire."

"The bullets were meant for Gini. How can anyone have sympathy for a character who survives because a priest takes the bullet instead?

"But that's what priests do. Like Jesus' sacrifice. It was symbolic – and very poetic, I might add."

Joe was exasperated, but luckily, the end of the commercial break once again allowed them to end an argument peacefully.

When the episode was finished, Nancy asked, "Feel like popcorn?"

"Yeah, that would be nice. I'll give you a hand."

By the time they returned, the next series was about to begin, but Nancy announced, "My turn."

He handed her the remote and she switched programs. The title screen appeared.

"*Departed Spouses* again?" he said.

"That's my choice," she said with her chin raised.

She was right; he had agreed to the rules. He refrained from saying anything more – at least until the second commercial break. "I actually like the setting, the widows and widowers meeting for grief counseling. In fact, when I first saw that, I thought, '*This is going to be a great series.*'"

"It *is* a great series," she replied.

"It could be, even with the partner swapping. But people switching from straight to gay, then back again? Sure, I can see someone discovering they're gay, but then rediscovering they aren't?"

"You're not a shrink. Maybe it does happen in the real world."

"That's a big *maybe*. Then we have the ghosts of the dearly departed coming back to advise each of them? Don't you think that stretches the rubber band beyond the breaking point? And do lines like, *'Don't be talkin' shit 'bout my ghost'* sound real? And what about the grief counselor turning out to be a terrorist who uses his counseling job as a cover? That takes bad writing to the stratosphere."

"Joe, you've never been in grief counseling. You've probably never even known someone who's been in counseling. So you shouldn't be deciding what's credible and what's not."

Once again, they were saved by the end of the commercial break.

The next night was a rinse-and-repeat. She got first pick, which was an episode of *Crypto Woman*, a series on the fantastic accomplishments of the world's leading cryptographer, Clarissa Labrador, who works freelance, often helping the NSA, CIA, FBI, ECSO and Interpol. In this episode, the CIA has captured a terrorist who knows where a small nuclear bomb is hidden, set to destroy some unknown city in Europe. Labrador helps with the interrogation using her mind-reading psychic powers, and in the end, the bomb is found and disarmed with one second left on the unnecessarily large digital-readout timer.

"There, now that was pretty good, don't you think?"

Joe Flinders avoided the eye roll, but his wife could see what he was thinking as he pursed his lips.

"Oh, come on, Joe!"

"Look, I can buy the world's greatest cryptographer. I might even accept the psychic stuff. But both together? And last week she had super-hearing ability. Next week she'll probably fly through the air."

They argued for another five minutes, ending with both of them standing, almost yelling at each other. The arguing finally stopped when she said, "Never mind, It's your turn," and handed him the remote as she sat down.

He smiled with delight as the title screen appeared: ROAD RAGE.

"What's this?"

"The guys at work were talking about it. It sounded fantastic."

The movie starred Vincent Dorsal as a man who works in an auto body repair shop. In his spare time, he outfits his friends' cars with lethal weapons. But, as he explains to his girlfriend, he wants "something more. I want to get out of the grease and make something of myself." He works his way through medical school to become a plastic surgeon. Most of his patients are women who have been attacked. He dedicates his life to helping them by modifying their bodies, turning them into lethal weapons. The action scenes include a woman who bashes in a rapist's head with her titanium arm, and another who uses her giant prosthetic breasts to smother her would-be attacker. The Bad Guy is a government agent who only wears black and convinces his superiors that Dorsal is recruiting and modifying women for some never-defined grand terrorist attack. In the end, Dorsal is exonerated and Bad Guy gets burnt to a crisp by his own wife, who drives a flamethrower-equipped car she purchased years earlier from Dorsal.

The movie triggered ten minutes of unusually acrimonious argument over its quality (or lack thereof).

"It's stupid!" she declared. "It's *Death Wish* meets bimbo, cross-fertilized with *Mission Impossible*. And the acting!"

"What was wrong with the acting?" he asked.

"Dorsal, as usual, delivers his lines in a monotone – flat as a corpse's EKG."

"But that's his character. It was a perfect example of method acting."

"Vincent Dorsal doesn't act. He just appears in movies."

By this time they were both standing and shouting their opinions.

The next night, he had first choice. "A movie?" she asked. "I hope it wasn't another of your co-workers' favorites."

"As a matter of fact, I found this in the Nightlife section of our newspaper. It was highly recommended by the reviewer."

"What's the title?"

"*Cool Man Pukes*. It's about…well, you'll see. I don't want to spoil the plot for you."

Unfortunately, the plot had already been spoiled by the screenwriter. It depicts a man named Les Moore, who can upchuck dry ice, which he uses to freeze his enemies to death.

At the first commercial break, she asked, "So how come the dry ice doesn't freeze him? Or at least his throat?"

Joe speculated about the possibilities – some far-fetched, some ridiculous, and the rest absurd. The movie resumed, with Cool Man killing off various medical researchers who work in the laboratory that had genetically modified him. Of course, the last guy to die is the director of the lab. In the final killing scene, Cool Man makes a speech about how the director was responsible for depriving him of marrying the love of his life out of fear that he might, at the moment of orgasm, inadvertently freeze his beloved on their wedding night.

Because only seven minutes separated the credits from the beginning of Nancy's movie, her many sarcastic comments only got him a little red-faced.

Loin and Coyn was a new series. It depicted the crime-fighting adventures of two robots recently purchased by the Kilo City PD. Could they work together? Could they fit in with the rest of the team? Would they be accepted? Or would they be destined for the spare parts department?

This time, there was no argument at the end of the movie. All the heated words had been expended during the commercial breaks. Besides, Nancy was disappointed, though she would never admit to having made a bad choice.

Her next night's pick was slightly better. *Lester And Pester* was about a talking horse and the 15-year-old daughter of its owner, nicknamed Pester by her adoring father. Together they battle the syndicate's attempt to fix horse races, then go on to save the losing horses from being turned into horse meat. In this episode, Lester kicks one of the bad guys into the meat grinder.

This triggered enough arguing to cut into the opening credits of Joe's choice for the night, *Conglomerate*, about a family that controls a chain of slider restaurants. They must battle the syndicate's attempts to blow up their restaurants and poison the meat during transport. Unfortunately, they fail to stop the syndicate from machine gunning the cattle herds.

"Just had to have blood, didn't you?" Nancy remarked, setting off a back-and-forth that got him walking in circles, waving his hands. This only encouraged some more digs at the series, and especially at his taste in video.

Psycho Minds, her choice for the following evening, focused on a team of former serial killers who have gone straight, and now help police track down current serial killers. The series subtitle, "Even their families aren't safe from them," elicited sustained laughter from Joe, which elicited sustained yelling from Nancy, which elicited sarcasm from Joe, which began the cycle yet again.

A week later, his choice was *The Neighbors*, a new series produced independently by Flix & Flack, their streaming service.

"Jesus, Joe! You know how I hate reality shows. They're all edited to distort the people's actual lives. They're for voyeurs, people whose own lives are boring and pathetic."

"I'll tell you what, let's watch it just this once. If it's bad, I promise I won't choose it again."

She accepted this, happy with his willingness to compromise. The opening shot was difficult to discern as the title screen and credits rolled in front. Then they saw the scene clearly.

"What the hell?" he said.

Nancy was quiet only because she was unable to speak, though her mouth could not have hung open wider. The image showed them both in their television room. A quarter-minute later, they begin arguing over some movie, first quietly and intellectually, then more angrily, and finally end up standing and yelling at each other. After several minutes, the scene jumps forward a quarter-hour to another argument.

"That was our discussion of *Pig Papoose*," she exclaimed. Except they weren't discussing; they were yelling and waving their fingers at each other. And the next scene showed another argument. And these continued, in a slow metronomic succession. Halfway through the show, she burst into tears.

He turned off the TV and consoled her. "Honey, we're going to get this fixed. We're going to sue them until the squeal like pigs – which is just what they are."

"But our reputations...what will our friends think, our neighbors?"

"Tomorrow, first thing, I'm calling Flix & Flack. And the second call will go to our lawyer. We're going to fix this, and fix them for good."

And, as was his nature, Joe Flinders kept his promise. After getting transferred three times and put on hold for 10 minutes, he finally got connected to a Ms. Broccoli.

He explained his anger and his issue, keeping himself as calm and self-controlled as possible.

"Mr. Flinders, I'm looking at your account on my screen, and it shows you explicitly agreed to allow us to use your audio and video images."

"What? We didn't agreed to this. We'd never agree to such a thing."

"It was in the terms and conditions you signed. It's what qualified you for a 33 percent discount."

"Where in the terms and conditions?"

"That would be part 17, paragraph five. "

"But how did you even get the images?"

"Oh, that's in your television. Most TVs come with cameras now," Ms. Broccoli added.

"Well, how do I turn the camera off?"

"I suppose you could find that in your owner's manual, but that would also void your contract. We would have to stop your service and renew it at the normal monthly rate."

"Christ! What if we had been in our underwear – or naked?"

"In that case, the episode would have been available only on our premium channel, at an extra pay-per-view fee."

That afternoon, Joe Flinders visited his lawyer, contract in hand.

Later, as the dinner was warming, Nancy asked, "What did the lawyer say?"

"He basically verified everything the Flix & Flack woman said. We don't have a case."

"So there's nothing we can do? No recourse?"

"He said we could cancel the service, or change the contract and accept losing the discount, which is substantial."

"I say we can do without the discount, no matter what it costs. Or change our streaming service."

"But then we lose their exclusive content. We both like some of Flix & Flack's shows. Besides, the lawyer says the other streaming companies are starting to do the same thing."

"Then let's lose the discount and get their filthy noses out of our lives."

Joe was surprised at the intensity of her response. "Yes. I agree. I'll call them tomorrow, and have someone come with a new contract. But..."

"But what?"

"But the lawyer says that any content they've already collected under the old contract belongs to Flix & Flack. They still have rights to it."

"Jesus!"

"I know. I'm angry too. You know, I was thinking. Maybe we shouldn't argue so much. After all I really love discussing movies and shows, and I know you do too. Maybe we should stop making it so personal."

Nancy nodded. "Yes. I was thinking the same thing. How did we get to that place?"

"I think it's because so many of the movies and shows are so badly written nowadays. We want to choose something good, but the pickings are poor. Then we feel the need to defend our choices."

"Anyway, I think we should step away if our" – here she made air quotes – "'discussions', become hot."

"Agreed," he declared with a smile. "Dinner ready?"

"Should be. Help me set the table."

As they procured the plates and cutlery, she said. "You know, *The Neighbors* isn't a bad concept. I mean, haven't you ever wondered what goes on in other people's houses? Like the Getson's two doors down. I'm not sure she's happy. Do you think he cheats? Maybe they have Flix & Flack. It would be interesting to know how they really act."

"I don't know. They don't seem that odd. But the Ellis family, I'll bet their son's up to something illegal. You ever notice how he looks around all the time?"

"I have," she said. "And then there's the Darbys, they…".

Stalker

Sarah Pope dropped from the power cable onto the roof with the grace and silence of a cat. She quickly cast off her one-piece ninjitsu outfit, darted to the roof access door, opened it and disappeared into the stairwell.

Peter Fress yelled, "Cut! That's a take!"

Everyone clapped. Sandra Cameron – a.k.a., Sarah Pope, hero and enemy of evil – returned from the stairwell smiling.

"Not bad," said Fress, director of *The One Against the Few*, this latest in a series of Sarah Pope movies. "Got it on the second take. Well done, as usual."

"Told you I could handle it just fine."

"I never doubted your martial arts skills," Fress replied. "I just don't like the risk. The insurance premiums on you are beyond the usual ridiculous. And if you get hurt – even a sprained ankle – shooting stops and we lose a hundred K a day."

"And if I don't stay in shape, I'm more likely to get hurt anyway."

"Your shape is just fine," he replied, embellishing an up and down eyeballing of her figure. Cameron laughed at his clowning, and walked to the makeup gal for a hair touch up. Fress turned to the crew. "Okay: Cameras ready for the exit sequence. Let's go! Before the sun gets too low." He spoke into his walkie-talkie: "Safety-net crew: pack up and clear the street." He turned to his assistant. "The bus ready?"

"In place with the driver waiting. Extras and cars too. Stan's got the cameras in place and is heading down there now."

The rest of afternoon went well. The scene where she exits the building – after killing two bodyguards and the bad guy, of course – was shot out of sequence so the daytime light level would match the one just recorded. Because of the many vehicles required, the level of coordination was greater, requiring an hour of rehearsal and five attempts before Fress was satisfied with the results. Between takes, Cameron's makeup had to be touched up, the vehicles reset to their start positions, and everyone's fingers recrossed in the hope the next take would be the last for this scene. It was the part of the job Cameron disliked most – even more than the smiling indulgences she had to give to studio heads and producers at boring social gatherings.

The final take of the exit scene wrapped up the workday for Cameron. The drive home relaxed her. As she turned onto her street, she was surprised to see police cars around her house. "Officer, what's going on?"

"Oh. Sarah Pope...I mean, Ms. Cameron. Your house was broken into."

"Burglarized?"

"Not exactly. Seems the guy was an admirer of yours. Not a smart one either. Didn't think there'd be an alarm."

"Jesus! Another stalker. Almost as bad as the paparazzi." She looked across the street. "Speaking of which..."

"Yeah. We try to keep them away, but legally, all we can do is push them back a ways. Say, would you mind autographing a card for my son?"

Cameron looked down at the clipboard, which held a generic movie-star autograph card. She knew that most officers in that precinct carried a box of them in their cars for their occasional encounters with celebrities. She didn't mind. It once got her out of a ticket, and besides, they did a great job of keeping her safe. "Sure. What's your son's name?"

"Neil. Neil Clippen."

He spelled it for her, and she wrote the name, adding one of the half-dozen 'personal' platitudes she had memorized for these occasions. After he thanked her with a broad smile, she strode over to a detective who appeared to be in charge.

He grinned when he spotted her and held out his hand. "It's a pleasure to meet you Ms. Cameron. Lieutenant Harper," he said.

"My pleasure as well. Do you have the name of the intruder?"

"Ron Kinder. Know him?"

"No. Never heard of him." Turning, she spotted him in the back of one of the cruisers. "No, doesn't look like anyone who works at the studio. Can you..." She stared at the stalker. Then she turned pale.

"Seems he was in love with you," Harper said. "We'll find out more when we question him. If you want, I can let you know."

"Sure...sure. Here's my card. You can reach my assistant at this number, in case I'm not available."

"Great. I'll do that. By the way, my wife's a complete fan of yours. Would you mind autographing a card for her?"

After the police were gone, Cameron sat in her living room for several minutes. Finally, she picked up her phone. "Talbot, how are you?"

"Very well, thank you. And you?"

"Not so good. I need to see you."

"As always, Sandrina, to the point. Why don't you come by tonight? Around 7:00? Leanne will be out with her mahjong group. I'd enjoy the company."

After she hung up, she smiled at his nickname for her. She made a cup of green tea and reminisced about her relationship with Talbot Balam, how it had grown over the years. He had evolved from her martial arts trainer to her mentor as she found herself increasingly drawn to MA, beyond its usefulness to her acting career. Something within her had resonated with the practice – no, not the practice, more like the discipline. And even more than that, Talbot had gradually led her to a philosophy... *'was that the right word? No, philosophies are too abstract'*. It was, rather, a new viewpoint, a way of organizing perceptions and of understanding the world and her relationship to it. She had originally been skeptical of his use of the word *spiritual* to describe the study of MA, but had finally come to see the accuracy of the term. In the process, their relationship had deepened. But he rejected the titles of *guru* and *follower*. He pushed all his advanced students toward independence, and insisted they not idolize him.

His house had no gates. She envied the fact that he, unlike her, didn't need them. The house appeared even more ordinary than hers. While she had gone to some lengths to avoid the typical star's mansion surrounded by barriers, she had gradually been forced to retreat from her ideal of openness, a fate predicted by several of her fellow actors. Considering that day's break-in, Cameron realized she'd probably be shopping for a new home, one with higher fences; or perhaps walls.

"Sandrina, good to see you. Have you eaten?" His beard was in transition – parts of it greying, part still inky black. She realized that once his beard went full white, it would lie in stark contrast to his swarthy complexion.

"Yes, thanks."

"A shame. I made a fine chicken and vegetable casserole." He paused as he led her into the kitchen. "This time, it turned out the way it's supposed to." They both chuckled at his honesty and humility – unfortunately well earned when it came to cooking. "Coffee?"

"Coffee would be great, thanks."

"Black, as I recall. Let me put on a fresh pot." He led her into the modest kitchen. The house was small – actually of average size for its era, before families became smaller and their houses larger.

As he prepared the drink and set out the cups and utensils, he continued the small talk, which she knew was protocol. Small talk was part of the ceremony – the practice of the art of relationship, a corollary to the art of fighting. She matched his chitchat with her own. She complimented the new wallpaper and the refinishing job he and Leanne had done on the chestnut cabinets. For her, chit-chat was also a well-practiced necessity, given her need to engage producers and directors socially as well as professionally. In fact, she had originally learned the art from Talbot's example. He never said it, but she was certain he had deliberately modeled the behavior to help her curtail her impetuous manner. In this too, he had been a teacher.

After they had both taken a sip, he said, "So what brings you here after so long an absence?"

"Yes. Too long. My career has swallowed my time. I apologize."

"No need. You know that."

"My home was broken into today." Talbot became very attentive, but remained silent. "Some stalker who apparently is smitten with me."

"And who could blame him?"

His raised eyebrows above a serious-looking mouth added to the irony, evoking her smile. "The police were alerted by the alarm, and caught him before I even knew about it." She took another sip before continuing. "What bothers me is that when I saw him in the back of the cruiser, I suddenly remembered: He had been in a café where I had lunch one day last week." Talbot slowly nodded, but remained silent. She resumed more slowly. "The thing is, I never sensed it. I never picked up the vibe. And I should have."

"Indeed, you should."

"My career keeps me running here and there. Not just making movies, but promotional appearances on TV shows, trade magazine interviews, charity appearances, and so on and so on." She paused as she tried to summarize her thoughts. "I feel like it's running me down – not physically, but spiritually."

"Do you meditate daily?"

"Not as much as I should," she admitted.

"Sandrina, you already know the answer."

She nodded, then switched to her more casual self. "You know, a ballerina begins practice as a child. Her profession often starts in her teen years. By her early thirties, age has changed her body, even if she's managed to avoid injury. At that point, her career fades, and by age 40, it's over. After that, if she's lucky, she might get a position as teacher or coach, but most ex-ballerinas have to start over, usually in a career lacking the thrill of their performance years." She looked down at the table for several seconds, then directly into his eyes. "The clock is ticking on me, Talbot. By the time I'm in my mid-forties, I'll be a back-burner actress. I feel I have to put money in the bank while it's there for the taking."

His gaze didn't shift, but she could see sadness flow into his eyes. Finally, he spoke. "I knew a man who had great artistic talent, even as a child. He could draw anything, and more important, anyone. And especially when he was a little older, his paintings showed great promise. But in his early twenties, he made a decision, a conscious choice to turn his back on art, and instead embrace a vocation that would earn him more money. For years I wondered why he didn't continue his art as an avocation, but eventually I understood: Within him, the two were mutually exclusive."

"Within him?" she asked.

"Some people can switch between their art and their career each day: Writers who practice their craft each evening after work; sculptors who engage their art on weekends."

"The thing is, Talbot, it would require me to reserve time out from a busy schedule. When this movie is finished shooting, I'm hoping to do a TV mini-series."

"Cancel it." He words were delivered as abruptly as a drill sergeant's. Then he casually took another sip of coffee.

"Cancel? If I cancel, they won't even consider offering me a spot in the future. You just don't cancel on a big network offer."

"Remember what I taught you about fighting someone considerably larger than you?"

"Of course: Use his force and weight to defeat him. Turn his advantages against him."

"Beyond that. What was the one main principle of all fighting?"

"Besides avoiding a fight? Maintain control."

"Sandrina, If you don't dare cancel on the network mini-series for fear of losing future offers, who is in control?"

She was struck dumb. After a half-minute, she said quietly, "My God. It was so obvious. How had I missed seeing it?" She looked up at him. "How did I get off the path?"

He enunciated each word separately: "Step...By...Step." He paused for a few seconds. "It is how everyone can wander into darkness."

They were both silent for a minute. He spoke first. "The important thing about the artist is that late in his life he tried to go back. He tried to find his art again, but he could not. Soil that is not watered doesn't merely dry out; it dies. The bacteria that make the soil nourishing die. The worms that keep it porous abandon it. And the chemistry, the crystalline structure of the soil changes. It would have taken half a lifetime for him to renew that soil, and his life was more than half over. You think you can put your soul on hold, and retrieve it later. But it will become as an unfamiliar terrain enveloped in fog. You won't be able to find your way back."

Her eyes began to moisten. At first, she had no idea why, but tears soon began rolling down her cheeks. She wiped them away, embarrassed. She recalled that when Talbot had been her teacher, sessions with him had frequently led to internal changes in her – shifts of perspective that helped her understand important facets of her life, of herself. Another shift had just occurred, though she understood this one. She had just regained a glimpse of her inner ground of being. She soon realized her tears rose from the recognition that she had been neglecting her spirit, that he had just rescued her from too easily losing it.

He grabbed her left hand and sandwiched it between both of his. "Make the time Sandrina, as if your life depended on it. Because it does."

She nodded. "I will."

He sat back. "And call me next month. Don't be a stranger. To me or yourself."

As she drove home, she realized the promise was a strange phrase. One can't *make time*. It was a budget. By the time she pulled into her garage, she had compiled a mental list of tasks for what she now called her *Time Diet*. During breaks in the next day's shooting, she got some real estate advice from Fress, along with the name of a reputable and discrete realtor. By the end of the day, she had made an appointment with Lou Narren, who came by her home the following Saturday. Familiar with paparazzi-avoidance methods, he arrived in a car registered to a fictitious law firm. She led him on a tour of the premises while he took pictures and a few measurements. Then she gave him a list of requirements for her new home – price, size, fences, gates, and perimeter walls.

"Thanks, Ms. Cameron, for availing yourself of our resources to upgrade your lifestyle; and also for such a complete and precise list of requirements."

"You are so very welcome," she replied, in an equally friendly/formal manner that 'availed herself' of a line from some 1940s movie, though she couldn't remember which one.

Cameron called her agent and told him she wouldn't be doing the TV series. She also cancelled several social engagements scheduled for the following month, but not the regular lunches with her friend Ronnie Crother.

***

"Moving? Where?" When Cameron told her, Crother was shocked. "But that's against everything you ever said – about career warping your lifestyle. You didn't want to be 'one of those big stars living in isolation in some walled-off mansion, etc. etc.' Or did I forget something?"

"Hmm. I think you skipped one more *etc*," Cameron replied, with more humility than irony. "I didn't anticipate how difficult it would be. I've had to make other changes as well. I'm reducing the number of social gatherings I go to."

"Aren't you concerned what it will do to your career?"

"I've become more concerned about what my career is doing to my life." She told Crother about the intruder.

"Good heavens! So that's why you're moving." She thought a second, then continued. "It's a bit of a paradox – a martial arts hero who worries about romantic stalkers."

"It's more than my physical safety. You remember I mentioned that MA is about more than physical fighting? Well, I discovered I was losing the mental conditioning part – the meditation, the instincts, the intuitive feel of the energies around me. According to the police, the stalker had been following me for weeks. Yet I never sensed it. I should have."

"Maybe you should get back together with Roger," Crother said, a mischievous twinkle in her eye. "He could stay at home, watch the house for you."

"A dog is much lower maintenance. Besides, whose side are you on?"

"Definitely yours. But he wasn't that bad."

"He treated me like a Maserati," Cameron said.

Crother chuckled. "A Maserati? You mean fast around the curves?"

"Well, I suppose there was that. He was good in the sack, but everywhere else? I was just his status symbol, his show-off trinket."

"Conspicuous consumption?" Crother suggested.

"More like a prize elk mounted on the wall." They both laughed.

"So what are you going to do?" Crother asked.

"Make more time in my life for meditation. And that means withdrawing from some of my peripheral activities – TV appearances, including the TV series – God! How that made me grit my teeth!"

Crother laughed. "You look like you just had your fingernails pulled out."

Cameron nodded. "And also most of the parties, though that part is easy. If it all reduces my career, so be it. Remember the saying, 'What if a man gains the whole world but loses his soul'? Well, I was losing mine."

There was a silence, then Crother said, "I hope this doesn't mean we won't be spending time together. I realize I'm not part of the Hollywood set, but we go back a ways, Sandra."

"Almost 15 years, Ronnie. And I want you to understand that I value your friendship more than I can describe. One of the reasons I like spending time with you is that you *aren't* movie people. You're my relief from them."

"Speaking of relief, your new home calls for an extra margarita," Crother said, as she signaled the waitress.

***

Over the next few weeks, Cameron kept her promise to Talbot – and to herself. She found time to meditate, and Narren found a couple of houses that met her specifications. After a few visits to each, she settled on one that had belonged to a 1950s movie star of the cowboy persuasion. It took her a month to unpack most of her things and to set up the house. Crother was the first person she invited.

"My goodness, what a lovely view." The home sat on a modest hillside, overlooking a tree-filled neighborhood. The vista was mostly treetops with a few tiled roofs between.

"Actually, the prestige and price rise with the elevation," Cameron said. "The homes at the top are for studio owners and their bankers. They have a view almost all the way to the ocean."

"If we want to see the ocean, we'll drive there. They can watch us. By the way, is it safe to sunbathe here? I mean with them looking down?"

Cameron laughed. "Not in the nude. The paparazzi use helicopters."

"Oh, that's right. Didn't you shoot one down in your last movie?" Crother suggested.

"I just wanted to have a bit of a green vista – not the neighbors' walls, but also not an airplane view."

"Well, this is certainly not suburbia." Crother looked around. "Who's your interior decorator?"

Cameron laughed, then said with gentle irritation, "Ronnie! I don't have an interior decorator."

Crother continued to scan the interior. "Wow. That's all I can say. Wow." She paused. "You know, you have a feel for esthetics. No one would know it from your movies. I've known you all these years, and never suspected it."

"Actually, most of the house was tastefully set up. And, I cheated a bit – lots of online advice on interior decoration. Also lots of pictures. And painting and hanging pictures is a wonderful way to relax after weeks of movie shooting. By the way, for lunch I picked up a salad with sausage and feta cheese. You'll love it. But first, I want to show you my inner sanctum."

She led Crother to one of the second-floor rooms that offered a clear arboreal view. "I call this my contemplation room. That mat along the wall is for my deep meditation, and the corner chair is for contemplation."

"What's the difference?"

"Meditation is about looking inward. Contemplation is for considering what you have observed or experienced. Kind of like digesting the meaning and significance of one's day-to-day experiences."

"Sandra, you know I'm not the envious type, but I do envy you – not just the nice house, but mostly that you're bringing your life back together. You seem so much more relaxed than before you moved."

***

Her second invitation went to Talbot and Leanne for the following week. "I brought this casserole. I think you'll love it."

"Thanks, Talbot. It smells incredible. What's in it?"

"Asparagus, a bit of cheese sauce, and chopped lamb."

"And this is for the your home," Leanne said. "I was making it for my grand daughter, but the timing worked out for your move. It will keep you warm in bed in the winter."

Cameron opened the bag and extracted a crocheted afghan. Her mouth opened as she took in the colorful pattern. "Leanne, it's heavenly." Cameron gave her a hug and declared, "But it's not going on the bed. This is perfect for one of my couches. Let me give you a tour."

Dinner went well and they delighted one another with their conversation. It wasn't until they were leaving that Talbot finally referred to their earlier meeting. "I am so glad you are once again on your path."

"My path?"

"You are very much more relaxed and self-possessed. You're finding your way back."

Leanne's attentive expression told Cameron that Talbot had kept their conversation private, even from his wife. Cameron knew he loved his wife deeply, but also knew Leanne understood that for Talbot to be a mentor, she had to respect his students' privacy. Cameron also realized their marriage benefited: respect for each others' separateness created more emotional space for their togetherness.

"I am, Talbot, thanks to you."

As they began walking down out, Leanne said, "Next one's at our place. Shish kebabs!"

"Sounds good, especially if it's anything like his casserole."

"It's not. *He's* learning to do the kebabs. But don't worry, by the time you come, he'll have it down perfect!" Just before she reached the car, she turned and shouted, "And we keep the take-out number handy!" Talbot grinned as the two women laughed.

***

Soon after, *The One Against the Few* opened with a very successful first weekend. She had been approached three months earlier about doing another movie for Walkathon Studios, but it was all part of the movie-business minuet: The next-movie offer comes early, to get the star hooked; but the studio delays sealing the deal until they've seen how well the current release does. As a major star, she could have threatened to walk to another studio, forcing Walkathon to sign her immediately, rather than risk losing her. Instead, Cameron had told them, "Not right now, Sam. We'll talk about the next movie down the road. I need some time off." Walkathon didn't understand that Cameron's delay wasn't a negotiating tactic; she wanted to slow down the merry-go-round. As a bonus, her willingness to wait sent a new message. 'Sandra Cameron is loyal; but she's also independent – less hungry for a movie than your bean-counters.'

She used the extra time for a meditation practice Talbot had taught her – one he revealed to only a few of his students. He called it *public meditation* – a discipline exercised when the practitioner was in a public place. It focused on detecting surrounding emotional states, rather than exploring her own. As his student, she had barely reached the edge of that kind of perception, but then her career had intervened. Now she had to reacquaint herself with the techniques and the tuning of her sensitivities. *'This is how the salmon must feel as it struggles on its return upstream,'* she thought.

It proved useful. One day, she was leaving a clothing store with a new sweater when she felt it. Her improved instincts took hold. She dropped the bag, crouched and turned as her arm came across her chest. She barely saw his shape before her arm rose to block his downward blow. A half-second later she realized the hand was empty, open – but not relaxed. It was a karate chop – probably a trained attacker. She rolled to his side in a ball, then jabbed her foot outward toward his knee, but hit the side of his upper leg instead. As he turned to restabilize, she caught sight of the bottom portion of a cane. She grabbed it, rose, and raised it high, as if beginning an overhead blow. The assailant raised his arm to protect, and as he did so, she dropped low and slammed the end of the cane sideways into the man's ankle. He went down like a stone, and as he did, she swung the cane again, this time into the side of his head. The cane broke – and, as the police later reported, so did the man's skull.

Cameron took a breath and looked at the broken piece of the cane in her hand. Only then did she think about its unknown owner. She turned around to apologize, but he was on the ground. "Oh my God. Are you alright?"

He wasn't. He was in his 60s, and his arm was broken. The wife berated Cameron, who was in tears. As the police took the report, Cameron interrupted to ask the ambulance driver for his destination. By the time she finished with the police and finally made it to the hospital, the man had been put into a room for overnight observation.

As soon as Cameron entered the room, the wife began castigating her again, declared an intention to sue, even to have her jailed for assaulting her husband. However, it was he who finally put an end to the tirade.

"Doris! What is the matter with you? This woman was attacked by a man! She could have been killed." Then turning toward Cameron, "What was he, your ex?"

"No. I never saw him before in my life."

"Well, then why did he attack you?"

"Well, maybe you recognize me. I'm Sandra Cameron." Both of them stared at her and blinked. "Sarah Pope?" she offered. The couple looked at one another, obviously still in the dark. "You never saw *One For The Many*? *The Woman In Black*?"

"We actually prefer BBC," Doris explained.

At first, Cameron was dumbfounded, then had to suppress a smile at the absurdity of the situation. "Okay, I've acted in a few films. I portray a martial arts fighter who defends the common people against…well, against powerful evil people."

"So, the man attacked you because he didn't like one of your movies?"

"Not exactly, Mister…"

"Venici, but call me Sam. And this is my wife, Doris."

"Have you seen many Western movies?"

"Sure," Doris replied. "We used to go to them all the time, but they don't make many of them anymore."

"Well, Gunfighter's Moon was about a famous, aging gunfighter who keeps getting challenged by a lot of young men – hotshots trying to prove they can outdraw the hero. Every now and then I get challenged to a match by guys who want to prove they can beat me at martial arts. That's what I think was the motive of today's attacker."

"Do the challengers succeed?"

"I never accept that kind of fight, though I sometimes enter matches to raise money for charity. But the fighters there don't really try to hurt each other – just pin their opponent to the mat. This time it was different. He didn't challenge me – just snuck up on me, and that tells me he actually wanted to hurt me."

"Why did you grab my husband's cane? You must have realized he could fall."

Cameron looked her in the eye and spoke slowly. "In that kind of a fight, you don't think. You don't have time. You have to act instinctively, or you will lose. I caught sight of the cane – just the bottom of the cane, actually. It was a weapon, so I grabbed it. I never even saw your husband until after I had put the attacker down. And I promise you, I will pay your medical bills and enough to compensate your pain and suffering."

"Just pay our medical bills," Sam said, "and I'll call it square." Doris began to object, but he raised his good arm and silenced her. "She was attacked by a man. I would hope if a man attacked you, that someone like Sandra here would do whatever was required to protect you."

Doris was obviously miffed at missing out on a chance at a windfall, but Sam was adamant.

"Thanks, Sam, but I do owe you something besides your medical bills – oh, and also a new cane. If you had not been there, I might have lost that fight. He caught me by surprise. I'm going to write you a check that will also include what *my* medical bills might have been." She extracted a check from her billfold and quickly filled it in. She handed it to Doris, who was obviously pleased, though probably still disappointed over the lost bonanza her imagination had created.

The next day, Cameron talked to the detective handling the case, who confirmed Cameron's assumptions about his motive. "The doctors say at least two months in the hospital before he can stand for trial."

"Looks like he'll have a chance to see if he can take on Jamal for a few months," she remarked.

"More like a year," the detective said. "It's a first offense, but it involved stalking. And it wasn't aggravated."

***

A few days later, she related the incident to Crother. "At least it shows me that I'm returning to my old self."

Crother looked perplexed.

"Getting back to the state of awareness I'd lost?"

Crother remembered, and nodded.

"Ronnie, are you alright?"

"I'm sorry, I'm terrible company right now."

"What happened?"

"My parents are going to lose their farm."

"Jesus! And here I've been rattling on. What happened?"

"You've heard of Bentham Agriculture?"

"The giant conglomerate? Sure."

"What most people don't know is how they became giant. They connive with commodity brokers to drive down the price of selected crops."

"How can they do that?"

"They've built hundreds of spare silos for the purpose of holding back specific harvests from the market. Then they target certain medium-sized farms – the ones that take on too much debt, enticed by the manipulated increase in crop prices. When the farmer is about to harvest, Bentham releases their grain onto the market, prices drop, the farmer goes broke, and Bentham picks up the farm at auction for a song. There are rumors that they pay off the auctioneers too."

"Let me guess: The authorities can't do anything."

"Or won't," Crother replied. "Some of Constable's relatives are in the state legislatures."

"Who?"

"Henry Constable. Grandson of the founder of Bentham – not to mention the CEO and chairman."

"What will your parents do?"

"They aren't sure. My dad's too young for retirement. I'm trying to convince them to move out to central California – maybe Merced or Modesto."

"Why there?"

"Well, they're not used to the city. They're country folk. And homes there are affordable. I'd have to help them buy a home, start over. He's good with fixing farm equipment. Besides, I had to give them hope. I made him promise he would keep trying."

"Keep trying what?"

Crother looked down as she paused. "I'm worried about him." Now it was Cameron who looked perplexed. Crother finally said it. "I don't want him to hurt himself."

Cameron was struck dumb. "Suicide?! Has he mentioned anything like that?"

"No. But a lot of the farmers have killed themselves – made it look like accidents by jumping in front of their tractors; stuff like that for the insurance."

Cameron's mouth hung open for several seconds. "Jesus! I never knew this shit was going on."

"Most people don't. Bentham has strong influence over the Midwest media. Only people like Shawn Quinn report it, and they're pretty much treated like loony extremists. Only the left-wing press pays attention."

"But they must have a lot of farmers in Iowa. Why don't they band together?"

"Wouldn't do much good if they could. The state government is in Bentham's pocket. Even if they did band together, they'd soon have state inspectors going over their operation with a magnifying glass. Everyone is violating some obscure regulation – labor, food safety, OSHA."

"What did you say was that guy's name – the reporter?"

"Jesus, Sandra. You never heard of Shawn Quinn?"

"I don't follow the news. When I'm on a shoot, I don't have the time. And frankly, the static interferes with my meditation."

"Okay. I get that, but what goes on out there in the big picture affects our personal lives too. Don't you think?"

"Last Tuesday could have affected me pretty badly if I hadn't improved my sensitivity these last several months. If I have to make a choice, I'll tend to the personal. At least I have some control over that."

However, when she got home, she went directly to her computer. She first focused on Shawn Quinn. Crother was correct. He was all over the internet, and not treated well by the press. That was understandable. The demonstrations he organized always involved some mild forms of violence – throwing rocks, tearing down fences, tossing paint bombs at people, including the police. When interviewed at those events, he came across as loud and volatile. In studio discussions, his manner was calmer, but his words were incendiary. Coincidently, his group, Many Against the Few – MAF – was reminiscent of her latest movie's title. Sandra picked up her phone. "Jeremy? This is Sandra…Cameron."

"Ah! Sandra! Of course! Long time no hear." Cameron disliked having to contact Jeremy, programming director for the television interview series *Uncover Hollywood.* He always pestered stars to appear. She wondered how big a ransom he'd demand.

"Yes. It's been a while. Listen, I need a favor. I need a contact number."

"Well, if I can. Especially if I can interview you about your next movie."

"Right now I'm taking a break. We won't be shooting till next year."

"Okay, then how about you telling our viewers about your hiatus. I could set you up with Howard. You and him always hit it off."

She hesitated before saying, "Deal. Have his scheduler call me."

"So whose contact number?"

"Shawn Quinn. Your network interviewed him three weeks ago."

"Shawn Quinn? You want to reach *him*?" He paused before saying, "Don't let this out of the bag. You'll lose fans."

"Strictly between you and me."

She heeded Jeremy's warnings, but not because she worried about her fan base. She had a far wider field of view in mind. She called Quinn and arranged for a late night meeting in an out-of-the way café, the Hanky Panky, an old diner in an old neighborhood, the latter sufficiently run-down to discourage the owner from renovating the former. The red counter chairs didn't go with the booths' orange upholstery, and neither went with the blue Formica table tops. Still, those were the newest upgrades in the place. It looked like an Edward Hopper painting, but with customers wearing drabber clothes – including her own. She had removed all traces of makeup from her face, and added a wig and horn-rim glasses. She waited in her car until she saw Quinn enter.

Her disguise accomplished its purpose. "You're Sandra Cameron? I didn't recognize you. You look a lot different on the big screen."

"Not really. I just thought it best no one else recognize me."

"Why? Afraid your ratings will drop if you're seen with me?"

"By the end of this conversation, you'll agree on the wisdom of my disguise."

"Okay. So what did you have in mind?"

"First we order…you know, like real people?" He didn't smile at her quip. She realized that in all the video clips she had seen of him, including his studio interviews, he had never smiled. '_So, possibly no sense of humor? Maybe a good sign – a serious person._'

He waved the waitress over and they both ordered coffee and dessert. "Alright," he said, "what is it you want?"

She found his gracelessness amusing, in a grating sort of way. "You've heard of Bentham Ag?"

"Obviously. I mean, you must know about my demonstrations against them."

"Yes, I've seen them. And how effective have they been?" She could see the question made his eyes squirm.

"Well, what do you want me to say? Or rather, what would you suggest?"

"Well, you've heard of the definition of insanity?"

"Offhand, I don't recall it," he replied.

"It's to keep doing the same thing and expect different results."

"I thought that was the definition of stupidity."

She repressed her urge to chuckle. "Either way."

"So, you've called me crazy and stupid. But back to the question. What's this meeting about?"

"First, where's your cell phone?"

He hesitated, then understood and removed it from his pocket. He showed her the screen and turned the phone off. Then he lay it on the table face up.

"To answer your question succinctly, erase the problem."

"Where's your cell phone?"

At first, Cameron thought his incivility revealed a sense of wit. But then she realized there were probably a lot of moneyed people out there who would love to entrap him. Perhaps a movie star? She took the phone from her purse, turned it off, and laid it on the table.

"Okay," he said. So you were saying?"

"I'd like to donate to the cause."

He paused, a puzzled look on his face. "Well, I'm certainly delighted to find support. We do have expenses."

"Yes. You travel a lot. How would you like to pilot your own plane?"

This pause was longer. "Well, a plane would be nice, but I don't know how to fly."

"I guess that means you're going to have to take flying lessons."

"What exactly are you proposing, Ms. Cameron?"

"Several things. First, call me Sandra. Second, I will pay for the flying lessons, but only if you are committed to the whole process."

"When you say 'whole process'..."

"It takes about 75 hours of lessons plus another few months of flying with an instructor. And there's a written test. Only after you've got your license do I buy your organization a private plane."

He was silent for about a half-minute, pensively tending to his coffee and dessert. "Alright, so what's the catch? What do you want out of it?"

"The same as you: To erase the problem." She let her words sink in, then elaborated, "There will be certain times that I will need you to fly me to particular places without a passenger listed in your flight plan. Those flights will be rare, and between them, you may use the plane as you see fit."

Quinn leaned forward. "In other words, you want me to help you transport drugs, right? Obviously, you do think I'm both stupid and crazy."

"I'll be happy to let you inspect my luggage for each flight."

He sat back. "You have money to hire a private pilot and go anywhere in the world you want. Why involve me?"

"Pilots for hire aren't interested in your cause. They would just as easily fly for Henry Constable as for me. You're committed. That's beyond question."

"Constable. What exactly is it you want me to do with Henry Constable?"

"You will do nothing but fly. I'll take care of Constable."

Quinn's eyes widened as the shadows in his imagination reformed into the shape of Cameron's idea. "What the hell!" he whispered. "You're talking about taking out Constable? Christ! And the public thinks I'm nuts!"

"Yes, and they think Constable and his company are sane. Go and figure."

He had no answer for that, so she continued. "He and his company have pushed people into bankruptcy and suicide. You already know that. So tell me: How would you save his future victims? Walk around with picket signs? Shout and throw rocks? How's that been workin' out for you?"

"You're talking murder!" he whispered.

"If Constable hired someone to kill your friend, and you had a gun when he snuck through the window, would you kill him?"

"That's different. That's self-defense, and for once the law would back me up."

"And also the threat would be immediate," she added helpfully. "But what if you knew who the would-be murderer was, but not when he would kill your friend? And before you say, 'Go to the police,' let's assume the murderer has bought the cops. How would you save your friend's life?"

Quinn sidled past the question. "You're trying to justify murder. A lot of people could use the same argument against me."

"How many deaths have you been responsible for?" Quinn's silence encouraged Cameron. "How many lawmakers have you bribed?"

"Sandra, if others had your attitude, everyone would be killing everyone else."

She had anticipated his line of reasoning – in fact, had asked the same question of herself. Spent days exploring it. "Why do you think Constable is allowed to continue his destruction? Driving people bankrupt, taking their farms, destroying their way of life – all that is accepted. And if he drives them to suicide, that too is accepted. Why?"

"People are apathetic. All my protests – the whole movement's protests – have been about waking people up."

"Okay, if you won't answer the question, I will: People accept a system that contains a measure of unfairness, as long as it works well enough for them to muddle through. And those who can't? They feel helpless. And even angry people – people like you – accept it because you and they believe you can energize the masses. So I ask you again: How's that been workin' out for you?"

Cameron wasn't sure if Quinn's silence indicated a weakening or a hardening of resistance. "Shawn, if you have another way of stopping the Constables of this world – not just making a lot of sound and fury, but actually turning off the bankruptcy machine and the suicide-maker, tell me now, and I'll finance *that*." She let the silence between them sink in. "Well?" She realized she had raised her voice more than she had intended, and was surprised at her own emotions.

"Let me think on it. I'll let you know tomorrow."

"I'll leave my phone on." She pulled a bill from her purse, laid it on the table, and walked out. Driving home, she reflected on the fact that she had become as passionate as Quinn. *'The difference is that I have better self-control,'* she thought.

***

Quinn didn't contact her the next day. It was three days before an unknown number appeared on her phone. She was about to block it, but remembered it might be Quinn.

"Hi. About that proposal you suggested three nights ago? I accept. Can we meet tonight? Same place and time?"

"Sure." But after Cameron hung up, she became wary. It was unlikely he would go to the police; but what if he suspected she was a tool of the establishment? A wealthy and famous actress – she *was* the establishment. Perhaps he suspected entrapment? Would he report her just to protect himself from conspiracy charges? She arrived an hour-and-a-half early, and observed the scene for any suspicious cars, but none appeared before Quinn drove up. She followed him in.

As was his habit, he got to the point. "How do I get started?"

"Here's a list of flight schools. Pick the one you want, let me know, and I'll write the organization a check. All the IRS will know is that I made a tax-deductible donation. Everything above the table."

Quinn sat up straight and raised his eyebrows. "Oh."

"Anything wrong?"

"No. I just thought...I thought it would be more dangerous. You know, James Bond stuff. Or Sarah Pope stuff."

She smiled, and nodded. "Nothing illegal. Everything above board...for now. Oh, and one more thing: Use your real phone. Movie stars habitually block unknown numbers."

He nodded. "Shall we order? I'm hungry."

"You go ahead. I've got to be somewhere." She didn't, of course.

***

Four months later, Cameron signed the contract for *Resurrection*, a movie to be shot in the middle of the following year, directed by Clint Hollis. She had kept track of Quinn from a distance, careful to avoid being seen or associated with him personally. All money from her had gone through MAF as donations, and all their meetings had been over coffee. By the time shooting for *Resurrection* was complete, Quinn had already soloed.

"Hi, Sandra. Listen, I'm having a little party to celebrate getting my license."

"Don't forget to wear your collar.

"Huh?"

Cameron realized his mind was too literal to decode the joke on his own. "I'd hate to see you get picked up by animal control."

"Oh, I get it. Very funny," he said with Saharan dryness. "Can you make it this Saturday evening?"

"Thanks, but I've got parties this weekend to celebrate the end of shooting my latest movie." She didn't, of course.

"I can't wait to pick out a new plane. I'm getting tired of flying bargain basement airlines. You thinking new or old?"

"I'm thinking near-new, Shawn. And I've already got it picked out for you. Can you meet me at the Lawndale airport next Wednesday?"

***

When she arrived, he was waiting for her, standing at the fence staring at a large 6-seater twin-engine plane.

"That's not the one I had in mind," she said.

"No. I was just admiring it. I'm only licensed for single engine anyway."

"Let's review this whole process. You understand the reason for this entire project?"

He nodded. "I've had a lot of time to think about it. In one way, it's crazy. I mean, it *is* murder, after all. But then, the indifference in this country – not just the establishment, but the people's – that's crazy too. You were right to ask the question – how it's been working for me. Frankly, it hasn't, and I'm frustrated. I would quit, except for the dedicated followers. They still care. They still believe."

"Is that part of the solution, or part of the problem?" He was surprised by her question. She let him ponder it for a few seconds, then tilted her head toward the terminal. "Let's go take a look at your plane."

The plane she showed him was definitely not one he had in mind. "It's a taildragger," he said, with a tinge of scorn. "That's from...like World War Two."

"Actually, it's a year old and has all the latest electronics – original equipment, I might add."

"But, I've never flown a taildragger; only a tricycle landing gear – you know, with a nose wheel, not a tail wheel."

"A couple of hours of lessons for takeoff and landing, and you'll have it down like a pro."

"But why a taildragger?" he persisted.

She turned toward him. "I've been doing my homework, Shawn. Taildraggers can land and take off on rougher terrain, and in shorter spaces."

"What exactly did you have in mind?"

"You will take off from this airport and fly to a small piece of land I own in Moreno Valley. The ground is flat but unimproved. You will pick me up and fly to the destination. You might have to gas up in between, but there are plenty of small airports for that, and we wouldn't need to go through security – just gas up and continue on."

"Which destination?"

"It will always be a double destination. First you'll land in a rural area – probably a farm road – and drop me off. From there, you'll fly to a small rural airport. Then you can take in the town or city, see the sights, relax, until I contact you."

"Wait, wait! What do you mean, 'it will _always_ be a double destination'? You're planning more of these?"

"How many different wrongs have you protested during, say, the past year?"

"Jesus!" he replied, without a tinge of religiosity. "Are you planning some kind of serial killing shit?"

"No Shawn, only those like Constable's case, where a great wrong has obviously been committed and cannot be corrected because the villain has bought the law and the lawmakers. Also, where only a handful of people are the cause."

"Hold on! We need to stop there! You never told me about others. Only Constable. So before you buy me this plane, we have to set one condition. I approve all targets."

She looked at him, unsure how to maintain control over the project.

"I mean it, Sandra. This here's a deal-breaker for me."

She hesitated, but saw something new in his eyes. He was calm and collected. And determined. For the first time, she understood: This was his source of strength for leading MAF. She also realized that at the very least, he had already agreed to eliminating Constable. If that proved to be the only accomplishment for this enterprise, it would be enough. "Okay, deal."

***

Their first operation began a week before the scheduled opening of *Resurrection,*. Cameron parked her car, removed her gear, and awaited the plane, now renamed *Maf Bird*. Quinn set it down two-minutes ahead of schedule. Cameron was impressed by the skillful landing as well as his punctuality. She had partnered with him for his commitment, but it now dawned on her that he was more than a passionate disruptor driven by anger. It took discipline as well as commitment to lead an organization, even one that had, unfortunately, not actually achieved much political success. He was tilting at windmills, trying to rouse an apathetic public. But perhaps he had fewer illusions about his chances of success than she had supposed. Perhaps he was driven by commitment, not expectations.

"What's that for?"

"Well, how do you expect me to get around?" Cameron asked.

"You're joking. A ninja assassin riding a bike?"

"I'm not a ninja. And don't call me an assassin."

Quinn had a great comeback, but then considered the eye-darts directed toward him. "There's plenty of room in the back." Their flight was mostly boring, especially if you define excitement as the one stop they made for refueling.

She hid under a blanket in the rear as he gassed up *Maf Bird*. The sun was near the horizon when he landed on the country road 10 miles out of town.

"Are you sure you've got everything worked out?"

"Shawn, I've been researching this guy for weeks. He has habits – you know, like game animals? Hunters learn the behavior patterns of their prey. I've learned his."

Quinn thought better than to comment on her coldness. "Okay. Well, good luck."

She unloaded her bike and supplies, and he took off for the local airport.

Her bike had an electric assist, and with the extra battery, had an honest range of about 60 miles. She only needed to travel a third of that distance to reach the public park Constable used for his morning jogs. She parked the bike in a rack, locked it, and jogged to some shrubs, where she caught some sleep.

Her watch alarm woke her a half hour before his usual jogging time. She walked up the path until she was in position. She sat down and waited. After 10 minutes, as he rounded the far bend, she leaned over holding her knee, as if in pain. He jogged right past her. "*What the fuck!*" she thought. She rose up and jogged behind him until she saw a bend thick with trees ahead. She caught up with him, and just as she passed him, she knocked him sideways into the surrounding shrubs. As another jogger stopped to look, she attended to him, apologized, and asked if he was injured.

"No, I'm fine. Just fine." He got up, and the other jogger went on his way.

"Here, you have foliage stuck to your back." As she wiped his back, she saw an opening – no one around. She stepped to his side and reached around his neck with one forearm and grabbed his head with the other, wrenching the top of his head into his shoulder. His neck cracked audibly, and as he went limp, she rolled his body into the base of the shrubs. She jumped after him and dragged the body into the spaces between the plants. She checked the view in the opposite side of the undergrowth. When nobody was in sight, she emerged and resumed her jogging, eventually making her way to a pay phone not far from her bike.

"Hi, I'll be ready to leave in an hour and 15." She retrieved her bike, switched batteries, and returned to the rendezvous point about 10 minutes before he touched down. She loaded her gear into the back and climbed in without a word.

Quinn took off without incident and gradually climbed toward cruising altitude. He turned toward her, and saw something was wrong. "How did it go?"

She held up one hand. "Not now."

He suspected the truth, and took the side of caution. Not a word passed between them until *Maf Bird* was refueled. After he got the plane back in the air, he yelled, "You can come out now." He looked back. She was still under the blanket. "We're airborne..." Finally, he understood. He was embarrassed at his obtuseness.

After a while, she crawled back into her seat. She looked exhausted. A thick silence pervaded the cabin until he had put *Maf Bird* down in Moreno Valley. As she unloaded her gear, he asked, "Are you going to call me?" He hated having to ask, as if, in her present mood, he was pestering her. "I'll need to know your plans and schedule." He turned to see her at the edge of tears. "Sandra, are you alright?"

She began sobbing. "Oh God! I never thought I'd feel like this. I mean, to actually drag a dead body..."

"If anybody deserved it…"

"I know. I know. But this is…hard…really hard." Both were silent for a while. Then she said, "I don't know if I can do this again."

Quinn was actually relieved to hear that. They were, after all, involved in serial-killing, but he felt bad for her. "Look, it's done, and the world is a better place for it."

"Don't you understand? Bentham is unlikely to change their ways until they connect his death with their practices. And one death won't make them see the pattern."

Quinn was surprised – not just at her revelation, but that he had been blind to it. Of course they wouldn't link his single death to their corporate sins. All they cared about was power – unless they realized they'd all have to pay a price. He also understood something about Cameron. Although her planning and determination were frightening in their coldness, her emotional detachment had been paper-thin. '*A façade? Or had she not understood the emotional toll of her intentions?*'

When she had unloaded the last piece of equipment, she stood there, looking at the ground, still holding her gear. "I'll call you. I'm not sure when."

She cried a bit on the drive back, more confused than sad, but she also knew what she had to do. When she reached home, her first act was to retrieve her phone from a drawer, and call Talbot. "I need to see you."

***

For once, Cameron found his small-talk protocol annoying, but it was his house; and, she suspected, also his way of maintaining control of the interchange. She kept up her end of the chitchat as best she could, and by the time they were sipping tea, had collected herself sufficiently to sound coherent.

"I hurt someone recently."

"How bad?"

"Very bad."

He nodded. "Huh. And why did you want to talk about it? Isn't that what you trained for years to do?"

"The thing is, I studied the moves. I studied the state of mind. I learned about human anatomy. The thing I couldn't study is how it actually feels to…to do that to another human being."

His eyes were clear and penetrating. Had he guessed she was talking about killing? Finally, he asked, "Was it self-defense?"

Cameron had already pondered that question a thousand times. "It was defending others. They were in great danger."

"And there was no other way?"

"None that I could see."

"You remember the principle of maintaining control. But I have also told you that if you get involved in a fight, you've already lost a measure of control."

"Tell me, Talbot, did you ever find yourself forced to fight? I mean, after you became a master."

He nodded. "A couple of times. Even a master cannot control everything all the time. So understand, Sandrina: I am not judging you; certainly not condemning. My questions are intended to clarify – more for you than for me. I can see you are troubled."

"It is a horrible thing to actually break…real bones in a real body. Not like martial arts bouts. Obviously not like the movies."

"I'd like to ask a totally different kind of question. At the moment you hurt this person, what was your state of mind?"

"My state of mind?"

"What emotions were you feeling."

"I don't mean to sound cold, but really, I wasn't feeling any emotion. I was focused entirely on my task. It was afterward that I…" here her voice dropped to almost a whisper, "…fell apart."

"Then your action was pure." He noted her quizzical look. "You weren't merely driven by emotion," he explained. "That would not be the way of a warrior. So tell me how you became upset."

"It was…" She refrained from saying, 'moving the injured person'. "It was seeing him lying limp, completely broken…"

"Could you tell me the extent of this man's injuries."

"No. I'd rather not."

Talbot raised his eyebrows.

She hated the silence. She had always confided in him in a completely open way. Did he suspect the truth?

He looked down, carefully crafting his question. "Let me ask you this: How precise were your actions?"

The question caught her off balance. "I don't know what you mean."

"Did you injure him *precisely* as you had intended"

She hesitated, but answered resolutely. "Yes."

"Then, you acted as a warrior." They were both silent for almost a minute. "Do you remember, Sandrina, what I told you when you first declared that you wanted more than mere lessons; that you wanted to become a warrior?"

She smiled. "You said that becoming a warrior wasn't fun; it wasn't even enjoyable."

He nodded. "Yet you still insisted you wanted to be a warrior. And when I asked you why, you said it was to have a purpose in your life. You wanted to be somebody...no, not somebody; something."

"I remember."

"I did not discuss it then, but we need to now. What you said was only partly true. The actual catalyst came from your childhood – your father's abandonment of the family, how you all had to live with your aunt."

"Yes, where we were tolerated. Nothing more."

"Childhood pains cut deep, Sandrina. For you, it was the helplessness before life's circumstances. When you came to me, what you were actually seeking was a source of self-reliance, a protection against the uncertainties of life."

"So, my interest in martial arts came from a neurosis?"

He chuckled. "Not at all. But the motivation went deeper than you were willing to admit to yourself. That doesn't mean it wasn't sincere." He paused as he collected his words. "Sandrina, everyone is either born off-center, or pushed there. We are supposed to find our way back. That's why we are all here. The warrior's path was your way back."

"I did feel in control of my life, thanks to you. But suddenly I'm lost, bewildered."

"The thing is, Sandrina, to act as a warrior, even after all the training and all the time and effort reaching toward perfection – to perform the acts of a warrior is also difficult. And as you have learned, even to maintain the warrior state of mind is work. That was the reason you came to me last year. By comparison, climbing high mountains is easy. For a warrior, there exists no endpoint like the top of a mountain. The only such point is death."

He nodded as the silence between them grew, but she realized it was a comfortable silence, one she had experienced many times before. *'That Talbot silence'*, she thought.

He looked up at her. "You *are* something. You are a warrior, one who, in this case, protected others. The question is, would you protect again?"

"I really don't know."

"Well, then," he said, with a sudden change in demeanor, "now you have something to meditate on."

Talbot had always called these conversations EOSs – Encounters of Souls. It was a play on the name of the Greek goddess of dawn. They always led both of them to a quiet internal place. That was his magic. His last statement and the attendant change in his bearing was an announcement: This EOS was over.

"Yes. And I will consider it carefully. Thank you, Talbot."

"And whatever you decide, Sandrina, don't be a stranger. I have a new recipe for curry chicken – one I've perfected. Let me know when you can come for dinner."

On her drive home, she considered his counsel. As usual, she would need time to digest the EOS. Midway through her study with him, she had had a period of resentment, misconstruing his control of the EOS as the action of ego. It took a few years before she understood the extent to which he exposed his own vulnerability in the process. It was when he told of his sadness over a close friendship he had broken unnecessarily. He had come near tears, something that had shocked her at the time. Her mighty warrior-teacher crying? It was then that she realized she had projected onto him her own cliché of a hero – a comic book version. In the end, he was just a man; one who had concentrated on a single area of life, one approach to living, which he continually polished to improve, and whose perfection was unreachable. But attaining perfection was not the point. One could sail north by the polar star without the illusion she would ever reach it. Still, every now and then, she wondered if he hadn't displayed that vulnerability on purpose, as a guide to her understanding, a means of diverting her from hero worship.

After several days of reflection and meditation, she called Quinn. "This has all been a giant mistake. I need to end the project."

"Then what was the point? All for nothing?"

"The plane will aid you in your own efforts, and I'll continue to pay the airport fees. I hope you can make good use of it."

"I'll keep your name in my phone, in case you change your mind."

"I won't"

***

Ten days later, she had lunch with Crother. As they began eating their salads, Cameron asked, "So how are your parents?"

"Oh they've settling in," Crother said with a look of satisfaction. "Dad doesn't have a full-time job yet, but I could tell he was feeling better. Last weekend I helped them hang some prints I bought for their home. Something to replace the yellowed ones they brought with them."

"Nothing makes a house into home as fast as putting something on the walls."

"When they first arrived, he looked like a whipped dog. But he's already met the neighbors. Seems to like them. I hope he can find full-time work soon, not so much for the money."

"You know if you ever need a helping hand…"

"I know, Sandra, and thanks. Luckily, I make enough as a dental hygienist. He just has to feel useful. You know, farmers are used to working – always something to do on a farm. That's what hurts most about big companies like Bentham. They never care about breaking people's spirit."

"Did I tell you Hollister studios wants to start a new series with me?" Her change of subject was meant to mirror her change of direction. She wanted nothing more of social activism, other than donations to worthy causes.

After lunch, they decided to shop for hats at a fashion store nearby. As they walked, the conversation paused. Cameron took in the sights, the sounds…and then she felt it. She turned around, but could see no attacker. Was she getting jumpy? But then she saw a tall man a dozen feet behind her turn off the sidewalk toward the parked cars. Behind him was a shorter man, whose eyes were locked on her. She sensed his intent and intuitively knew he had a gun.

She quickly pushed Crother through the door of a tobacco shop. "Run to the back!" Crother hesitated. "Run!" she shouted. As Crother finally responded, Cameron jumped back to the side of the door. As the man entered, he saw Crother running and didn't look to the side. He was reaching for his gun just as Cameron leaped at him and swung her elbow into his neck. The blow stunned the man. He let loose of the gun, but before it hit the ground she punched him in the kidney, then pushed his head into a cabinet. He dropped to the floor, insensate. She grabbed the gun and turned to the clerk, whose mouth hung open.

"Call the police!" By this time Crother was returning from the back of the store. She was also open-mouthed. "It's okay," Cameron said. "Everything's under control."

"What the hell? Who is this guy?"

"We'll find out later."

She visited the police station the next day. Detective Lou Patrillo led her into a private room. "Well, the perp's name is Trevane. George Trevane."

"Does he have a record?"

"Yes and no. He has no priors, but he's all over the internet. Right-wing blogs mostly."

"Right wingers? I'm not involved in any politics, except for voting every couple of years. And I often think of giving up on that. What does this have to do with me?"

"He hasn't said much, Ms. Cameron, but we got a little out of him. The gun was legal, but carrying concealed was not. And there were three witnesses, including yourself, so he's going away."

"For how long?"

Patrillo frowned. "Not long enough, as far as I'm concerned. He'll be out in a year – two at the most."

"And his motive? Why did he come after me?"

"Let's just say he uses the word _feminazi_ a lot in his blogs. Apparently, he thinks your movie depiction of – if you'll pardon the expression – an ass-kicking woman is a political statement. Like you were trying to convince the women of America to rise up and attack men."

Cameron shook her head. "Jesus! Are people crazy, or what?"

"I see it all the time; just not against movie stars. Their stalkers rarely go beyond throwing paint."

"Thanks for taking the time to explain all this, detective. Obviously, if you need me to testify, I'll be happy to oblige."

"We'll contact you. By the way, Ms. Cameron, my wife loves your movies. Would you mind autographing a card for her?"

When she returned home, she did an internet search on Trevane. Patrillo didn't exaggerate – he was a major poster on at least a half-dozen far right-wing blogs – most of them with tinges of anti-feminism, along with a dozen other 'anti' gripes. Her name came up a couple of times, though not in postings by Trevane. She turned off the computer and sat in her contemplation chair for two hours. And two hours on the next day too; and the next. And then she made the call.

"Sandra! Hi. How are you?"

"Hi Shawn. We need to talk."

***

After takeoff from Moreno Valley, Shawn asked, "You feeling alright?"

"You don't have to worry about me. I'm totally settled."

"What changed your mind?"

"I was attacked by some whacko. Right in the middle of a peaceful American city."

"Attacked? By who?"

"Some anti-feminist who decided I was the enemy."

"Wait. You mean in La Cienega?"

She nodded.

"That was you? I had no idea."

"I asked them to keep my name out of it. Or had my lawyer ask them. He got it suppressed somehow. He's good with that legal gobbledygook."

"So, *that* changed your mind?"

"It's like my teacher said: I am a warrior. More than a movie star. And there's a war on. Bentham is part of that war, just like that anti-feminist fruitcake. Who else is going to fight on our side?" She turned to him. "I've always criticized you for being ineffective. And that was true, but I've come to realize that you fight in your way, as I fight in mine. We need fighters who lead demonstrations just as much as we need people who battle physically."

"Yet here I am, not exactly following the law. If my followers discovered what I'm doing, the movement would fall apart."

"Then don't be their leader, Shawn. Teach them to be independent activists."

"Funny…Cassie said the same thing to me last month."

"Cassie?"

"Cassie Adams. She's our logistics chairwoman for MAF."

Cameron noted a slight change in his demeanor, a softening of his features. She was glad he had this connection to someone. She began massaging her hands, a nervous habit. "The thing is, Shawn, we each bring something to the battle. If I have this skill and if fate has provided me with money, it's my obligation to use these gifts for the greater good. We're all here temporarily. It's not just the money, not just the risk, and not just the time. The horror of my acts is also part of the burden I must bear."

He looked at her. "If you're all in, so am I."

She nodded, realizing that they had both come to understand each other's complexities.

That night, she climbed a gate and turned off the water supply to the home of Myron Lukas, recent VP of Bentham Corporation, now the new CEO. She went around to the east side of his two-story mansion. She lit the wicks on her two bottles of gasoline. The first one broke the window and landed a few feet inside. The second went through the hole and landed near the far wall. The fire spread quickly, setting off the alarm. Everyone exited the house and waited on the front lawn for the fire trucks. When they arrived and began putting out the blaze, all eyes were fixed on their noisy efforts. She turned on her burner phone and dialed him.

"Hello? Who is this?"

Cameron spoke softly and in a slightly garbled voice. "This is the dispatcher at the Rincaid Fire District. We have a report…"

"Could you speak up please?" he asked, as he moved away from the commotion of pumper trucks and yelling firemen.

When he had walked far enough away from everyone else, into the darkness, she leaped up and placed him in a rear choke hold. As he struggled and kicked his feet, she dragged him deeper into the shadows until she had reached the edge of the property. By that point he was dead. She pulled the body behind some small shrubs, then snuck to the rear of the yard and over the fence. Before the sun had risen, she had reached the pickup point. Fifteen minutes later, Quinn brought the plane down in an impressively smooth uphill landing.

No words passed between them as she loaded her gear into the plane and he got airborne again. Only then did he take a good look at her. "How did it go?"

"Okay. Mission complete."

"I mean, how are you holding up?"

She nodded. "Better then last time. This one was tougher – not an instant death. But I was better prepared. Emotionally, I mean. It's still hard, but I'll be alright."

"And if this doesn't get them to change?"

"I've got a third target in mind, and worked out the method. If the third one doesn't get results, I'm not sure what I'm going to do."

"I've got to be at a national meeting of MAF next month. I absolutely have to go. The organization depends on it."

"Okay, I'll make sure to leave the date open. Which hotel are you staying in?"

"I'll be doubling up in one of our member's house."

"I could pay for a hotel."

"Thanks, but they have a spare bedroom. It'll be fine."

Cameron looked at him. She suddenly saw the consequence of operating a movement for years on a shoe string. Even though it was her money, he was unable to imagine luxury. She felt a bit sorry for him, realizing his frugality had become ingrained; that he would probably never develop a sense of art or style, even if he attained success and wealth. He had become an activist machine – attuned to empathy, but not esthetics. '*What was that line? "All men are changed by what they do…"* ' She tried, but couldn't remember the name of the poem, or even the author.

She began to wonder how she too might be changing. Her movie career had led her astray from the warrior path; Talbot had helped her return. But to where would her deadly actions pull her? She could not reveal them to Talbot. How would she avoid becoming lost? The maybes and mights flowed through her mind like a rippling stream until she drifted off to sleep.

***

Her third mission finally achieved results. The corporation publicly announced changes to their business practices. She was glad, not only for the million-plus small farmers; not only for the freedom to end her horrible actions, which had pervaded her sleep and disturbed her dreams; but also for having given corporate America a warning: *There are limits to the public pain you may cause. Your wall of lawyers can be pierced.*

She called Quinn and took him to dinner to celebrate.

"How did you know I like Thai?"

"Everyone likes Thai," she said.

"I'm surprised. A normal restaurant. Not some secret retro diner at a late hour."

After they had ordered, she moved from chitchat to the heart of the matter. "We've won; I'm done. You can keep *Maf Bird* and I'll continue to donate to MAF so you'll be able to pay the fuel and airport fees.

"Actually, Sandra, maybe you're not done."

She raised her eybrows. "Shawn, you *do* understand that it's my decision to make."

"Of course. But you did what you did because the world is a cesspool. You got a whiff at one end of it, and cleaned it up. Do you really think that will be the end of it?"

"It is for me."

"Well, if I had any money, I'd bet you'll change your mind down the line. I've watched you. You're just as passionate about injustice as I am. I'm just louder about it. And...I don't know...you were probably right. Pretty ineffective."

Cameron leaned forward. "Shawn, what you do – the demonstrations, the histrionics, the crowds you raise and the news coverage you get – those are just as important as what I did. Some problems can't be solved that way, but some can – especially if the perpetrators aren't sociopaths; or if they actually care about their public image. In that case, they'll change behavior eventually. If every problem was solved by killing, the whole society would degenerate into chaos. Every time you and your followers step out and exercise your right to demonstrate and speak, you strengthen the public acceptance of peaceful change."

"Wow," Quinn said. "Maybe you should run for office. That was really stirring."

Cameron smiled, realizing she'd gotten carried away. "No. I'll stick with movies. I'm done fixing society."

"Considering the stress I saw it cause you, Sandra, I hope you're right."

***

A few months later, at the hair stylist, she saw the front page of a folded newspaper. "Vital Drug

Unaffordable," it blared. She usually avoided the news. It tended to deflate her centeredness. But, she thought, with her money, perhaps she could help people. However, the story was far different than she had anticipated: The cancer drug manufacturer had been bought by Gargoyle Pharmaceuticals, who then raised the price by ten-times.

That night, she spent a lot of time on the internet, an activity she despised because of its thievery. In her view, it robbed her of meditation and contemplation time. The next day, she called Quinn.

"Let's have coffee."

"Thai or diner?" he asked.

"Diner." After she hung up, she realized her choppy speech probably told him as much about her purpose as the choice of restaurant.

Their discussion was more relaxed than their earlier diner conversations. Quinn was familiar with Gargoyle's Gouge, as the public was calling it, and was in full agreement with her plan.

Cameron realized how far he had come. *'Did I pull him to a different mental space? Or did the success of our previous operation? Or has he been getting frustrated with his own work – a lot of effort for meager results?'* She did not voice her questions. She needed him to be focused, not distracted by psychological doubts.

The operation went smoothly, both of them familiar with their procedures – *'Is this what it's become? A routine? A routine to be killing people?'* The thought chilled her. But they were successful. The vice-president of the company replaced the deceased CEO. He immediately lowered the price to ten-percent above the original amount, and also offered discount subsidies for the poor. Cameron was glad that the operation required only one killing. *'Maybe the*

Bentham deaths sent them a message.' Whatever the reason for their quick response, she was relieved. She could get back to her own life.

Or so she thought, until she read about Kenneth Cook, director of a charity that aided starving people in central Africa. It seems the charity was mostly aiding Kenneth Cook. News organizations told of overhead costs of 40-percent, three-quarters of which were paid to Cook. The Cameron-Quinn team ended that problem with what had become a well-practiced efficiency.

'*Will this horrible burden ever end?*' she asked herself. '*Or has God or the gods or the Tao or whatever, have they created me for an unending horrible purpose?*' The second question would remain forever unsolved, but the first was soon answered. She had just finished for the day on the set of *P Is For Punish*. It was near the end of the shooting, and she was looking forward to another year off.

Chris Fernwood approached her. "Sandra, there are two men who need to see you – in A-building."

"A-building? Who?"

"I don't know." Fernwood, seeing that Cameron was about to refuse, said, "Bottoms insisted."

Bottoms was the nickname of the studio head, a nickname that described both his ample anatomical sitting equipment and his authority: His word was the bottom line.

Cameron exhaled, then said quietly, "Okay." She got in her cart and drove to the administration building. Waiting outside were two men who looked like they had just stepped from the set of *Men In Black*. Except their suits weren't black. '*Are they doing a new series? Men In Gray?*' she wondered. Even their hair was starting to turn.

She tried to imagine how colorless they would appear in 10 years.

"Ms. Cameron. Can we have a word?" They led her to an office with an oval table. Cameron surmised it was used by the studio for their most private meetings. After they were all seated, one of them said, "My name is Bill, and my partner here is Robert."

"Bill who?"

"Bill Smith."

"And Robert Smith," the other one added.

"You guys selling cough drops?" she asked.

Despite their deadpan habit, they seemed perplexed. _'Guess they never heard of Smith Brothers Cough Drops,'_ Cameron surmised. _'Or they don't get humor. After all, the initials of one of them is BS.'_ She smiled. "What can I help you two gents with?"

"Eighteen months ago you bought a plane for an organization called _Many Against The Few._"

Cameron instantly shed her fatigue. "Are you with law enforcement?"

"Let's just say we work for the federal government." BS said.

"In that case, I'll want a lawyer before I answer any of your questions."

"That won't be necessary Ms. Cameron," RS said. "We won't be asking you any questions."

Cameron was intrigued. "You just asked me about the MAF plane."

"Actually, Ms. Cameron, I _stated_ that you had purchased a plane. We don't need to ask you anything."

"That is wonderful!" She decided to play her version of their game – a pretense of civility with a dash of pepper. "Because I won't be making any statements."

RS raised his eyebrows. Was that a slight smile? BS continued. "The plane is piloted by Shawn Quinn, who flies to various places around the country. For instance, here's one place he flew last year – in April, I believe." He slid an eight-by-ten photo toward her. There was *Maf Bird* sitting on her piece of land in Moreno Valley, taken from a very high altitude – satellite photo, Cameron conjectured.

"This particular stopover wasn't listed in his flight plan. Here's another one in June."

The two photos easily made his point. These men obviously had access to high-level intelligence photos. They had an open-and-shut case against her. What they could not have known is that from the beginning, she had already dealt with the possibility of getting caught. In a hundred contemplation sessions, she had accepted that possible fate, and was prepared to face life in prison, even death with total equanimity. And this was the reason she could surprise BS and RS with a simple, "So?"

"You don't deny it?"

"You said you weren't going to ask questions."

RS spoke up. "Then take it as a statement. An observation."

"Okay," Cameron said. "Then I'll ask the same question: So?"

"The reason we are not asking questions, the reason you don't have a lawyer beside you, the reason we're not conversing in an interrogation room of a jail is not for lack of evidence," RS said. He gestured toward the two photographs in front of her, and the pile that remained in the folder in front of BS. "We are not interested in seeing you punished for the five killings – yes, we know there were five. We have allowed your rampage...excuse me. Rampage is the wrong word. I do not mean to belittle your actions. Frankly, their precision and efficiency impressed me. As I intended to say, we have allowed your actions to continue because they have helped reset the system."

He let the words sink in as Cameron absorbed this unexpected turn, carefully trying to unfold the full meaning of his words.

RS resumed. "Corporate interests have used lobbying and campaign contributions to accumulate huge amounts of power – including more money and more lobbyists, not to mention many reductions in government oversight. It had gone far enough to destabilize the system. I like to think of it ecologically: One species – say, foxes in the meadow – becomes too numerous, and eventually they eat up all the rabbits; the next year, with no rabbits to eat, they starve. You end up with no rabbits and no foxes."

"So you used me to get rid of some of the foxes?" Cameron asked.

"Used you?" he responded. "No, we had no idea of your actions until they occurred – at least, until the Lukas killing. Then we began an unofficial investigation. Let's just say you created a useful set of circumstances. The public will accept a system that contains a degree of unfairness, as long as it works well enough for them to get by."

Cameron was surprised at the similarity of his words to her own at her first meeting with Quinn.

RS summed up: "Their methods had gone too far and the system was becoming increasingly unstable – approaching the point where the people would no longer be able to get by; the point where they might rebel."

However, Cameron had noticed a glimmer of light. "Unofficial investigation? Then you're not FBI. You're CIA." She waited while BS and RS attempted to hide their reactions, but she discerned the slight straightening of their postures. "Officially, you're not allowed to investigate domestic matters."

BS spoke up. "Actually, Ms. Cameron, the law states that if we 'inadvertently'" – he displayed air quotes – "come across information within the purview of the FBI, we're supposed to turn it over to them and let them carry it to whatever conclusion they see fit."

By this time, Cameron had figured out that RS was the one with the more astute intellect. However, even though BS's threat was probably at the outer limits of his subtlety, it was still valid. "So what happens now?" she asked.

"Now?" RS responded. "Nothing. You continue to make movies and go on with your life. However, when I say 'nothing', I mean specifically no more killings. Continuation of your actions could create its own kind of instability – copycats, small private armies, and the public's expectation that only violence works. You've put enough fear into corporate heads to alter their behavior. And our occasional conversations with them, as well as with a few politicians, will reinforce the changes you've set in motion. From now on, they'll keep their greed and their lust for control within acceptable boundaries."

Cameron realized they wanted a promise. She also realized that if actions similar to hers were needed in the future, BS and RS would find some other means to make them happen. "I can agree to desist, but only if Shawn Quinn is untouched; and if he is allowed to continue his demonstrations and organizing activities."

"Absolutely," BS answered. "As long as they are legal, we have no interest in them."

"In fact," RS added, "his activities provide both hope and an outlet for individuals with…let's call them 'heightened political passions'. And also, they do provide a slight brake on the activities of the powerful."

BS retrieved his photographs, and closed his briefcase. Cameron was relieved. The ordeal was over.

"And by the way, Ms. Cameron," RS said, "my whole family loves your movies."

"I'm glad. Perhaps you'd like my autograph?"

"On the contrary. Since this meeting never took place and we've never met, I could never have gotten your autograph. But thanks, anyway."

Defeat of the Croutonians

"Hi, Lester. How ya doin' there?"

"Well, I'm not so sure, Travis. That's why I'm callin'. Maybe you could give me a bit of advice."

"Sure 'nuff, Lester. What's the problem?"

"Well, 'bout five minutes ago this object came out of the sky…"

"Now hang on, Lester. Are you pulling my leg? Because if you are, I got to git back to helpin' Sally pick some apples. I'd love to talk with ya, but let's do this later."

"Travis, this isn't no joke and I might as well add, I haven't been drinking. Haven't had even a beer since last night. So don't lay this on brew, either."

"OK, I'm a listenin'"

"This object came down from the sky and is sitting in my field right now."

"When you say object, what exactly do you mean? Like a meteor?" Travis said.

"This isn't no meteor. It's like a cylinder, about 20-foot diameter and at least 50-foot tall, and looks man-made. And it didn't fall, like fast. It dropped down quickly until it was a hunnert feet above the ground, and then it settled down nice and slow."

"Maybe it's one of them government space devices. What's it doing now?"

"Nothin' right now. But what I wanted your opinion on is this: Should I call the authorities? I kinda hate to have government people lookin' 'round the farm."

"Understood. Not with your pot patch out back. Look, I'll be over in 15 minutes."

A quarter-hour later, the two men stood silently a hundred yards from the mysterious object. Finally, Travis said, "Lester, it don't look like no Muslim thing, but still, I think we need to play it safe. Better call Sheriff Decker."

A half-hour later, three men stood silently a hundred yards from the mysterious object. Finally, the sheriff said, "I don't see no Chinese writing on it, but that don't prove nothin'. I'm calling Sam Pouch at the FAA."

An hour later, four men stood silently a hundred yards from the mysterious object. Finally, Pouch declared, "Well, I'll be."

The crowd continued to grow a bit faster than the wheat surrounding the mysterious object. By the next morning it comprised two dozen men and women, including agents from the FBI, NSA, and a couple of military generals. Given the small size of nearby Lebanon, Kansas, this activity seemed frenetic. Word reached the media, and soon the police were spending more time keeping the hundred cameras from the mysterious object than placing a cordon around it in case it did...what? But at exactly noon, it did what it did.

From the side of the cylinder, a door opened downward, forming a ramp. A single man, thin and swarthy, walked down and approached the circle of soldiers. His appearance seemed mostly normal, except for his large eyes and his head, which was abnormally tall; and, of course, his mode of transportation.

General David Whiteman stepped forward. Noting the brown skin, he searched back in his distant memory to his high school classes. "¿Como se llama?" The brown man just tilted his head, obviously confused. Whiteman tried switching languages. Pointing to his chest, he said "Me General Whiteman. You speakee English?"

"A damned sight better than you, apparently. Where is everyone?"

Whiteman looked at him suspiciously. "Just who were you expecting to meet here?"

"According to our geo-locaters, this is the exact center of your country. So where is everyone?"

"Yes, it's the exact center. So what's that to you?"

"We come bearing gifts of knowledge and technology, but we expected the center of your country to be the most populated and most advanced part of it – like the hive of an ant colony; or a fungus in a petri dish."

"Just who are you and where are you from, mister?" demanded Whiteman

"My apologies. My name is Gropik, and we are from the planet Crouton in the planetary system around the star we call Uneeun."

Whiteman was startled. "What do you mean 'we'? How many others aboard your ship?"

"Oh, it's just me and my copilot," Gropik replied.

Whiteman was perplexed at Gropik's lack of understanding. "And just what is this technology, Mr. Gropik?"

"No offense, General, but we intended to make our announcements to a larger audience. You understand: PR and all that."

"Well, Lebanon has about 250 people – not exactly the size you probably had in mind. I suggest you try one of the major cities – Los Angeles, f'rinstance."

"And would you be so kind as to point me in the correct direction?"

"It's mostly thataway," Whiteman said pointing west-by-southwest. "Out by the edge of this country."

"Many thanks," Gropik relied cheerfully.

"Happy to help. And also, I have to ask you not to land here again. I'd rather not have to arrest you for trespassing. You're welcome to use our public parking in town, if you like to come back. It's right across from the Country Central diner. Their pie is a killer."

Gropik rolled his large eyes, turned around, and reentered the cylinder, which quietly rose and disappeared into the sky.

A few minutes later, it landed in Los Angeles. Gropik departed his craft with Zartlik, and the pair quickly become the bullseye of concentric rings of police, television crews, and onlookers. They turned to face the cameras. "Earthlings," Gropik announced, "we come bearing gifts of knowledge and technology. They will save your planet from the coming catastrophe."

The two of them attempted to walk toward the cameras, but were blocked by the police. One man walked past the ring of officers. "I'm Chief Myron Hardman of the of the Los Angeles Police Department. I'm afraid you're not going anywhere. You're under arrest."

Gropik and Zartlik looked at each other. Then Gropik asked, "For what?"

"For...hang on a second." After conferring with the DA for about a minute, he said, "For entering the country illegally...unless you can produce a green card."

He thought his statement had not been picked up by the media. But the cordon of officers were useless in the era of modern technology. Unknown to him, electric drones had flown the hundred yards beyond the media line to record both his image – which, given his bald head and the view from above, was not flattering – and his words, which also were not flattering.

The public responded with a great commotion. The next day's headlines read, "Even Little Green Men Need Green Cards?" and "When Jesus Returns, Will He Get Arrested?" The DA tried to soothe the public's indignation by announcing, "The illegal immigration charge has been dropped, but the two suspects have been charged with landing an aircraft illegally, and failure to produce proper identification when requested by police."

That stratagem lasted for almost an hour, battered by public demonstrations that acclaimed "…these emissaries from the heavens." Talking heads on radio and television praised, "…our brothers from the stars." And social media went viral with millions of "likes" attached to helium-light discussions about, "…our last chance to save us from ourselves." But perhaps what ensured their release were the quiet phone calls from a few specific people: From CEOs stressing the importance of the unknown technologies to their respective companies, which, coincidentally, were big contributors to election campaigns. The governor reminded the mayor of the jobs the new technologies would mean to the state. The president called to remind them of the importance to national security: The alien technologies might give us a jump on China and Russia. Local defense companies publicly hinted at jobs the new weapon systems might create, based on "the visitors' advanced technologies". And the wives of both the DA and chief called to remind them not to be late – they had to drive their sons and daughters to baseball games, school plays, music lessons, etc.

After Gropik and Zartlik were released, they announced that they would make a public proclamation the following day at noon. By 10:00 am, a huge crowd had gathered to hear this first announcement of technology brought to Earth from beyond our solar system. By the time Gropik and Zartlik arrived, the crowd had grown to 50,000 people, who cheered them as frenetically as any rock concert audience. The occupations among the crowd were probably a full spectrum mixture, but the most coveted places – those closest to the two 'stellar emissaries', as they were now officially named – were reserved exclusively for politicians and leaders of the largest corporations. By previous arrangement, several of the politicians made introductory speeches.

Mayor Crotch declared, "We proudly welcome these stellar emissaries to Los Angeles, the diamond of the west coast, the sapphire by the sea, the…blah blah…"

Governor Nacho praised, "These two saviors who have chosen the Golden State as the portal to humankind…blah blah…"

And so the drone continued through a dozen more politicians until the truly important people stepped up to the mike. Robert McLouch, chairman of FireAnt Industries, a military contractor, praised, "our new allies in the battle against tyranny and terrorism, the twin evils of our times."

Steven Evan, CFO of OFC Technology commended "these two angels who have come from the heavens to advance our technology beyond anything our competitors can even imagine."

Larry Sackless of Whizbang Worldwide spoke of how "this contact with a higher civilization would advance our entertainment not by months or years, but by centuries."

During all this official boredom, within the crowd, scantily clad, green-painted women kicked their legs cancan style, which made the spring-mounted eyeballs on the top of their heads bounce in every direction. Gropik looked at Zartlik, but he was equally mystified.

Finally, Gropik was given a chance to speak. "Earthlings, we have come to help you. Your civilization, your very planet, is facing catastrophe. We will give you the means to avoid that, and in the process, live happier and more fruitful lives."

The politicians and corporate chiefs seated at the adjoining tables led the crowd in applause.

Gropik continued. "Each month, we will release to your world one piece of technology. After 30 months, you will have sufficient technology to transform your planet to a paradise. I will take questions now."

"Sir, George Grub of KBC news. Why only one per month? Why not give us the whole 30 and get it over with? You know, like a package deal."

"After we reveal the engineering drawings and formulas, it will take at least a month to confer with your scientists and engineers. We will need to explain the principles to your technicians, and also assist your governments in decisions regarding integrating the devices into your infrastructure. Further, some of the technology is sequential. You will need the previous devices to make the subsequent ones functional."

"Mr. Alien, will your technologies come with instruction manuals; and in how many languages?"

Gropik looked at Zartlik who looked equally perplexed. "Uhh, that will be up to Earth scientists."

"Mr. Gropik, the people of Earth want to know…"

After the third question, the crowd began to chant, "No more questions! Release an invention! No more questions! Release an invention!"

Eventually, the press was cowed into silence. Gropik finally announced, "Technology number 1 is being transmitted at this moment. We will leave you now and confer with your scientists and engineers."

Everyone switched to their cell phones and tablets. After a half-minute, they could see an image of a large box with mostly smooth sides and rounded edges. Two large cables protruded from the top. The crowd was disappointed at its apparent lack of a camera – in fact, not even a screen – but the experts were not. Scrolling through the pages, scientists, engineers and reporters discovered it was a power generator. What was truly shocking was the table of specifications: The package, approximately the size of a sedan, would produce over 1600 megawatts of power – as much as an entire utility generating facility! Even more important, the device used nuclear fusion, a goal that scientists had been attempting to achieve for decades. And perhaps best of all, it could use any substance for fuel, converting the forces binding atomic particles into energy. A single rock the size of a fist could power a town for a month. The environmentalists especially loved it, because it produced no CO2 and no radioactive waste; every gram of matter was converted into energy.

The media went wild. Television talk shows could discuss no other subject. Soap operas were preempted by a new genre – science operas, where men and women grew passionate with talk of 'dirty energy' vs. 'good, clean heat'. The music group *DT3* renamed themselves, *Radioactive Rocks*, only to be sued by an online porn site of the same name. And comedy shows were preempted by panels of engineers and scientists discussing with Saharan dryness the manufacture of the new generators.

However, within three days, the flaw in the entire plan became evident. The newly-formed group URGE – Unemployment Risk to a Good Economy – warned of the threat to jobs if the new devices replaced the, "good old American can-do generators" that had "traditionally provided the electrons that made America the most powerful country on Earth." Television commercials featured hard-hatted workers with remarkably clean fingernails who talked of losing the ability to feed their families – presumably the dispirited-looking ones in the background wearing tight-fitting jeans and pristine straw hats. Ordinary-looking men and women in front of *Dawkins Hardware Store* and *The Goodfellow Cafe* talked of their small cities – the one where their dads and granddads grew up – turning into ghost towns. CEOs of oil companies talked in breaking voices of, "the terrible burden of laying off our workers, with whom we have shared a long and rewarding relationship". Coincidentally, a madame in North Dakota used identical language regarding her customers.

Meanwhile, Stanley A. Tzap, chairman of Sparkland Power LLC, a major electrical utility, spoke of the dangers of fusion reactors. "If this reactor core overloaded even once, it would destroy our entire country – and the rest of the world with it." Other power companies sent letters to shareholders – which included government pension funds – warning of the costs of replacement of their current equipment, along with the elimination of dividends for several years. And Rick Santelli redirected his usual rants toward the "threat of a radioactive economy".

Eventually, the president and various members of congress spoke reassuringly of their commitment to, "defend America from this alien assault on the American way of power." By the end of the month, the people had turned against the "new energy gizmos", and congress passed a law forbidding the building of fusion reactors for commercial purposes.

"Can you believe it?" Gropik said. "They're rejecting our energy generators. It took our ancestors a whole century to create a working model."

"This is a really strange species," Zartlik observed. "One day we're heroes, and a month later we're villians."

Gropik nodded. "Well, there's no point in presenting them our technology for worldwide wireless transmission of power. I think we should just skip that one."

At their next press conference, the crowd was only about one-fourth as large.

Gropik had decided the best approach was to begin by defining the problem. "The population of the world is increasing and within a century will reach at least 10 billion. Simultaneously, your world is losing 38,000 square miles of arable land each year. Our calculations show that by the end of this century, half the people of this world will starve. We will provide a solution to prevent that catastrophe. Technology number 2 is a machine that utilizes a new method of agriculture. It will allow growing food in cities and in rural areas of the world currently suffering drought. This advanced form of agriculture will ensure that no one in your world need starve. It's design and specifications are being transmitted at this moment. As before, we will leave you now to confer with your scientists and engineers."

Once again, radio and television time was fully booked with talk of the "third agricultural revolution". Foodies cheered the coming end of GMOs; food banks welcomed the day their vital mission would no longer be needed; ministers spoke of the end of starvation, and with it, the end of poverty as, "well-fed humanity could become productive, enterprising people the world over."

And the praise extended beyond the West. Within a few hours, African leaders were sitting before cameras, praising the Crutonians in general, and Gropik and Zartlik in particular. Weighty discussions among weighty African leaders provided hope to millions of their skinny, starving people.

"You know," began Kwambu Zinizit, president of the Republic of Eskoto, "in the Bible, the Israelites are fed by Manna from heaven. The Crutonians have come from heaven, and their farming methods will provide our manna."

Lamuda Rikikaka, president of North Regalia, disagreed. "The Israelites then and the Israelis today were never favored by God. However, President Zinizit is correct: These new farming methods will cut the bonds of dependency on American-grown food. We will become self-sufficient. Allah has blessed us with these prophets from the stars."

President Dolomento of the South-Central African Republic was more cautious. "I see only one problem with the optimism of my esteemed fellow African leaders. The information provided us has been examined by our engineers. They all agree that we lack the sophisticated technology to manufacture the devices. That means we will be dependent on the richer countries to build them. And what terms will they impose on us?"

He need not have worried. Within two days, CRAP – the Coalition for Raising Agricultural Prosperity – pointed out that widespread implementation of the new devices and methods would eliminate jobs. "What will the two-million farm workers do? Their families will starve." Fertilizer and pesticide companies' ad campaigns encouraged people to stick to "food raised as nature intended". And corporate agribusinesses warned of "possible radiation from the mysterious devices." Television commercials featured cowboy-hatted workers with remarkably clean fingernails who leaned on combine machines and talked of losing the ability to feed their families – the dispirited-looking ones in the background wearing tight-fitting jeans and pristine cowboy hats. Ordinary-looking men and women in front of *Hawkins Hardware Store* and *The Goodwoman Cafe* talked of their small cities – the one where their dads and granddads grew up – turning into ghost towns.

Senator Vernon Fernwood of Kansas reminded people of Jefferson's belief in the yeoman farmer tilling his land "as the backbone of democracy", and although Senator Yeaman of New York pointed out "that Jefferson also believed in the backbone of Sally Hemmings," in the end, Congress passed a law restricting, "the building or shipping across state lines of any of the aforementioned machines, their parts, or their engineering drawings."

In effect, the plan was dead. Gropik and Zartlik found it all incomprehensible. "I think we should go directly to number 30," Gropik said.

At first, Zartlik was confused. "Number 30? Why would we do that?"

"The reactions I've seen on their visual devices and printed materials all seem to hark back to money – you remember seeing all those little pieces of green paper."

"You mean the ones they need to get services and objects?" Zartlik asked.

"Exactly. Well, as near as I can determine, our first two attempts failed because they would have interfered with large amounts of money from very large enterprises. But number 30 only interferes with waste disposal companies. They aren't that big, so they can't move their government to ban our gifts to their planet."

"Well, that's just it," Zartlik said with disgust. "We offer them priceless gifts – ones they need to save their putrid civilization – and they reject them. They act as if accepting them would be doing *us* a favor.

"I'm a bit frustrated too," Gropik admitted, "but I think we need at least one victory – one thing they love – to get them on our side. It will make them more receptive to the rest of the list."

The next day, the crowds were small, and only two television crews and two newspaper reporters bothered to attend. The local mayor was the only politician to speak, and his talk was uncharacteristically short.

Gropik spoke in a tone that imitated as closely as he could that of the politicians he had seen on television.

"Technology number 3 is the most tremendous, hugest, grandest and most American technology devised since the founding of this glorious nation. It is a form of nanotechnology we call *Red, White, and Blue Recycling*. Using these patriotic RWB devices, literally 99% of your hard-working Americans' trash will be broken into its individual molecules, separated and sorted into purified raw materials, to be reused in the manufacture of new goods. No longer will foreign countries take advantage of this generous nation by selling you *their* copper, *their* titanium, or any of *their* other materials."

"Sir, Ted Lipschitz of Sticktown Gazette. My question is, will we still have to separate paper from plastic?"

Gropik was struck dumb, so Zartlik spoke up. "Only if you want to."

"Sir, Marie Erie from KLAM TV. How much radioactivity will the machines produce?"

By this time, Gropik had recovered sufficiently to speak. "None, Ms. Erie. Why would you think they would produce radioactivity?"

"Well, your power generators would have if the government hadn't intervened."

Gropik was about to argue with Ms. Erie when Zartlik announced, "The design and specifications are being transmitted at this moment. As before, we will leave you now to confer with your scientists and engineers."

Almost immediately, environmental groups lauded the new technology. "Finally, we can stop polluting the oceans," stated John Erikson of the Save Our World foundation. Robin Murphy of the Save Our Manufacturing foundation spoke of, "...our ability to lower prices as the cost of raw materials drops to nearly zero." Zelda Markus, president of the Save Our Oil Refineries foundation praised, "...this new device, which will make pollution control a thing of the past. Residue chemicals will be reduced back to their original elements, to be reused repeatedly. The costs of EPA regulations will drop to nearly nothing, saving us billions annually." Even politicians commended the technology. Senator Dreg of Kentucky stated, "Reducing our dependency on foreign nations – including many who don't like us – will make us more secure."

However, within three days, lobbyists from several companies made appointments with members of congress, pointing out the main defect in the devices – they would halt mining operations across the globe as manufacturing industries recovered and recycled the minerals used in their goods. Shipping companies would have to scrap their vessels. Ore refineries would be shuttered. Ports would have to close many of their berths. Ultimately, unemployment across all these sectors would rise. And who would be blamed? Why, the very member of congress sitting opposite each lobbyist. And who would help them get blamed? Why the very company the lobbyist represented.

Almost overnight, newspaper editorials had reversed their opinions, warning now of the threat posed by the new devices. Sunday talk shows featured old talking heads possessing new expertise. George Willy quoted statistics from the American Hernia Institute estimating unemployment rising to, "between five and eleven percent." Ann Crackers declared, "Our founding fathers knew something like this would eventually threaten our freedom." Television commercials featured hard-hatted workers with remarkably clean fingernails who stood next to belching ore smelters and talked of losing the ability to feed their families – the dispirited-looking ones standing outside a chain-link fence wearing tight-fitting jeans and spotless baseball caps with American flag emblems on the front. Ordinary-looking men and women in front of the *Squawkin' Hardware Store* and *The Good Ol' Boys Cafe* talked of their small cities – the one where their dads and granddads grew up – turning into ghost towns.

And Senator Dreg of Kentucky opined, "These devices would destroy valuable trade ties with our friends overseas, encouraging them to form alliances with other nations – including many who don't like us."

Zartlik turned off the television. "Do you think we'll ever be able to help this planet?"

Gropik paused for several seconds. "Time to go home."

"What? Wait! What about the mission? If we leave now, we arrive home as failures."

"How do you compute that?"

"Well, it's obvious," Zartlik replied with irritation. "Our mission was to save this planet from the coming disasters. According to our mathematicians, climate change will collapse civilization in approximately three centuries; collapse of other animal populations from pollution will eventually expand to humans in a century-

and-a-half; and resource depletion will begin shrinking the global economy within less than a century. Our assignment was to prevent all of these. If we leave now, we fail at all three."

"Do you remember the history of the Maclons? How our ancestors advised them to poison all the ectsins that were eating their jharush crop?"

"Yes, of course," replied Zartlik. "That was one of the early courses in our training for missionary certification."

"The point of it being...?"

"Well, in attacking one problem, you might be ignoring the bigger picture. When the ectsins were eradicated, the jharush spread so fast, it destroyed several other food crops. They didn't understand that the jharush itself could become a bigger problem."

"Exactly."

Zartlik was silent for several seconds. "I think it's a bad analogy. Our efforts were specifically designed with attention to the rest of the planet's ecology."

"However," Gropik said, "what if the problem isn't just the numbers of humans and their ecological footprint? What if that's just a symptom?"

"Of what?"

"Of...of...of whatever we should call their kind of insanity."

Zartlik was very still. "At the moment, I can't think of a name either; but you're right. It is a strange kind of madness. But how did such a twisted mentality produce an advanced civilization?"

"I don't know, but I do know this is more than just a technical problem."

Zartlik was silent for several seconds, then looked at Gropik. "Yes. Time to go home."

Eden and the Sugar Tree

Of course Charlie was nervous. He'd never stood on that side of a television camera. And he certainly never imagined he'd be on Wendy For Women, his image and words streamed to millions of viewers. As he waited behind the side curtain, he followed the advice from a web page: deep breaths held for a count to five, then slowly released. He waited for her cue.

"And now I want to introduce you all to a fabulous cook I recently discovered in the city of Eugene, Oregon. The restaurant he oversees is only slightly upscale, but the food is incredible. More important, it turns out this chef has a deep concern for healthy eating. So at this time, I want to present to you Master Chef Charlie Krale."

With that, she held out her hand toward Charlie, who emerged onto the stage with the smile he had practiced in front of a mirror – not too wide; a modest display of teeth. He sat in a chair kitty-corner to Wendella Brolin, producer and host of the most popular daytime show in the world. The hundred or so audience members, mostly women, all smiled enthusiastically.

"I want to say that when I stopped in your restaurant, it was not because of any reviews or even word-of-mouth. I was just hungry and on my way to the Eugene Airport. It was pure serendipity."

"It was for me too, Wendy. When Nancy came back and told me you had entered our restaurant, I was sure she was ribbing me."

"And I want to tell my audience that not only was the food fabulous, but Charlie gave me a tour of the kitchen. His attention to the healthfulness and purity of the ingredients is remarkable." Turning back to Charlie, she said, "Perhaps you could tell us how you decided to become a chef, and why you chose to focus so strongly on the health aspect of cooking."

With this prompt, Charlie went into his personal history, telling of childhood angst over his mother's illness, of his years observing friends' and relatives' medical problems. "I became convinced that at least half the ailments could be remedied with a proper diet. I'm not just referring to avoiding antibiotics and pesticides, but more important, sugar and white flour. One of my cousins was able to improve her hormonal imbalance through diet alone."

"Are you saying that sugar and white flour are more important than pesticides?"

Turning toward the camera, he said. "I want to be clear. Avoiding pesticides and antibiotics is important. But Americans eat colossal amounts of sugar. Sugar puts heavy stress on the body's biology – we're talking the pancreas and the liver, and also, it can cause permanent damage to nerve tissues. And white flour is harmful because during the digestive process, the body transforms it into sugar very rapidly. Both of those foods might be organic, prompting people to think they're wholesome, but they're inherently unhealthy."

"So, your original motivation toward cooking came from observing others' illnesses," Wendy prompted.

"Watching others control or even correct medical problems through dietary changes was rewarding, but I could also see how unpleasant some of those healthier foods could be. It made me understand the difficulty people have sticking to healthy diets. I made it my mission to do something about that – to make food that was both healthy and tasty."

The interview continued until the commercial break, after which Charlie put together a quick dish – vegetarian, so none of the viewers would tweet about Wendy 'aiding and abetting animal suffering' – created the sauce, and combined the ingredients. During the 10-minute process, he kept up a well-prepared dialogue about the unique health qualities of each ingredient. Portions were then passed around to audience members, who oohed and awed appropriately.

***

"How did it go?" Amanda Krale asked.

"Just about perfect," Charlie said. "Once I began the walk-on, all my nervousness dissolved. And you were right. Nobody was wearing woolen slacks."

"As I said, just be yourself. People today want authenticity." She paused as she reconsidered. "Then again, some celebrities work pretty hard to be 'authentic'," she said with air quotes.

"And afterward, Wendy said it was the smoothest first-time rollout she'd ever seen."

"She probably says that to all the guests. This is Hollywood, after all. Anyway, I hope it will boost the restaurant."

"We'll know in a week, after it airs. But there's more." He waited till her anticipation had peaked. "She wants me to come back next month."

Amanda's mouth opened wide. "Wow! That is great." She paused. "I don't know if I can take more time off. You might have to do it alone."

"I can handle it. I'm thinking, maybe this could do more than increase our restaurant traffic."

"Like...?"

"Like if I could get my own show. You know, like *Mike's Cuisine*? I saw a photo of him in a magazine. Inside his house. Honey, I don't know the square footage, but the place looked fit for a king. It was gorgeous."

"Aren't you getting ahead of yourself here? It's only one more appearance, right?"

"Sure. But maybe something bigger comes of it. I'm just sayin'."

"Okay. Doesn't hurt to dream. For now, lets do some celebrating. Hollywood has got to have some nice restaurants."

But Charlie's dream became prophetic. His return appearance was as successful as the first, which prompted a third. Within six months Lax Broadcasting had contacted him about doing his own show.

***

"How much?!"

"You heard right," Charlie told his wife. "And more than that, they'll pay all moving expenses and provide us a rental for two months so we can find a house."

"I guess I could find a teaching position in Los Angeles. I'll probably have to take the state exams there, but that shouldn't be difficult."

Charlie said, "And, the sale of the restaurant and our home should bring us a wad of cash. Honey, this is the dream of a lifetime."

Amanda looked over the top of her rectangular glasses. "Do you realize that once you become a celebrity, our lives are going to get a lot more complicated. It's going to be difficult to go to a movie without people wanting your autograph."

"Makes sense. But that's a problem I'd love to have."

Leonard Morris, Charlie's producer, suggested *Health In Charlie's Kitchen* for the show's name. Unfortunately, the media would eventually abbreviate the title to HICK, but what would they have done with Charlie's original idea, the *Anti-Sugar Show*?

Morris also referred Charlie to Pierce Acton, an agent with two decades experience handling the careers of several famous celebrities. Acton pulsed with intensity. He leaned forward most of the time, elbows on the desk, eyes peering over his glasses. His dark complexion increased the effect of his stare. Though Charlie didn't know it, he was receiving the standard introductory speech. "I know where you're coming from. You're only thinking of a show. You visualize cooking, giving out recipes and a few cooking tips. I hate to say it, Charlie, but you're thinking way too small."

"Okay, Pierce. So, what should I be thinking of?"

Charlie's response pleased Acton. So many of his clients had begun their relationship overawed by their own talent. He usually had to patiently steer them toward possibilities they could not envision. It was like trying to turn a giant oil tanker traveling at full speed. But Charlie had immediately asked for advice. "Charlie, every show host makes money based on his ratings – the number of viewers. You get viewers by promotion. You promote through several paths. Your first path is appearances on other people's shows – Ellen, Jimmy Fallon, The Daily Show, and so forth."

"Yeah. Leonard mentioned that."

"Did he mention magazines?"

"No."

"Merch?"

"What?"

"Merchandise," Acton explained.

"Like…"

"Okay. Here's a standard summary of bases we'll need to cover." He handed Charlie a half-inch thick folder. "First, you do the show tour. In the meantime, we'll compose a profile on you – bio highlights, basically. After the show circuit is done, you'll begin a series of interviews with journalists. In no time, your face will be on all the magazines at the supermarket checkout counters."

"Does that include *Guns and Ammo?*"

Acton had to check Charlie's expression to be certain he was joking. Some of his clients actually *were* that dumb. "In the meantime, I'm going to set you up with a web developer. You're going to need an online presence too."

Charlie began shaking his head. "Okay, Pierce. Looks like I have a lot of work ahead – I mean besides the show."

"It's going to be a hectic first six months. We've got to hit it hard at the beginning, because if your numbers aren't good for that period, you get canceled."

"What? I have a one-year contract."

"Read the fine print. You're guaranteed only three shows."

"Tell me the truth, Pierce. What are my odds?"

"Way better than most. First, you've got the Wendy for Women audience at the starting gate. And from what I see, you're smarter than a lot of my clients. Plus you know your stuff when it comes to healthy cooking. And you got me. Not to brag, but my record is better than average."

"Yeah, Leonard said you were the best. You mentioned merchandise?"

"We wait on that. It does little good to bring that out early. It comes after the talk shows and magazine interviews. The whole process is choreographed. Everything's explained in the folder."

When Charlie got home, Amanda asked, "How did the meeting go?"

"I've got two full platters of tasks ahead." He recounted everything that had transpired with Acton.

"Charlie, what good is it if you burn yourself out? You'll need some downtime."

"Honey, it's like Pierce said: 'You've got to stoke the coals while they're hot.'"

"Huh? That doesn't even make sense. If the coals are hot, you don't have to stoke them. It's when they start to cool."

Over the years, Charlie had learned to expect her linguistic critiques. He took it as a sign of affection that she never took issue with his own common vernacular. "Hollywood speak, I guess. Anyway, he's got a lot more experience than us. He's also going to get me into merchandise."

"Merchandise?"

"You know, like tee shirts, recipe books, cookware, and who knows what else. And did I mention the driving? It took me almost an hour to get home on the unfreeway."

"I know. It takes me 45 minutes to get to the school. And that's assuming no one decides to run into someone else."

***

Three weeks later, Charlie answered the doorbell.

"Charlie Krale?"

"Obviously"

"Uh, okay. I'll take your word for it. I'm Benny Nerdson. Pierce said you'd be expecting me." The pale complexion and indifferently combed hair told Charlie he was a work-at-home kind of guy.

"You've never seen me on TV?" Charlie asked.

"Actually, I don't watch cooking shows. I usually settle for frozen dinners."

"I see."

"My web work keeps me pretty much glued to the keyboard. Though I do stream movies. Have you seen *Pork Papoose* yet?"

"I think I missed that one. I keep pretty busy myself."

"Anyway, Pierce pretty much filled me in with what you guys are looking for. I'll just need you to look up the bio notes he gave me, add or subtract as you want. Oh, and I'll need some photos – any family pictures, childhood photos – anything you'd like to have on one of the web pages."

"Honestly, Benny, I haven't given much thought about a website."

"No problem. They're standard templates. We just fill in the blanks – which photos to use, color preferences. Oh, and Pierce mentioned recipes. He wants a weekly recipe page."

"Just out of curiosity, Benny, who's paying you?"

"Well, indirectly, that would be you. But you don't have to worry. The bill will go to Pierce. He'll pay it out of the promotion fund. You won't have to be bothered with it."

"It seems my entire new career revolves around things I'm not supposed to be bothered with."

"Yeah. I get that a lot from celebrities."

"It's beginning to seem like I'm just everyone else's puppet. Guess I shouldn't complain. The money's nice."

"Oh, one more thing: My name gets posted at the bottom of each page. Small lettering in the corner that links to my commercial page. Helps me drum up more business."

"Seems fair enough," Charlie said. He led Nerdson into the dining room, and motioned him to a chair. As Nerdson began removing objects from his laptop briefcase, Charlie said, "Can I get you some coffee or tea?"

"No thanks, just a Coke Classic."

"Uh, I only have the sugar-free."

Nerdson looked at him with raised eyebrows. "Seriously? Okay, that'll be fine."

After they were both seated, Nerdson said, "So let's get to it. I've got some great ideas for wallpaper."

"Wallpaper?"

"Yeah. That's the background that appears on every page of your website. Obviously, for yours, it should be food. I have three ideas." Nerdson turned the laptop. Three images were on the screen. Nerdson clicked on the first, and it expanded.

"Those are donuts and maple bars," Charlie observed.

"Yeah, looks delish, huh? This one's even better." He clicked and the next image appeared.

"Cream cake? Really?" Charlie brought his head close to Nerdson's. "Are you aware that my show is about *healthy* cooking? As in low- to no-sugar?"

"No, I wasn't. So, sugar's not healthy?"

"I'm curious, Benny. What do you do to protect whales?"

"Huh?"

"Well, you're wearing that lovely *Save the Whale* tee shirt." In truth, it wasn't lovely, though it might have been three years earlier.

"Oh, this was just a gift from my girlfriend – actually, my ex. She's an activist. Not that I don't believe in saving the whales. It seems like a good thing."

"Well, I'm as passionate about healthy eating as your ex is about saving whales. So, no sugar, no pastries, no junk food. Okay?"

"Well, what else can we use for wallpaper?"

"I have some photos that will be going into a cookbook I'm assembling. Why don't I email them to you, and you can choose some of them?"

"Hey! That's tidal, man."

An hour later, right after Charlie's ordeal had ended, Amanda arrived home. "Who was that who just left?"

"That was our hope for the nation's future. And I should mention, God help us."

***

After several months of promotions, the name *Charlie Krale* was as familiar to Americans as Wendy's. Even the summer reruns of his shows brought in a fortune, and the new line of Charlie Krale TV dinners sold almost as fast as the markets could stock them. As Acton had predicted, his photos were on several magazine covers. The _Grease and Grass_ cover depicted him in knight's armor fighting off some kind of sugar cookie; and _Vacuous Vegan_ showed him machine-gunning the Pillsbury Doughboy. And still the rollout continued.

"Charlie? Pierce here. Can you come by tomorrow afternoon. Say 3:00?"

"Sure, why?"

"I need you to meet someone."

Charlie didn't ask for more details; he had learned to trust Acton, who always delivered as promised. As usual, Charlie tried to arrive a few minutes early, but traffic had been even worse than its usual horrid mess.

"Charlie, I want you to meet Jack Ditter. He's going to write your autobiography."

"What?"

"Your autobiography. It's in the folder I gave you at our first meeting."

"I thought _auto_biography meant I was supposed to write it."

Ditter answered. "I don't do much cooking, Mr. Krale. How many books have you written?" Ditter's magenta scarf suited his profession, though not the warm day. Charlie considered complimenting his 'nice uniform', but that would have to include his unnatural tan. '_Chemical or tanning bed_?' Charlie wondered.

Instead, he nodded and said, "I get your point. And call me Charlie." Then turning to Acton, he said, "Isn't this fakery? I mean, if my fans found out I misrepresented..."

Acton raised his hand. "Relax, Charlie. That's not how Hollywood works. Nobody in this town actually writes their autobiography."

"You mean, Seaborne's autobio was ghostwritten?"

"Actually, I won't be ghosting," Ditter said. "The cover will say, 'by Charlie Krale with Jack Ditter'. That way, you can never be accused of deception – provided the narrative you give me is reasonably close to actual events."

"Well, I'm not sure my life was at all interesting until my Wendy For Women appearance."

"That's no problem," Ditter said breezily. "I'll make it interesting. We don't have to lie, just dress up the facts a bit. Think of it as a fairly plain woman donning a low cut dress and applying makeup, and voilà! She looks stunning. I do it all the time."

'I don't doubt that,' thought Charlie.

Later, he told Amanda of the meeting.

"But you'll get to approve it after he's written it?" she asked.

"No, actually, Pierce reads it first. He'll decide on whatever corrections are needed to promote my image. Then he'll send it to me, though apparently, that's just a formality."

Amanda opened her mouth, but said nothing at first. "A formality? Charlie, that's becoming the story of your life. Your opinion should come first, not last."

"That's not the way Hollywood works, honey. When you think of it, it makes sense. He's been doing this for a long time, and that's why he gets a cut of the action. Besides, I won't have the time."

"It's like you no longer control your life," Amanda said. "You're supposed to be a star not a stooge."

"I know. It's curious. You'd think with more fame and more money, we'd have more control. But it seems to work opposite. Anyway, once the merchandise is in production and the bio is released and the recipe book is published, we'll be clear of most of the static. By that time, most of the talk show promotions will be done, and I can get it down to just a couple per year."

Amanda sighed. "It will be nice to do things together again."

***

Amanda was proven correct about the downside of fame: Within nine months, they had to move to a second home – not only larger, but surrounded by gates and walls. He had become famous.

"Listen to this," Amanda said one day, while reading *Cooks and Crocks* magazine. " 'Charlie Krale's career trajectory has seen a meteoric rise'. Do you believe that?"

"Well, it has, hasn't it?" he said with an air of pride.

"No. That's just more Hollywood speak. Besides being cliché, it's also incorrect. Meteors are bright because the fall downward through the atmosphere. If they had said it rose like a rocket, it would have been more accurate – though still a cliché."

He looked at her, but stifled his anti-nitpick impulse. It was just how her mind was hard-wired; she was a teacher down to her toes. Besides, he realized his cookery was equally concerned with details. "Honey, if the money arrives on a rocket or a meteor, I'm not about to quibble."

***

As the money rolled in, Acton rolled out his appearances all over the world. Both New York and California adopted him as their Official State Chef, and he was wined and dined by other governors as well. *Fondling Fondue* magazine christened him America's Cook. Others tried to imitate him, but were immediately subjected to negative comparisons. Twiggy Hamm's show was described as "...a knockoff, like a 20-dollar imitation of a Louis Vuiton." *The Vain Vegan* with Loreen Peeps wearing a bikini was pronounced "tasteless". Every bad imitation served to brighten Charlie's star.

He was lauded even more during his international tour. The Saudi king asked him to oversee the food preparation to celebrate the end of Ramadan, an honor never before bestowed on a non-Muslim. Afterward, he called home to tell his wife about the event.

"They awarded me the Order of Abdulaziz al Saud."

She was unimpressed. "When will you be coming home?"

"Amanda, they only give that to heads of state."

"When will you be coming home?"

"And only to a few heads of state."

"When?"

"Only two more cities. I'll be preparing a meal for the French president, then on to London to help celebrate the Queen's birthday."

"The Queen. Wow. When you were young, did you ever think you'd meet the Queen of England?"

"You know what I'm planning? Next summer, when things cool down, we can both visit Britain and France. I'm talking as tourists, not celebrities."

"I'd like that – a lot. In the meantime, say hello to the queen for me," she said.

The Paris trip was a rousing success, with the president and his entire Council of Ministers proclaiming the meal as, "the best French cooking we have ever experienced." And the Queen's welcome was indeed royal.

"I hope, Mr. Krale, you will find my chefs' preparations to be a decent comparison to your own."

"Your Majesty, I'm certain they will exceed mine; and I'm most grateful to be a guest instead of the chef for a change."

The meal was excellent, though in his conversations with the chef, Charlie had to refrain from suggesting minor improvements. At the end of the meal, the press was allowed to witness the cutting of the birthday cake. Charlie was impressed by the confection.

He ended the international tour with a last-night stay in one of London's grandest hotels, and flew home the next day. The flight was long, with a stopover in New York. He got in late and went straight to bed.

"It's Saturday," Amanda said. "Where shall we go for breakfast?"

"Honey, I've been on the road so long, I'd just love to have a simple meal around our kitchen table."

She smiled. "Okay, I'll scrape together some leftovers."

"And I'd like to spend the day here too. I hope that's okay with you. We have this magnificent home, and I hardly get to spend any time in it."

"How about we turn off our phones for the day, and stream a couple of movies?"

"Great idea. And I'll turn off the buzzer for the front gate. Let the world find someone else to bother."

The movies and a couple of glasses of wine made Charlie sleepy. It was the first time he'd been able to truly relax in months. When he awoke on the couch, he joined her on the back porch to watch the sunset.

"You had yourself quite a nap," she said.

"Yeah. The trip was great, but I sure needed a recharge."

The next morning, they turned on their phones. He had 27 messages, five from Acton with some variation of 'CALL ME ASAP'.

"What the hell were you thinking?!"

"And good morning to you to," Charlie replied. "You want to tell me what this is about?"

"What? You been living inside a crock pot? Haven't you seen the news?"

"Actually, no. Amanda and I decided to hibernate for a day. What's the problem?"

"Jesus. It's all over the internet and the TV news." Charlie had never heard Acton sound exasperated.

"What is all over the...whatever?"

"You want to explain what you were thinking when you ate the cake?"

At first, Charlie thought Acton was using sexual wordplay. Then he remembered. "You mean at the Queen's birthday party?"

"Yes. With all the press cameras around."

"But it was the Queens birthday. What was I supposed to do? Refuse to join in? There's something called etiquette, you know."

"There's also something called Facebook and YouTube and a whole bunch of celebrity gossip TV shows. Charlie, they've already called to warn me. They're going to make mincemeat of you."

"For eating a piece of cake? I was just being courteous, for crissake."

"Charlie, you're a great guy and a great chef, but I've got to warn you. You used poor judgement. You're going down."

Charlie went into the kitchen, where Amanda was fingering through her phone messages, her jaw hanging open. She looked up at him. "Charlie..."

"I know," he said quietly.

They went to his computer. The news was bad. Very bad.

When his phone rang again, all he said was, "Hi, Leonard," and after a long silence, "Okay."

He looked at Amanda and quietly said, "Leonard want's to meet with me tomorrow morning."

"This isn't good. Do you think they'll cancel."

"I don't know."

He did know, but preferred hope to reality. They cancelled, and even Wendy repudiated him at the beginning of her next show. Jack Ditter called, threatening to sue him unless Charlie completely and publicly exonerated him. Benny Nerdson quietly removed his name from Charlie's website.

Charlie realized he couldn't go out in public – not for shopping, to eat, or even to gas up the car. Amanda went for him, wearing sunglasses and a wig.

One day, on her return, she said, "Charlie, it's awful out there. You know what they have on the magazine covers?"

"I take it my picture's been removed?"

"Oh no. It's still there. But with different banners. Hateful, in fact. They label you "Fried Food Fake", "Sugar Sneak", "Hotdog Hoodwinker", and all sorts of other awful things. One even shows you as a Roman soldier spearing Christ with a skewer."

"I've seen the morning talk shows, and they're ugly too – beyond the edge of reality."

"Jesus! Think of all the scandals other celebrities have created. That woman doctor who beat up her husband's girlfriend, and the shrink who set his ex's car on fire. They still have their shows."

He nodded. "Yeah, remember that guy with the pricey medical supplement that turned out to be cheap ingredients you can buy in any store? Or the Slim Susie show? Where her brand of powdered breakfast mix contained insecticide? The people still love her."

"And the back-stretcher that Joe what's-his-name was praising on his show? Turns out it damaged nerves? His show got renewed."

"And what about the pastor who was caught with some other woman?" he said. "His followers forgave him and he's still on the air. All I did was eat a piece of cake."

"At least now they can use the term *meteoric* correctly." He was evidently confused. She explained. "Remember? Bright because of falling through the atmosphere?" she explained. Then, in a schoolmarmish manner, "Your fall is *meteoric.*"

For a moment, he hated her sardonic humor. Then he realized it was all that was left for them. He joined in. "How about Icarus flying too close to the Angel's food cake?"

"Charlie, what are we going to do?"

"Well, we're obviously done in California. At least we have plenty of money. We can go back to Oregon, and start over. I'll open another restaurant. You shouldn't have any trouble getting back into teaching."

But Charlie's infamy had spread very far, and with it, a virulent anger that perplexed them both. Southern California was everywhere. Oregonians didn't want him back: The administrator of Amanda's old school district refused to see her; and Eugene City Hall refused him a business license because of his record of "violations of ethical and moral standards". Property managers recognized him and refused to rent to them; and realtors recognized him and refused them as clients. Even flying there had entailed angry stares. After a month of disappointments and rejection, their emotions were ragged.

Beneath her eyes, dark circles had formed. "Jesus, Charlie! What are we going to do? Sure, we've got money, but we can't even show our faces."

He nodded. "That's exactly what we're going to do."

"Huh?"

"Not show my face. I've been thinking a lot this last week. I've got a plan. First, we've got to change our appearance. We'll both wear wigs, and I'll shave my goatee and wear horn-rim glasses. Then we move to Mississippi."

"Mississippi?" She was incredulous. "Why Mississippi?"

"Because that's where my show consistently had the lowest ratings. People there would happily eat roadkill fried in lard and dipped in corn syrup. It's unlikely I'll be recognized. Hell, most of them probably never even heard of my show."

"But who wants to live in Mississippi?"

"People who like roadkill." He smiled, prompting hers in return. It was the first real joke he had made in two weeks. He continued. "It will only be temporary. Then we'll request a legal name change. Finally, I'll have to have plastic surgery. After that we can move back to civilization."

"We can't to go back to California," she said. "Some of the magazine photos were of the two of us."

"You're right. And Oregon's out for the same reason. Eventually, someone would recognize you."

Amanda paused for several seconds before raising her forefinger. "Hawaii!" she said.

"Hawaii?" He was incredulous. "That's a tourist trap. Thousands go through there every week. Someone's bound to recognize us – or at least you – eventually."

"Hawaii – the Big Island, not the state." He looked confused. She continued, "Tourists go to Oahu, even Maui, but few go to the Big Island. It's sparsely populated."

He was skeptical, but her plan had two advantages. One was the gleam in her eye; for the first time in weeks, she looked hopeful – in fact, truly excited. The other was that he had no better idea.

Eighteen months later, as they sat on their porch overlooking the palms and the bay a hundred feet below, she said, "We have a beautiful backyard."

"Yeah. It is."

She paused for a few seconds. "You know, I suspect some of our neighbors recognize me. I see some odd expressions now and then."

"Any remarks?"

"No. They're very friendly. They seem to be very live-and-let-live around here. Just like their driving."

"I love how they practically insist on letting others go first at intersections," he said.

She was silent for several second. "I do miss teaching."

"You can't apply. They always do background checks. But you could be a volunteer."

"Yeah. I could. I think I'd like that."

They were both silent for a while before he said, "Amanda, what the hell's the matter with me?"

She stared at him with a furrowed brow. "What?"

"We had a good life in Oregon. There was nothing wrong with the restaurant. I liked my work as a chef, and you loved teaching."

She relaxed as her gaze returned to the bay. "You wanted something better. All of us do."

"Not anymore."

She turned her head and looked at him, but decided to say nothing.

The Shape of Salvation

After President William Dickerson had spent 20 minutes delivering his 10-minute message, he turned toward Charles Lukason. As previously instructed, Charles stepped forward on this cue, then turned toward Dickerson, who said, "For saving the world from runaway climate change, I award you this Medal of Freedom. Your country and your world are grateful."

After shaking the president's hand, Charles stepped to the mike. "The honor bestowed on me today belongs to the entire staff at X-Sequel Labs, including its president, Peter Ardent, who gave his full support for our entire team of researchers and for the project. The CF1 bacteria will consume atmospheric CO_2 as soon as the necessary vats are fabricated and become operational. Their capacity to transform CO_2 to cellulose will also provide material to the paper and composite wood industries. And finally, I want to commend President Dickerson for his commitment to build thousands of vats in this country, and for convincing other nations to follow our example. It will be all of us, all of humanity working together, who will save civilization for future generations."

As he backed away from the podium, all of the 300 persons in the West Wing room stood and applauded.

That night, Ingrid Lukason was all smiles. "You actually looked great on TV. I guess you're famous now."

"Just before I left the White House, Dickerson told me he just received word that the EU had committed to build 2000 vats a year for the next decade."

"Is that all you care about? For once you're making your mark in the world, and you want to talk about vats?" She shook her head and went back to preparing the salad.

"What? You think the vats are unimportant? Like, saving civilization is just a side issue with you?"

"I've never said that, but I've always hoped you would tend to your career status a little more. It looks like you've actually achieved fame, in spite of yourself." She turned around. "And why did you have to say the germs were created by your team?"

"Well it was. And CF1 is not a germ, it's a bacteria."

"Why even mention the team? Without you, they'd be a bunch of aimless lab techs."

"That's terribly unfair. They thought of a lot of ideas that made success possible."

"All I'm saying is stop avoiding fame. This is your chance to shine. I get so frustrated seeing you avoid the limelight. A little modesty is attractive, but this is ridiculous. I have no idea what my coworkers are going to think."

"I suspect they'll be more understanding. After all, Morganic Pharmaceuticals employs scientists too."

"That's not what I mean. I've never told them you were a scientist. I always said you were an engineer."

"An engineer? Why on earth..."

"Say *scientist* and people think *nerd*. Engineers actually...well, you know. Engineers design things – cars, planes, computers. They create actual stuff, not just ideas."

Charles mouth hung open, words blocked by the revelation. Finally, one word passed his throat. "Jesus!"

At this point, Robert came downstairs. "You two arguing again?"

"Did you see your father on TV this afternoon?" Ingrid asked as she chopped the spinach.

"On TV? What for?"

"For the Presidential Medal of Freedom. I told you about it two days ago."

"Guess I forgot."

Ingrid shook her head, swinging her auburn chignon back and forth. "And tonight he'll be on the David Godwin show."

"You mean, the *Who's Happening Now* stuff? Boring. He hasn't a clue what's happening."

"Well, tonight it will be your father happening. You could tune in for this one show."

"I'll record it. Basketball game's tonight."

"Anyway, your father is now famous. Don't be surprised if your high school mates ask you about him."

"Did they mention the name of the company? I mean, like, X-Sequel Labs?" Robert asked.

"Of course," she answered. "Why?"

"Like that's a real name? Sounds like 'X equals.' What kind of a name is that? Or even X-Sequel? Who came up with that one?"

Charles was exasperated. "What difference does that make? We just made a breakthrough that might save civilization."

"Okay. Whatever. I just know what my friends are going to say. Dinner ready?"

"The casserole will be done in 10 minutes. We can start on the salad."

In the following months, most of Charles' family conversations were equally ridiculous. '*But then, maybe they always had been. Maybe I'd been buried too deep in my work to notice.*' On the other hand, sex had been resurrected – not like a messiah after three days; more like a cicada emerging after years underground. Its song was loud enough to drown out her chatter.

***

The next day, Ingrid bronzed in the light of her co-workers admiration. They each came by her desk to congratulate her. The only sour note came when Maria remarked on how handsome he looked for a man his age; he was 41, Ingrid 42. Other employees stopped by her desk regularly – to compliment her husband's interview, how much they admired him, how they would like to meet him, yada, yada. Even the warehouse workers stopped by her cubicle. Driving home, she wondered if she felt more like a star than her husband.

Two days later, Charles and Peter rang the opening bell at the New York Stock Exchange. That event enticed even more investors to buy X-Sequel stock. The price, which had languished around the 10-dollar level for years, had already shot up to 100 dollars in a few weeks.

A month later, after several interviews for more television shows, newspapers, magazines, online journals, and a book, the Norwegian Nobel Committee announced that the Nobel Prize would be awarded to Charles Lukason. And the following week, he was awarded the Einstein Peace prize.

Ingrid was riding on a cloud for the entire month. Even Robert was basking in the fame. His science teacher explained the significance of Charles' achievements, and called him a hero – as much a revelation to Robert as to the rest of the class. And the girls all wanted to chat with him.

In the Science 103 class, Dan Hollis raised his hand. "Mr. Pontil, are you saying that global warming is a threat to society?"

"Uh, no. Actually, to civilization."

"Excuse me, but I don't remember you mentioning it before."

"That's because we haven't gotten that far. It's in chapter 18."

All the students in the class turned toward Robert.

"What...What?!"

"You never said anything about this," Dan said. It was practically an accusation.

Robert looked down at his desk. "Well, he never mentioned it to me." He nodded for a few seconds. "He's cool that way."

The following week, Peter asked Charles into his office. "I've got some news, Charles, but I'm not certain if it's good or bad. You know how our stock price has soared the past few months?"

'Sure. Since we became a famous company."

"Actually, there's more to it than that. The shares were scooped up by a conglomerate."

Charles tilted his head. "I'm not sure I understand."

"I didn't either, until this morning. We've been taken over by Leech Holdings International."

Charles tried interpreting this news. Finally, he asked, "How will that affect us or our work?"

"No way to tell. X-Sequel no longer makes its own decisions. Leech does. As for me, I'm out. But I can't imagine you losing your job. After all, you're the jewel in the crown. You're famous. They'd want you as a part of the company, even if only for your name and fame."

The following week, Leech made the public announcement, and CEO James Dodgson met with Charles. "The entire board and executive committee are delighted to have you on board, Charles."

Charles tried to ignore his first impressions of Dodgson – the thin reptilian lips pressed together to prevent his thoughts from escaping. '*What would they say?*' He also ignored the pictures on the wall – the yacht, presumably Dodgson's; and the small mansion on the edge of the lake, also presumably Dodgson's, though Charles wondered whether that applied to the lake as well. The vanity that infused the room went beyond it's gold objects on the oversized desk.

Charles wasn't a political animal, but he understood his status. "And I'm equally glad. Would you like me to bring you up to date on our latest research?"

"That won't be necessary. Your work will be absorbed into one of our labs."

"Which one?"

"Oh, we haven't decided. The important thing is we have a huge promotion for you, with a compensation package to match."

Charles now realized that he did *not* understand his status. "Promotion? To what? Mr. Dodgson, I enjoy what I do, and our discoveries and inventions have made X-Sequel...will make Leech famous and rich."

"Please call me Jim. And Charles, in case you haven't noticed, we're already rich." His mouth smiled, but his eyes squinted.

Charles didn't know what to say. He certainly couldn't express his intuitive dread at Dodgson's attitude. Couldn't, because at the moment, he didn't fully understand it. And couldn't because he did understand that Dodgson's concerns were different than his own. He realized this 'promotion' was going to take something important from him – his work, which had always given him a sense of purpose, and a kind of nobility to his life. For Charles, science was a lamp leading humanity forward through the darkened hall of our weak perceptions, and away from our primitive instincts. It revealed reality to the world, and made modern civilization possible. And he had the honor and privilege to be one of those people holding the lamp.

"To be honest, Charles, this company needs you for one main function, and it isn't the science. Leech can buy scientists from all over the world with a snap of its fingers. No, Charles, what you can do for us is add your name and fame to our enterprise."

'Name and fame. What Peter said.' Charles realized that the decision had already been made. "In that case, Jim, what position did you have in mind for me?"

"How does VP of the Bedding and Environmental division sound? You'd be working right under Steven Dyer."

Charles realized it did not matter one worm turd how it sounded to him. "That sounds fine, he said." He tried to imitate Dodgson's corporate smile, but only half succeeded.

"Great! Now first we have a few papers to sign. Let's begin with the non-disclosure agreement..."

***

Ingrid was delighted. "This will be good for you – tick another box in your career."

"No, Ingrid. It's a dead end. I'm obligated to remain for five years, and I'm not even allowed to do research."

"Then why did you take it?"

"I had no choice. X-Sequel is gone."

"So what did they give you?"

"VP of the Bedding and Environmental division."

Ingrid opened a wide smile. "Vice-president! A whole division? Fantastic! See – I always knew you would make it to the top."

About two months into his new divisional do-nothing job, he was surprised by his phone beeping. It was Dodgson. "Can you come to my office?"

When he entered, he saw a woman in her mid-thirties seated in front of Dodgson's oversized desk. Charles, I'd like you to meet Danielle Colleen, a researcher in our Ocean and Housewares Science division"

After the two of them had exchanged greetings, Dodgson continued. "She has some disturbing news. Go ahead and explain it, Danielle."

"Sure." She turned to Charles. "About two months ago we discovered a decline in phytoplankton off the coast of Madagascar. Shortly afterward, an expedition off the coast of Spain discovered the same anomaly. Naturally, we were alarmed by the second instance."

Charles leaned back in his chair. "Of course. As I recall, phytoplankton helps reduce algae blooms."

"More important, it's one of the bases of the food chain across all the oceans."

He nodded. "Oceanography is one field I haven't studied."

"One of the few. I've read your professional bio. Very impressive. If anyone's going to solve this problem, it will be you."

"A phytoplankton problem? This is worrisome, Danielle, but what does it have to do with me?"

"We took samples of the plankton, as well as the water in the area." She took a breath. "We found the plankton had been starved of CO2. Further, we found the water contained concentrations of the CF1 bacteria."

Charles abruptly brought his chair full upright. "But, that's impossible. They're a freshwater bacteria."

"Apparently, some have adapted. The question is, how did they get out of the vats?"

Charles began tapping the table with his fore finger. And tapping. Danielle shifted in her chair. Finally, Charles stream of consciousness became audible. "Even if some had clung to the cellulose as it was removed, their concentrations would have been too low to survive...certainly too low to adapt to saltwater...and if Madagascar had dumped some vat water, how did it end up off the Spanish coast...and ditto for a Spanish leak reaching Madagascar...other side of a continent...and ocean currents don't go..." He looked up at her. "I don't know."

She said nothing, but raised her eyebrows at his circuitous route to nowhere.

"I'm sorry, Danielle. I just don't know. The vats are filled with freshwater, and ordinary air is bubbled into the tank."

Dodgson spoke up. "Danielle, perhaps you could explain the problem to Charles more fully. What you told me."

"I'm sorry Mr. Dodgson, but you said..."

"Yes. Mention it to no one. But you can tell Charles. And call me Jim."

"Charles, if the CF1 bacteria spread across the ocean, they will eat up all the CO2."

Charles started to open his mouth, but nothing came out for several seconds. Finally, "Jesus!"

"That's right," she answered. "Another ice age. Not to mention, our farm crops would diminish, which would mean global starvation." When she saw his complexion go white, she felt his pain. "I'm sorry to lay this on you."

Dodgson smiled. "Anything you can do to help us here?" he asked cheerfully.

"Actually, we kept a worldwide database of the vats." He turned toward Dodgson. "Please tell me Leech retained the X-Sequel databases."

"I'm sure they're here. Somewhere."

"One of the tables was a list of all CF1 vats in the world. We can notify all governmental CF1 offices to check their vats for leaks. I'll make certain to tell them it's urgent."

Dodgson leaned forward. His smile was gone, his stare was intense. "Yes, but governments only. No press. And no scientific organizations. You do understand?"

Charles nodded. "Sure." He paused, thinking, then said, "The only way this problem is going to be solved is to eliminate the CF1."

"Of course," Danielle remarked.

Charles leaned forward, tapping his chin. "And the only way to do that is to develop a bacteria that will attack the CF1."

Danielle lifted her head. "Yes. That would work. An anti-CF1."

"That means a bacteria that will be antigen-specific for the CF1."

Danielle nodded. "So, you're saying it's a job for the gene-splicers."

"Absolutely!" Charles looked at Dodgson. "We need to get Leech's genetic labs working on this. It's the only solution."

Dodgson looked at Danielle, and she nodded her assent. He jumped to his corporate smile. "I think that for now, it's more important to locate the source of the leak. There isn't much point in creating another germ if the original ones are still getting dumped in the ocean. I'll leave the search for the leak in your hands Charles. Let me know when you have something. Meanwhile, I'll be calling the president."

***

A week later, Charles heard from Jidda Paresh in India. Indeed, one of their vats placed along the Son River had a leak from a bad weld.

"The Son river? Does that empty in the ocean?"

"Not exactly, Dr. Lukason, but it empties into the Ganges which very certainly does empty into the ocean,"

"The Ganges? The most polluted river in the world."

"Be pleased to not insult the Ganges. Most sacred to us. And I could point my finger toward some of your rivers in America."

"My apologies, Paresh. I simply meant that the pollution that exists there might have placed evolutionary pressure on the CF1 bacteria. That could have accelerated their adaptation,"

"Apology most accepted, Dr. Lukason. And your point is well taken. And allow me to add that the Ganges is a slow moving river as it approaches the ocean. That would increase the ability of the CF1 to adapt."

"A good point. But I'm curious. Why on earth would your scientists choose a location near a river?"

"It was to be near a place for transporting the cellulose to a paper factory downstream. But I have very good news for you. I can report that the bad weld has been most thoroughly repaired. Everything is working perfectly."

Charles rolled his eyes, then said goodbye as patiently and gracefully as his mood allowed.

***

He immediately went to Dodgson with the news.

"I see..." Dodgson replied.

Charles was confused. "Is something wrong?"

"No. Why do you ask."

"I just assumed you'd be happy to hear the news."

"Oh, I am...I am. I guess this solves the problem?"

"Not really," Charles replied. "The CF1 are still in the ocean. I just got off the phone with Danielle, and she says they're continuing to increase."

"Really! I see." Dodgson's voice had suddenly and strangely shifted. For some reason, Charles was reminded of Julie Andrews on a hill, breaking out in song.

"We're not out of the woods. Not even close. We need to get Leech's bio labs working on an Anti-CF1."

"Oh, yes. Yes," Dodgson said. Yes. Of course. I'll talk to Arthur."

"Arthur?"

"Arthur Turesh. He heads our Lichen Lab division. One of these days, I'll have to introduce you to him."

"Yes. Given my background in gene splicing, perhaps I could assist him."

From Dodgson's lack of response and another one of those corporate smiles, Charles intuited that Dodgson had no intention of anyone talking with Arthur Turesh. *'But why?'*

***

In the following week, Dodgson called an executive meeting, where he announced that Leech Holdings had recently purchased some coal mine companies.

"Without consulting the executive committee?" Ron Doe asked.

"I apologize for keeping you all out of the loop. Let me explain. I recently received privileged information from the president that our government will be subsidizing the operation of these mines. And I was able to confirm this with the leaders of both houses of congress. These mines will become a key part of the government's Save The Future United program. Once the formal announcement is released, the value of those mines will triple. We had to move fast."

Mary Smith raised her hand. "Excuse me, Jim, but what part will the mines play in the STFU program?"

"The federal government will pay us to set the coal on fire to replace the diminishing CO2," Dodgson replied. "And we'll avoid the expense of refining it. We are also looking into subsidies from individual states where each mine is located."

"Will it be enough?" asked John Jones.

"Of course. Our calculations indicate it will bring in hundreds of millions of dollars directly to the bottom line."

"No, what I meant was whether it would be sufficient to replace the CO2 which the germs are destroying."

Dodgson appeared thoughtful for a few seconds. "Probably."

***

As mere VP of division, Charles was not in attendance. When his boss, Steven Dyer, told him – with the appropriate patina of enthusiasm – of the meeting, Charles was incredulous. "But burning coal, especially directly from the mine, will throw huge amounts of pollution into the atmosphere."

"There it is again, Charles. You're always so negative. Always looking at the dark side of things."

"Coal is dark."

Of course, the joke was lost on Steven. It was useful only to relieve some of Charles' tension, which had begun to produce headaches for the previous two weeks. '*Or is it my constant eye-rolling every time someone says something stupid about the problem being manageable?*'

***

That night, Charles watched the president make a special broadcast to the nation. He explained the problem, and held the Indians fully responsible for endangering the world. "We need to replace the CO2 that the subversive sea-borne germs are gobbling up." It was then that he announced the proposed STFU program.

Charles again rolled his eyes, but he would have been wiser to do so at his own innocence, for in the morning, he found the media and public blaming him, not the Indians, for the dilemma. It was all over the web. So was his picture, like a wanted poster from the Old West. It seemed the web crowd – despite the president's speech, despite the facts, despite the webosphere's own former praise of CF1 – it seems they now blamed Charles for the threat to civilization.

He had invented this germ, hadn't he? The world was talking of little else, including Ingrid, who called from work.

"My God, Charlie, what have you done?!"

"We'll get the problem fixed. We've got our lab working on an Anti-CF1. The climate will be safe." He knew it was likely a lie, but could he really sit down and have a rational discussion with her?

"The climate? Who gives a shit about the climate? Half the people in the office won't talk to me. And nobody joins me for lunch anymore. They treat me like a leper."

"Is that all you think about? The fucking planet's in danger and you're worried about your status at work?"

"Not just at work. I noticed the way our neighbors looked at me this morning. I thought you finally had made something of yourself. I was proud of you. And now you go and pull a stunt like this."

"I've got to hang up now, Ingrid. My staff is waving me over."

She didn't know enough to ask, 'What staff?'

And for the rest of their time living together, he knew better than to suggest sex. The cicada had flown away.

***

The call from Robert hurt worse. "Thanks, Dad." The sarcasm was acidic enough to eat the phone's plastic casing.

"Robert, it's not my fault. The newspapers have it all wrong. The Indians caused it and Leech Holdings refuses to take the steps to fix it."

"Newspapers? Who reads newspapers? I mean BuzzFace, InstaWhat, HooHuh – all of them make me look like Son-Of-Hitler. And getting a date? I've given up trying to get girls to even look at me. I'm just hoping the profs aren't going to bias my grades down."

"I'm trying to save the world, and all you can think about is dating?"

"Not just dates. My roommates practically sneer at me."

"I'm sorry, but I'm sure when we solve the problem, they'll treat you like a hero again."

"I'm sorry too."

The phone went silent. So did something inside Charles. It wasn't the scientist, but the science tunnel. He felt the change, but could not identify it, perhaps because the dissolving thought pattern had been his image of life? Or was it because the picture had just become a window looking out upon an unfamiliar landscape?

A deep anger took hold. He checked the company directory. "Hi. Arthur Turesh? I'm Charles Lukason. James Dodgson referred me to you."

"Oh, Dr. Lukason. I'm honored to talk to you. How may I help you?"

"I was wondering if Dodgson has mentioned anything to you about an Anti-CF1 bacteria."

"A what?"

Charles repeated the question, though he had his answer. "It's the solution for the CF1 problem – a genetically engineered bacteria that will target the CF1 in the ocean."

"No, he hasn't, though that sounds like a brilliant idea. Maybe your lab and mine could combine our efforts."

"Uh, Arthur, I don't have a lab."

"Really? Well, where are you working?"

"Actually, I work for Leech Holdings. I'm the VP of the Bedding and Environmental division.

After a pause, Arthur said, "What the fuck is that?"

"A parking lot," Charles said with an acerbic edge to his voice. "They just wanted my name, and intend for me to do nothing."

"Let's meet for lunch – say tomorrow? Today is completely filled."

However, before the day was done, Charles got a call from Dodgson. "Can you come to my office?"

Charles suspected nothing, even when he noticed a uniformed person sitting in the outer office – not until he entered Dodgson's office and saw the head of human resources sitting beside a man in a dark blue suit.

"What do you mean by calling Arthur Turesh behind my back?"

Charles guessed that Arthur had called Dodgson to protect his own butt."Behind your back? Why would I need your permission to call him?"

Dodgson pushed a paper toward Charles. "Do you remember this paper?"

It took a few seconds before Charles could recall it. It was the non-disclosure agreement.

Dodgson continued. "You violated these terms when you informed Arthur about our private discussion."

"Actually, the CF1 is not a private matter. Even the president has publicly discussed it. And Arthur is a part of the company. I've never discussed company business with outsiders, even my wife."

Mr. Blue Suit leaned forward. "Technically, which is to say, legally, any discussion about any subject that takes place in this office is considered *private*. Mr. Dodgson is a member of the executive committee, and you are not. Neither is Mr. Turesh."

Dodgson pointed toward the blue suit. "This is Mr. Simms, one of our corporate lawyers. I assure you that if he says you violated the non-disclosure agreement, you did. At least, I'm taking his word for it."

The HR manager spoke up. "I'm afraid that this is cause for dismissal, effective immediately at..." she looked at her watch "...2:47 pm. She wrote it down, then handed the paper for Charles to sign.

"I'm not signing anything."

"As you wish," Dodgson said. He pressed a button. "Marie, could you send in the security guard?"

The latter was polite, but diligent about accompanying Charles back to his office, watching him pack his possessions in a box, and accompanying him all the way to the exit.

***

"Fired? What for?" Ingrid was indignant, but toward her husband, not the company.

Charles outlined the internal politics of Leech Holdings, Intl.

"Well why would you be talking to the lab tech? You're an executive. Or were."

"He's not a lab tech. He's in charge of the lab. And it was the only way to push the Anti-CF1 program forward. Dodgson has no interest in it."

"Then why should you?"

"Uh...how about to save civilization."

"For God's sake, Charles. Talk about self-aggrandizement! I liked it better when you were a wallflower.

"Ingrid, this is a serious thing. It's a threat to the whole world."

She rose and walked away shaking her head.

***

By the following week, Charles had decided on a course of action. The decision alone galvanized his spirits, and resuscitated his withered hope for the world. He called Rick Epstein of Fiddle Genetics, an X-Sequel coworker before he had decided to venture out on his own. They met for lunch at Arpeggio's.

Rick gave a strong, friendly handshake. "I was so sorry to hear you were let go."

"You mean, 'kicked in the ass.'"

"Yeah, I heard. Word gets around. Well, the way it looks to me, too bad for them."

"Rick, I'll get straight to the point. I'd like to come work for you. I have an idea for solving the CF1 problem."

Rick paused, took a sip of coffee, then paused again before looking up. "As much as we've always been friends, as much as I'd like to hire you, I simply can't."

"Why?"

Rick paused again, this time like an adult trying to explain that Santa wasn't real. "Charles, when Leech bought X-Sequel, they bought all the patents as well. That means all the knowledge you gained working at X-Sequel."

"Sure, but we would be working on something new, an anti-CF1."

"Doesn't matter. They can claim it was based on your knowledge of the original CF1. Any breakthrough, any invention we make with you at our labs will automatically trigger a suit from Leech. I can't risk that."

"What if I wasn't employed by Fiddle Genetics? I mean not officially. You wouldn't have to pay me. We could do it all on the sly."

"Charles, that would only delay their suit by...maybe a couple of weeks. The first thing they would think of is you. It wouldn't take them long for investigate."

"Rick, you realize, don't you, that civilization itself is in danger? If we don't fix the problem, patents and suits won't matter."

"Even if we do discover a fix, Leech will get a court injunction. We'd never have a chance to get any anti-CF1 to the field."

"Rick, this is insane. We're talking survival here."

"It's not just my company, Charles. How many labs do you think would be willing to go up against a platoon of corporate lawyers?"

"It's either that, or die."

"No. It's die. Period. If it wasn't for Sarah and the children, I'd be preparing my own quick exit."

Charles sat back, staring, silent.

Rick's brow wrinkled. "What else is left for us, Charles? One way or another?" His eyes welled with tears.

Charles slowly shook his head. "I created the CF1. This is all on me."

"I wish it were that simple, but it's not."

"How so?" Charles asked, partly as a moral question; partly as a drowning man grasping at any stick of wood that floated by.

"People invent things. Other people apply them. Steel makes skyscrapers, but also cannon. One builds, the other destroys. Chemistry created medicine and poison gas. One heals, one kills. It's been that way since the first caveman decided to use a limb for a club." He looked down as he collected his thoughts. "Frankly, this, 'it's all on me' stuff sounds a bit egotistical, though I know you didn't mean it that way. No, it's not on you. It's on all of us, a remnant of our simian past."

"True. Our cleverness exceeds our intelligence."

"The thing is, Charles, I'm no better. I'm protecting my lab, I adhere to the rules that keep the system running, because I'm part of that system. I've read of German soldiers who hated the SS and their death squads. But they kept fighting. Perhaps they could have defected, but we're all wired to support whatever group we belong to, whether family, tribe, or country."

They were both silent for a minute as Charles contemplated Rick's words. His friend's hopelessness and shame saddened him. He rose, and patted Rick on the shoulder. "That's alright. I've experienced the same feelings. I've been trying to figure a way around the impasse, ignoring the obvious. There isn't any." He stuck out his hand. Rick grabbed it, then rose to embrace Charles. Charles returned the hug, but the two men did not – could not – say anything.

As Charles drove home, he realized how much his spirits had descended from the morning's anticipation. He was finally resigned to the inevitable. But as he pored over the pieces of their conversation, he had an idea. He stopped the car and checked something on his cell phone. He turned the car around and drove into the city.

He was surprised it wasn't larger – just an ordinary office building. He entered and walked directly to the reception desk. "I need to talk to the director."

The lady looked up, surprised, but after a bit of back-and-forth, she complied. A man came out, introduced himself, and said, "How may I help you?"

"My name is Charles Lukason."

Surprise crossed the director's face as he broke into a smile. "Ah Dr. Lukason. I recognize you from the television. I'm honored to meet you. How can I be of service?"

"I hope to be of service to you. I wish to defect to China, if your country is interested."

The director's expression turned to shock, then a very wide smile. "Please, have a seat while I talk to the Consul General. I'm certain he will want to speak with you."

The Pleasant World of Mrs. Peeples

"How did the bake sale go?" asked Paul.

"Excellent. There were so many nice people to talk to." Calli Peeples put the empty trays on the kitchen table and hung her coat in the closet.

He looked up from his magazine. "How much were the sales?"

It was the question she had expected from her husband. Numbers were his nature, and also his career before retiring from Gregory Accounting, LLC. "Oh, we won't have the figures until next weekend. You know, we had people there who aren't even church members."

"The committee must have done a good job promoting it. Or do you think Pastor Hammond got help from the other Methodist Churches?"

"Actually, we had people from other religions. I had a wonderful conversation with a couple of Jewish women. And one gentleman was an atheist."

"Really? Was he actually a gentleman? Or did he just come to argue?"

"Surprisingly, he was very nice. In fact, I only found out about his lack of faith when I asked if he was Methodist. He said, 'Actually, I'm agnostic.'"

Paul looked at her. "I thought you said he's an atheist."

"Well, you know – same thing. But he said it in the nicest way. And we talked about our families, the weather – all sorts of things. He even bought some of my bear claws. It just shows how everyone can be friendly despite differences."

"That's true," Paul said as he turned the page. "The important thing is to be pleasant. Too many people want to talk about serious things."

Calli nodded. "Absolutely. If we all just ignore our differences, everyone can get along with everybody else."

Paul nodded as he continued reading. "Yep. That's what made America great."

The next day, Calli Peeples was pulling some impertinent weeds from her flower bed, when she heard, "Good morning." Martha Bradshaw was carrying a trash bag.

"Morning, Martha. Nice day, isn't it?" Calli admired how the sunlight brought out the red undertones in Martha's dark-brown pixie-cut hair. _"Such a nice color. Too bad she cuts it so short."_

"It's lovely." Martha deposited the bag in the bin and walked over to Calli. She looked at Calli's fairly new, stylish print blouse, much nicer than her own plain magenta shirt. '_Upscale clothes for gardening,_' she thought. "Weeds, huh?" she remarked. "We get them all the time. But your yard has very few of them."

"Paul sprays a lot. And they have a new kind that won't hurt the grass. We don't want it looking like the Darnell's house. I'm surprised the HOA hasn't issued them a warning. I've thought about complaining."

"Didn't you say 'getting along' was the most important thing? What was it – 'live and let live'?

"Actually, the HOA keeps names of complaint filers secret. That way, I could still be friendly with them."

"Uh huh…Anyway Calli, I hate using chemicals. They wash into the gutter and end up in the ocean."

"Really, Martha, you worry too much about such things."

"I worry about my great grandkids. I don't think anyone can be too concerned. I mean, they're the whole point, aren't they?"

Calli looked up with a wrinkled brow. "The point of what?"

"Of...of...everything." She stretched her arms outward. "What is this all for?"

"Gosh, Martha, you do fret. Every generation has had its challenges. Why not just keep things simple and enjoy?"

"I can see why you voted for Murtaugh. He doesn't give a damn about the environment, either."

Calli looked up. "There you go again, turning everything into politics. Politics is so divisive. Like Rodney King said, 'Can't we just get along?'" She returned to her work.

Martha wondered how the Rodney King incident could be considered non-political, but instead said, "Sure we can, Calli. But Murtaugh gets along with no one. He tells a Black audience they should worry about Hispanics. He tells Hispanics they're threatened by Blacks. How's that 'getting along'?"

"No. I'm talking about you and me. We get along just fine. Let's just ignore politics."

"Calli, I'll just say it direct. If you truly believed in that 'getting along' philosophy, you wouldn't vote for someone who pits groups against each other."

"Speaking of generations, how are Moira and Ron doing."

Calli's diversion was clumsy, but Martha took the hint. "Moira called last night. She's switching her major to physics."

"Physics? That's quite a change. Wasn't she going for a degree in literature?"

"She was. Now its physics. She says she finds it interesting. Jerry and I are just glad she decided on something that might actually be lucrative."

Calli was pulling the last few intruders from the ground. "Sounds like a better choice. I've met only a few scientists." She looked up. "They talk different. I hope Moira won't talk like them."

"Like what?"

"Oh, I don't know. Not as friendly. No – that's not it. They're friendly, but not really warm. They don't smile a lot."

Martha tilted her head to the side, but, in the interest of détente, withheld her thoughts. "Well, I'd better get started with the vacuuming."

After the last weed had been expunged, Calli went inside. "That Martha. Always wanting to talk politics."

Paul was dusting his collection of World War II models. "Complaining about Murtaugh again?"

"Of course. Talking about his rallies, saying he pulls people apart."

"They're already apart," Paul declared as he ran a soft cloth over the P-50 aircraft model. "Murtaugh is just honest enough to state the truth."

As usual, around 3:00 Calli took Freddy for a walk. A block into her route, she saw Lena Holden, but didn't bother waving to her. She'd given up after several snubs.

Ever since Calli mentioned her approval of Murtaugh, Lena had refused to even acknowledge her existence. *'Such a shame.'* After another few minutes, she ran into Verna walking her boxer.

"Hi, Calli. How are you?"

"Fine, Verna. Thanks. How is everything? How's Boxy?"

Verna smiled down at him. "He's chipper today. I tried a new brand of dog food, and he seems to like it better." Freddy and Boxy sniffed and rubbed against each other. Though very different in appearance – Freddy was a terrier – they got along like twins.

"Paul and I are very particular about Freddy's food too. Good dog food is a bit pricey, but nutrition is important. Just like with people."

"Yes, it is. Roger and I always make sure the kids have a good breakfast before they go off to school. Not just a bowl of cereal – you know, starch and sugar."

"You're right. It affects their learning. Paul read an article just the other day about how good nutrition improves kids' attention span. They learn better."

"That's true. But then how can you still support Murtaugh after he cut the school nutrition program?"

"I like Murtaugh for his other actions, like cutting taxes and increasing defense spending."

"But Calli, if you do those two things, you have to cut somewhere else – like the school nutrition program."

Calli managed to ease her way out of the conversation. When she got home, she recounted the exchange to Paul. "Honestly, Paul, I tried avoiding politics, but she just redirected our conversation. I mean, we were having such an interesting conversation about dog food, and she just had to bring in politics – totally irrelevant."

Paul nodded, but kept on reading his newspaper. "People just don't care about being friendly and upbeat anymore. Here's a front page article on some protest somewhere about something or other. Too many people don't realize how much better it is to get along with each other."

"Exactly. So many people can't see it."

After dinner, they watched the evening news with Leonard Glaze

"Good evening. President Murtaugh addressed a rally last night in Cryptville, Georgia, where he made some surprising statements about the poor." Glaze's image was replaced by a video of a large crowd, then one of President Murtaugh at the podium.

"Now people will tell you – I've heard it myself – that the poor are victims. Maybe some are. Maybe not. I don't know. You can decide for yourself. You *should* decide for yourself. You're smart. You can make up your own mind. Don't let the media treat you like idiots. 'Cause you're not. That's why you're here tonight. Isn't this a wonderful place to be, Cryptville? Huh? Isn't this a terrific place?"

(Applause)

"Just terrific. But the poor aren't victims. They want to make *you* the victim. They're planning revolts. Right now. Even as we speak. Revolution. They want to rise up and take from you real Americans what you worked so hard for. That's right. They're jealous. Very jealous. Completely jealous."

Glaze's image reappeared. "Journalists from our network, as well as other news sources, asked the White House for confirmation of the president's claim that the poor were planning some kind of revolution. Press Secretary Louch claimed the president never said it. The attorney general's response was even more mysterious."

An image of the attorney general appeared, confronted by several microphones. "The president said 'revolt', not 'revolution'. Technically, those are two different things. Under the law, a revolt is not a revolution."

"Actually, sir, he used both words."

"Well, there you are. He offered you two choices, and you chose the one that put him in the poorest light. Perhaps now you can

understand why he accuses
you news fellas of bias."

The image of Glaze at his desk
reappeared. "And when we return, we'll
have the results from yesterday's
elections in Italy."

Paul shook his head. "Will you listen to that?"

"I know," Calli said. "All those people at the rally
looked like they were enjoying themselves just fine. And
the media has to come along and throw a fly in the punch
bowl."

"They aren't happy with tearing down our president.
They have to go after the guys who work for him. Those
poor people, just trying to do their job."

"Which is to protect and defend the president. I really
admire their loyalty."

Paul shook his head. "What I don't understand is why
the media think they have the right to do that."

The next evening was mahjong night at Tina Hayes'
house. As usual, the guests brought appetizers and the
hostess served dinner. After dinner, they set about the
game.

"Did you see where they ended the Foody Club
program at the Greasy Grocers chain?" Tina asked.

Leona nodded. "I did. I shop there all the time. It's too
bad."

"I only started shopping there because of the club
discounts," Dorothy remarked, "Now I think I'll go back to
buying at Stuffy's."

"I'm not happy about it," Calli agreed, "but their prices are still pretty good. And it's right next to our townhouse complex."

Tina shook her head. "You wouldn't think they could just end it all of a sudden. I mean, it's just bad PR."

"Well look, the president breaks treaties left and right," Dorothy said, "and his supporters to care a whit about the country's PR."

Leona tried to play the peacekeeper. "Now Dorothy, let's not get into politics."

Dorothy persisted. "It's true. People see the president do it, and it influences them. It becomes acceptable."

"He has to protect America," Calli pointed out.

"Part of protecting America is protecting it's image," Dorothy said. "Breaking our word tarnishes our image."

"Come on. It's not like we have to care about a bunch of foreigners."

Everyone looked at Calli.

"Well, we don't. We're the United States of America. We're the deciders."

"You honestly think breaking our word…" Dorothy began.

"Let's get back to the game." Again, Leona was the peacemaker.

"Yes, let's," Tina agreed.

***

"How'd the game go?" Paul asked when his wife arrived home.

179

"The game went fine. I won by a big lead. But that Dorothy was so annoying."

"Is that the one who hates the president?"

"She's the one. Always carrying on about his breaking deals with other countries."

"Really? Whose side is she on anyway?" Paul said.

"Indeed. I half thought of telling her that if she likes backward countries like France or Holland, she should move there."

"Damned right. Maybe you should just drop the mahjong. There's no reason you should have to put up with the likes of Dorothy."

"But why should I let one narrow-minded person force me out of the group?"

"I don't know. Murtaugh set a good example. He's dropped out of a few international organizations. If he thinks it's the right thing for the country, it's probably right for us."

Calli laid her forefinger on her lips. "You know, Paul. You've given me an idea. Instead of me leaving, why shouldn't she leave?"

Paul raised his eyebrows. "Now, that's a heck of an idea. Who's the one most likely to agree?"

"Let's see. Leona is always the one to quell the arguments. But then again, Tina never discusses politics. I'm not even sure of her political party."

"Who's the one with the most money?"

"That would be Tina. Their house is lavish, and her husband drives some kind of expensive sports car."

"Okay. So she's the one you should approach first." Paul leaned forward, excited at his plan. "Once Tina's on board, you approach Leona. If she's reluctant, you can point out you already have half the group in favor."

"I don't't know, Paul. Don't you think that's a bit aggressive?"

"Remember Murtaugh's speech, the one we saw last Thursday? When he told us how he reveres the bald eagle, symbol of our country? He said it was a ferocious predator that tears apart its weaker prey. And he's right. That's what made our country great."

"Yes, it was very moving. Especially with *America The Beautiful* playing in the background. Paul, I think you're right. We'll just push her out. And I know a gal, Haylee, who's been looking for a mahjong group."

"Great. Let them both know about Haylee. That should put them over the line."

***

The plan worked perfectly. At the first meeting of the reorganized group, they made clear to Haylee that political talk was forbidden. From then on, the mahjong gatherings were pleasant.

A week later, on the evening news, Murtaugh was conducting a press briefing .

> "Today, we have realigned some African countries. Two weeks ago, the country of Spitistan voted against us at the United Nations. We warned Spitistan beforehand, but they thought they could just ignore us. I talked to the prime minister, but he

thought he could thumb his nose at us. This little postage-stamp country thought they could ignore our warnings. That's what he thought. Just ignore us.

In the two weeks since, I've been talking with President Umgole of Lickistan. I convinced President Umgole to break his treaty with Spitistan and invade them. I'm a great talker. I know how to talk. Talking is what I do. I want to report to the nation that the country of Spitistan no longer exists. It's gone. Disappeared. It now belongs to Lickistan. Everything – every hut, every cow, goat – whatever they've got there.

Let every nation understand. The time when other countries could thumb their noses at us is past. No more thumbs. The time when others could ignore us is past. Nobody pushes America around anymore.

Paul nodded. "Now that's telling 'em. No one pushes us around anymore. It's about time!"

"That's why we wanted him," Calli said. "He's doing what he promised."

"I wonder how the liberals are going to spin this."

"I just don't see how they can criticize him this time."

The next day, Calli was refilling the bird feeder on the front porch, when she saw Jerry Bradshaw watering some potted plants.

"Hi, Jerry. How are you and Martha doing today?"

He walked over. "Hi, Calli. How's Paul?"

"The same. And Ron, did he find a job?"

"Yep. His first out of college. Pays decent, though they don't provide health insurance."

"Well, he'll find something better. Besides, he doesn't need health insurance at his age."

"That's easy for you to say. You have Medicare. If Murtaugh had his way, we wouldn't even have that."

"There you go again. Why do you and Martha always have to bring up politics? What is it with you two? Can't we just talk about other things?"

"Like what?"

"Like…I don't know. The weather, the flowers, things happening with the HOA. Something that doesn't involve politics. Politics divides people."

"You know, Calli, you're just like a fish in an aquarium."

She looked at him and wrinkled her brow.

He explained. "Someone above is dripping poison into the water, but you want to ignore it. You go into your nice little cave in the plastic rock in the corner, and pretend the poison isn't important."

Calli tilted her head sideways. "What are you talking about, Jerry? Who would put poison into an aquarium?"

Jerry paused, then decided against a fuller explaination. "Murtaugh," he replied, then turned and went back to his yard.

After she had gone inside and washed her hands, she said, "Paul, that Jerry is getting really weird."

Paul was carefully polishing the windshield on his Messerschmidt model. "Why? What happened?"

She sat down. "He tried to drag me into a political argument again, and when I objected, he switched to aquariums."

"Did they buy one? I don't remember seeing one in their home before."

"Then he said Murtaugh wanted to poison his fish."

Paul paused his work and turned toward her. "You think he might be smoking pot?"

"Or maybe early-onset dementia. I don't know. All I know, is everybody is a hater. And you know who's the worst? Lena Holden. She won't even look at me when we cross paths."

"From what I hear, she does seem to be more passionate about Murtaugh than most haters. Always ranting on about him."

"You know, Paul, that's a good point. Maybe she's the one turning people against us."

He paused his cleaning and turned toward her. "Come to think of it, yesterday I saw her talking to Marissa what's-her-name as I was about to pull into the driveway. They were looking in the direction of our house."

"God only knows what tales she might be spreading." After another minute, she got up from the chair and walked over to him. "You know, it all fits. Jerry and Martha didn't start making remarks until shortly after Lena found out I liked Murtaugh. I wish I hadn't mentioned it. And the same with Verna."

Paul set the Messerschmidt into it's proper place, and took out the P-38. "So, Lena must be talking."

"That's it! She's turning the neighborhood against us. We've got to do something."

Paul looked up from his work. "Like what? We can't stop her from talking."

"I'm going to complain to the HOA at their next meeting. I'm going to lodge a formal complaint. I'm going to get her kicked out of the development."

"Can we do that? What would the grounds be?"

"She must be violating some section of the CC&Rs." She went to the file cabinet, found the papers, sat down and carefully perused them. After a half-hour, she announced, "Here it is, Paul."

He came into the den and sat down beside her.

"It says here, 'Nuisances: Members found to be in breach of any rule three times can be declared a nuisance by a majority vote of the board. Also, a member can be declared a nuisance by a vote of three-quarters of the owners for any reason. Members found to be a nuisance will be fined until they are declared to be no longer a nuisance.'"

"Paul, we can use this to stop Lena Holden from gossiping about us, or drive her out of the complex. Either way, we win."

"But how?"

"I'll make up a petition about Lena Holden being a nuisance by shunning us and gossiping about us. And I can add a paragraph about injecting divisive politics into our peaceful community relations."

"Yeah. Maybe drive her out, just like you did with Dorothy. Let's see. They've got 92 townhouses here, so you'll need...69 signatures."

"I think I can do that. Obviously, the Bradshaws are out, and so is Verna, but everyone else will sign. Whenever I meet anyone except those two, they're very friendly. We all get along fine. Even if they voted against Murtaugh, they're not the type of people who like dissension. They never discuss politics."

However, after four days of collecting signatures on the petition that she had personally composed – with some help from online examples – she had only 23 signatures.

"I'm really disappointed, Paul."

"I know you are, but it's not your fault. You tried your best."

"What irritates me is that several people who refused to sign told me they didn't agree with Lena's behavior. The Garths said they just didn't want to create any ripples. And they told me – after swearing me to secrecy, mind you – that they voted for Murtaugh. Can you imagine that? They didn't have the courage! Why can't people stand up for what they believe?"

He shook his head. "Cowards like that are as bad as liberals."

"Well, I'm going to the monthly meeting next week, and present my petition."

"What good is that, Calli? You don't have enough signatures."

"To register a complaint, and to show the board that I'm not the only one having a problem with Lena."

At the HOA meeting, after the old-business and treasurer's reports, she raised her hand. "I'm Calliope Peeples. I'm having a problem with one of our members. And just to show I'm not alone, I have a petition here signed by 23 other members. I know that's not enough to get Lena Holden declared a nuisance, but I thought you should know there's a problem. I also want it to be shown in the record."

At this point, someone else rose. "Excuse me. I'm Susan Pickering. I too have a petition. After Ms. Peeples went around with her petition, several of us were angered and decided to circulate our own petition declaring Calliope Peeples a nuisance." She walked forward and handed the sheets to the board president.

"How many signatures did you collect?" the president asked.

"Seventy-one," Susan replied.

"In that case," the president said, "I move to impose the minimum fine of $100 on the Peeple's residence. In one month, we'll poll the members again. For each month the member remains in violation, the fine will increase by $100."

***

"They did what?!" Paul said. "That's un-American."

"That's what our country has become, Paul. Why can't people just get along?"

The Latest News

Hank Blount's whole face was one casaba melon of wrinkles, but those now on his forehead deepened beyond their habitual furrows. "What do you mean hacked?"

Nate Morris had not been able to devise a way to soft-pedal the bad news. "This is the second time it's happened. I gather most of the facts, write the rough draft and transfer it to our server. Within two days, it's up on the web."

"Where on the web?"

"CogInGear," Nate said. His boss looked even more perplexed. "CogInGear dot com," Nate explained. "It's a website that purports to expose stories supposedly suppressed by the 'old media', as they call us. Basically a knock-off of Wikileaks."

"I see. And who runs this site?"

"That's just it. Nobody knows."

"Well, maybe he's using the same sources. How did we find out about the story?"

"That's what I figured on the first story," Nate replied. "Just a coincidence. But this makes two in a row, and the timing is identical — two days after I transfer it from my laptop to the server."

"This was the naval commander story? Garrison was it?"

"Garrister. Naval squadron commander making it with a Pentagon playmate — someone in the admiral's office. The thing is, it even had her name. And that came from a totally separate source. CogInGear would have had to reach both sources right after I did."

"You're sure nobody could have hacked your laptop? Or your home Wi-Fi?"

"The thing is, the playmate's name came from my D.C. source. I didn't work on the Garrister story after I got back from D.C. It was late and I came directly here the next morning and downloaded it to the server. Two days later, we get scooped."

Blount nodded. "Okay. I know you're careful. We have to look at all possibilities."

"Of course," Nate said, though he knew his boss. Blount's middle name was *Paranoia*. He never trusted anybody when it came to keeping a lid on a story.

Blount looked at his oversize desk for several seconds. "You're right," he finally said. "Too coincidental. I'm calling in a computer expert. If we've been hacked, he'll find the leak. Special investigations are the cherries of the *Philadelphia Lighthouse*. If we lose the lead time on those, we lose a big chunk of our readers. In the meantime, continue writing your next story, but keep it off our servers until the computer guy's done with his work."

***

By the time Nate got home, his headache had spread from his eyes to his temples. He knew he had damaged his creds with his distrustful boss, but it would have been worse to say nothing. Nate's production would have sagged, and Blount would have eventually found out, anyway. *'What would he have thought then?'*

Catherine was busy in the kitchen. "Dinner's gonna be a little late. I had to run an errand for the boss on the way home."

"That's okay. I need a few minutes to unwind anyway." A half-hour later, he entered the kitchen. "How's dinner coming?"

"Just getting ready to put it on the table. Can you get the plates and silverware?"

As he arranged the two place settings, he thought, *'Maybe it's time for a better table to go with the new plates.'*

Once they had started eating, she asked, "So how long you back for this time?"

"A few days. I've got to put together what I know to figure out what I don't know. Then I'll have to travel to fill in the missing pieces."

"Something big?"

"Well, I don't think it will bring down the administration, but I suspect the president's going to be making some cabinet changes."

"Really? That big?"

"Yep. That's what journalism's about. Changing the world. Keeping people honest. That's what I love about it. How are things at your place?"

"Pretty busy, actually. Koln is probably going to pick up some work from MIT."

"MIT? Hey, that's big game. Capture a trophy like that, and Koln could attract other big league clients. Maybe Harvard or Princeton?"

"Yeah. Maybe." Her lack of enthusiasm bordered on indifference.

"Honey, I realize you don't think your job is important, but MIT and all those colleges and museums function only because of a lot of other elements that don't seem important. It's the same with the *Lighthouse*. The people who work at the ink manufacturer probably don't think their job's important, but without them, there'd be no newspaper. Koln Publishing is one of the pieces for MIT and others."

"Yeah, that's true. Good point."

After dinner, he took his briefcase to his work room, and worked with his laptop to refine his project's outline. It was a small room, which he liked after spending a day in the large open floor space at the newspaper.

She did the dishes, then watched television alone for the rest of the evening.

***

Randall Bodine rotated a pencil between his thumbs and forefingers. "I'm satisfied with your work, and I've heard compliments from associates in other sections. Your handling of the department is competent. However, I'm wondering what you think you could do to make it more efficient."

Catherine hated annual reviews. It wasn't from any expectation of criticism – she worked extremely hard to track the details of her tasks. No, it was the charade: The praise followed by the inevitable request for suggestions on what you could do to improve. Of course, that should raise embarrassing questions: 'Why weren't you already doing those things?' Or, 'Why didn't you make this suggestion before?' And she really hated that pencil-rotating thing. "Well, I could use a better headset. The one I have is old, and the newer ones have a longer range. Sometimes I have to access file drawers, and they're in the next cubicle, and I have to put the customer on hold."

Bodine switched from his two-handed axial rotation to the one-hand propeller twirl. "Hm. I guess we could look into the cost. Hm. Yes, good idea. Anything else?"

"No. Everything else seems to be running smoothly."

"Very good. As I said, we're very satisfied with your performance and the performance of your department. I'd like to be able to offer you a larger increase, but things are a bit tight now in the academic publishing business. Education institutions nowadays are struggling with their budgets, so we have to as well." He handed her the envelope.

She thanked him without opening it, already knowing it contained despondency; hoping it didn't hold humiliation. But then, the annual review process had already hardened her to those. In fact, her whole job had long ago habituated her to Thoreau's "quiet desperation." *Director of Customer Service* was just an obfuscation, a long title pinch-hitting for a short paycheck in a fixed game. She long ago realized she was a glorified customer service operator, the gal you got on the telephone when you wanted to be transferred to someone else; or worse, the one you bitched to when the system broke down. The only thing that made it tolerable was the class of customer. Academic people were relatively polite and capable of understanding plain English. Still, it seemed to her a pale reward for four years of college and seven years of working off its debt. She returned to her 'department', which was her.

***

The following week, Nate strode into Blount's office without bothering to knock, which told Blount that the story was big. "Morning, Nate. How did your trip go?"

"Fantastic. Not only are our suspicions true, but all three were willing to talk."

"On the record?"

"Two of them, yes; one, no."

"Two? That's good. Really good. This could be the biggest story of 2009. Finish up the story and log it on the server."

"Has it been fixed?" Nate asked.

"Oh yeah, that's another thing. Our hacking expert couldn't find any evidence of an intrusion. Still, just to be safe, he added some encryption safeguards, and some new procedures. The big one is that from now on, no Wi-Fi anywhere in the building. We've got Ethernet cords at every station."

"Okay. Got it."

"And one more thing: Here's your new user name and password." He pulled a piece of paper from his desk drawer and handed it to Nate.

Back at his desk, Nate logged on and created a new folder titled *VesicleBribesNotes*. He transferred all his notes and records for the story into that folder, then created another, which he named *VesicleBribesDraft*. He created an outline for the story, and assigned outline sections to each item in the notes. Once these preliminary tasks were complete, he began writing the story. At 5:30

he called Catherine. "Honey, I'm going to be late...I know, and I'm sorry. I got buried in a story, and lost track of time...I'm uploading my progress right now. I'll be leaving in two minutes." After he hung up, he reflected on the fact he hadn't called her sooner. He felt guilty leaving her alone so much with all his traveling, and now he was going to be late in getting home for the evening. But then, he'd written almost the entire story, one that would shake things up in the political world. As he walked out, he thought of saying goodnight to Blount, but saw that he was in conversation with Mel Trenchant, the _Lighthouse's_ reporter-at-large. '_Mel staying late? Must have a special story in the works too,_' he thought.

After dinner, he got back on the project, and made considerable progress.

"You coming to bed?" she asked as she got up from the couch in the TV room.

"In a few minutes. I've just got to make a couple of notes on fact-checking for tomorrow's phone calls. I'll be there in no time."

When his head finally hit the pillow, he had no trouble falling asleep, happy at how much he'd accomplished for the day. He knew Blount would probably give it front-page exposure – a nice feather in Nate's career cap.

The next morning, after a shower, he wolfed down an abbreviated breakfast and headed for the office, eager to get back to the article. Would this make his career? No. But it would be another link in a someday chain that would lift his reputation in the news publishing world, and hold his name up high enough for public recognition. Not that he was doing badly. The Philadelphia Lighthouse wasn't some lightweight local news-sheet. It was a 137-year-old prize-winning newspaper famous for uncovering scandals. And who was it's main scandal ferret these days? Nate Morris. '*Maybe I should change that to* Nathan. *Give the public persona more gravity. Then again, he doesn't call himself* Robert Woodward. *Maybe in Europe that would work better, but here in America, Nate sounds more...more man on the street. Yeah, just keep at it for a few more years, and then find a way into television, starting as a guest on some of the morning talk shows.*" In Nate's internal screen, he pictured his career as a Jacob's ladder, long, but inevitably leading to a golden light, provided he continued step by step by step. The Vesicle story was just another rung, but an important one.

By three-o'clock, the story was complete, except for his edit. He always did his own editing, even though it would have to be cross-checked with another writer in the office – probably Emily James. She was good, but Nate had learned that the more errors he could iron out of the article, the fewer details the cross-checker would amend. At half-past four he emailed it to Blount, then called Eddie. "Hey Eddie, how about we get together tonight?...Ranchero's? Nah. We ate there the last two times...Ramblin' Rosies? Sure, that sounds perfect. Five-thirty work for you?...Great. See you then."

Eddie Penster worked for the *Stelladium Herald*, a competitor, but they got along too well to let that get between them. They never discussed ongoing or upcoming stories – only old or dead ones. They had never formally agreed to those conditions. It was an understanding between professionals who bore respect for the other's craft; and also friendship rooted in their college days.

"Hey buddy, good to see you."

Nate gave his friend a hug. "Yeah, it's been a while. Great to see you too." He always marveled how Eddie's wide smile could light up a room.

"Two months, hasn't it been?" Eddie asked.

"Something like that. I've been traveling a lot."

The hostess welcomed them and led them to their booth, past the crowded tables in the noisy room.

"So where've you been traveling to? Anyplace interesting?"

"Naw," Nate said, "mostly grunt work. You know, second-sourcing, verifying names and places."

"Exciting ones, I hope."

"More frustrating. My last story got scooped by CogInGear. Somehow they hacked into our computer system."

"Hell, Nate. That can be a journal killer. It's hard enough to get people to pay for online access to our papers, and if we can't scoop the freebie cowboys, it'll become impossible."

"And we spend all the money and do all their work for them. But we got it fixed. Blount brought in a hacker expert to armor-plate the system. Still, I already lost the exclusive on two stories. So what have you been up to?"

"Oh, you know. We have our struggles too. I just lost a story, too."

"How come?"

"Empty air."

Nate nodded. "No there there. We get plenty of stories that don't pan out. But that's the nature of the beast."

"True, but this one actually swallowed up a lot of hours. The boss was not happy."

"So, what was the story? I mean, as long as it turned out to be nothing..."

"Sure, I can tell you about it. It concerned Russian embassy personnel. A guy named Andrei Slovodakov. Works in the Commerce section of the embassy."

"What? A spy?" Nate asked.

"Well, sort of. Not spying on us, though. He was supposedly a member of the Estonian Mafia who had somehow infiltrated the Russian Foreign Office." Eddie noticed his friend's quizzical look. "I know, I know. And I approached it as skeptically as any wildass story I've ever been told. The thing is, when I fact checked the records, there were some odd things. Then my State Department contact did some checks and discovered they've got Slovodakov's file red-tabbed."

"What does the file say?"

"That's another thing. My contact's security clearance isn't high enough to read it. So now the red light's really blinking, and I get sucked in even further. Eventually, I find out he's just some guy who's in tight with a Russian plutocrat – which explains how he got the job."

"And also explains the red-tab and security level. Most of the plutocrats have Putin's ear."

"Exactly," Eddie said. "So, almost fifty hours of investigation time wasted. Like I said, I had a very unhappy boss."

"Consider yourself lucky. If it had happened to me, Blount would have accused me of doing it on purpose."

"Hi. Beef stroganoff I believe is yours…" the waitress set the plate down in front of Eddie, "…and the crispy chicken for you. Careful. The plate is hot. Anything else I can get you for now?"

After she left, Eddie continued, "So your boss is hard on you?"

"You bet. After the second hacking…"

"Second hacking?! You've been hacked twice?"

"Well, on the first one, we figured we just got scooped. But on the second…well, that was too much of a coincidence."

"So, why's Blount blaming you?"

"He might think I'm investigating on the newspaper's dime, then selling to CogInGear."

"Double-dipping?"

"It's how his mind works. Always worried about every little thing, almost expecting that something's going to go wrong."

"Well, I know you, and you're the one thing that won't go wrong. I remember you in college, Nate. You were always out to change the world."

"I'm trying to build a reputation, Eddie. That's why this thing's giving me a double whammy. I've learned to read Blount. He's starting to have some personal doubts about me, and I'm losing some damned good stories too."

Eddie raised his glass to signal the waitress for another beer. "The computer guy's work should stop all that."

"Yeah, I feel much better about my next story. Just submitted it today. It should put me back on track."

***

Except it didn't.

Two mornings later, when he walked into the office, the indoor season was winter, coated with dark ice. Everyone looked at him like he was a displaced refugee from a war zone.

"Blount wants to see you."

"Okay. Thanks, Mel."

Blount just looked at him for several seconds. "Don't sit down. Come around here and look at this."

The computer monitor was already on the CogInGear website. With the Vesicle story. Nate's legs started to give out and he slumped into Blount's chair. "Some of the same words. But...I thought you said the encryption software was upgraded."

"It was. Can you explain it?"

"No." He looked at Blount. "I...I have no idea. I sent you the story just yesterday."

"Did you write any of it at home?"

"Well, sure. I did some of it at home, but…"

"You got Wi-Fi at home?"

"But how would anyone…"

"Jesus!" yelled Blount. "If we got rid of Wi-Fi here, you sure as hell should have realized yours was potentially vulnerable too." He turned away. "Christ!"

"But Hank, the Garrister playmate story – I never worked on it at home after I got the name."

"Look Nate. It's real simple. They didn't get it from our system, so it has to come from yours. And now it's been picked up by The Harmon Report on TV – as a CogInGear story, not as ours. By tomorrow it will be in half the newspapers in the country. I don't care how you fix this, but you better God damned well secure your end of it." Blount took a breath and paced back and forth. "Okay. Here's the rule. While you're working at home, you turn off the Wi-Fi. Is that clear?"

"Yeah."

"And you don't turn it back on till your computer is off. For all we know, the bastards are reading stuff right off the hard drive. And don't back it up to your server or another computer or any system backup drive. Got it?"

"Yes. I got it. I'll only back it up to a memory stick."

"And immediately remove the stick."

"OK, Hank, I got it. By the way. Did we even get a chance to edit my story?"

"Yeah. Mel completed it before he left yesterday evening. Why?"

"I just feel bad that it got scooped when we were so close."

Blount looked at him for several seconds, but refrained from commenting. "Just get out of my office and find us another story," he muttered.

Nate returned to his desk, ignoring everyone's sidelong glances. They obviously regretted not being a fly on the wall over the previous 10 minutes. For once he wished his cubicle wasn't in the front of their common office space. It was the most prestigious place, but also the most visible. He found himself envious of a previous era, one of semi-private offices, or at least taller partitions. He pulled himself out of the reverie, disgusted at his mushiness. _'Might as well wish the internet would evaporate. You handle the cards you're dealt.'_

But how do you play this hand? He felt helpless, uncertain how he could stop the hacking. Perhaps get another laptop? One they could never identify as his? Then, another thought occurred to him, one that had been hiding unrecognized in the back of his mind. _'What if it was one of the staff? He looked around. Emily? No, she's competent and works hard, but she's no back-stabber. Lenny? He does sports and entertainment. Maybe he wants to expand into more serious journalism? Then again, he relishes sports. Not just a fan. Fuckin' fanatic. Mel...hmmm, doubtful. Officially reporter at large, maybe hungry to make a name for himself? But Mel's totally straight-arrow.'_

Nate spent the rest of the morning pretending to write, but really doodling; or more accurately, thinking hard while his hand drew squares. Lots of squares within squares. And circles within circles, and squares inside of circles. Finally, he went to lunch. At Yoto's Sushi bar, he took a table instead of the counter. He wanted to be alone.

"Good afternoon, Nate. How are you today?"

"Fine, Ken," he lied. "How're things with you?"

"Very good, thanks. You want a menu?"

"No, I'll have the tekkamaki and the nigiri."

"And green tea, as usual?"

"Yeah, thanks."

As he stared at the garish wallpaper with its cliché scenes of Mt. Fuji and huge ocean waves, he remembered his trip to Japan, where sushi bars had plain-painted walls with wood screens for decoration. Most American sushi restaurants were American's fantasies of Japan. *'Then again, so's the sushi.'* He remembered reading how the fish are fake, except in the most expensive sushi restaurants. *'What was it…red snapper's actually dyed tilapia…or was that rockfish?'* But it was delicious, and he didn't care about the food fakery or the wallpaper fakery or… *'Fake. Hmm.'*

He grabbed his phone. "Hey, Eddie. How you doing? Remember the story you told me last night about the Russian Embassy? What was that guy's name? Andrei something?…How do you spell the last name?…Slovodakov. Got it. In the commerce section, right?…No, no. You've already discovered there's nothing to it. I just wanted to tell Catherine about it. She always enjoys a good story. Lifts her spirits after a day at work…Yeah, you too. And thanks."

He ate the sushi slowly, but hardly tasted it as he mentally constructed the story all through the meal. And on his walk back to the office too, barely aware of the passing cars and people. Back at his desk, Nate began typing like a speed demon. It was easy. He didn't have to reference any notes. He already knew the whole story – the whole fake story. But then he wondered, *'Is there actually a mafia in Estonia?'* He checked on the internet, and there was. *'Perfect!'* he thought. And after he returned home that evening, he continued writing the story, making certain the Wi-Fi was *not* turned off. The 'report' included everything Eddie had mentioned to him, plus a lot more. To protect Eddie's creds with his State Department contact, Nate's article mentioned an anonymous NSA source. Other changes made the story even more alluring. It was late by the time he finished with the spell-check. When he finally got to bed, he fell asleep quickly.

The next day, he arrived early at work, logged in and uploaded the story onto the server. Then he put together a notes document, with fake sources and dates. In truth, he wasn't certain of the source of the leak, but whether it was his home Wi-Fi or the newspaper's computers, he was determined to cover both bases. CogInGear would run the story and be totally discredited on an international basis – by the Russians, the Estonians, NSA, State Department, and finally, by the public. Their website would lose fans across the globe. It was Nate's only remedy. *'Remedy, with a liberal dose of revenge,'* he thought. If he couldn't plug the leak, he could make certain it would drown whoever had created it. He was also confident that he could construct a string of such stories in the future. *'A lineup of fiction as long as a snake, and as poisonous,'* he thought.

Once he had completed the Slovodakov story, he went back to one of the actual stories he'd been investigating. His work seemed to return to normal. He checked the

CogInGear site each night, and as expected, the story popped up the second day afterward. By the next day, other media were reporting it, with CogInGear fully credited. Nate was pleased. He knew that the wider the story spread, the more damage to CogInGear's credibility when the public learned it was false. Watching television that night, Nate smiled, a reaction television news rarely evoked from him.

***

Two weeks later, two agents from the FBI showed up at the Philadelphia Lighthouse and escorted Nate to their local office.

As a news investigator, Nate knew which questions to ask. "You said I was here to 'help you with an investigation.' Could you be more precise: Am I here as a witness, a person of interest, or a suspect?"

Special Agent Peter Truman pursed his lips. "I appreciate the fact that you're not some greenhorn, Mr. Morris. Frankly, at this point we're still trying to make heads or tails of this. So for now, you're a possible source of information. Let's call it, 'a witness' for now."

"Okay. So, how can I help you?"

"Do you know anyone named Allen Spengler?"

"No. No never heard of him."

"Either professionally or personally?"

"Understood, agent Truman. The name's unfamiliar."

"How about one Francine Rickards."

"No, never heard of her either."

"Spengler and Rickards were found murdered two days ago in a house in Bodine."

"Ah, yes. I remember now. There was a story on the evening news. But what does this have to do with me?" What Nate was also wondering was why the FBI would be involved in a local murder. Was there a story for the Lighthouse in this?

For the first time, agent Robin Fletcher spoke. "Mr. Morris, we're wondering if you or anyone at your newspaper was working on a story concerning Rickards or Spengler?"

"No. As I've said, I never even heard the name – well, I heard it on the newscast, but I certainly didn't remember it. You'd have to ask my editor about our other reporters' stories."

"The reason we're asking you is because of the memory sticks we found in the house. They contain news stories with your byline."

For the first time in the interview – which appeared to be evolving into an interrogation – Nate was lost for words. He shifted positions on his chair. Finally, he asked, "What were the titles of the stories?"

Fletcher looked at a printed sheet. "One was titled, 'Corrupt Commerce', and the other was 'Russian Spies Out-Spied.'"

Nate said nothing. His inner feedback began to rumble. He realized he wasn't breathing. Fletcher and Truman looked at each other, baffled by his silence. Finally, Nate said, "I think you just caught the CogInGear network."

After a long pause, Truman said, "Actually, we've come to the same conclusion. The question is, how did your stories end up in their possession?"

"We were hacked." Nate realized how improbable it sounded, even before he noticed their skeptical expressions. "Look, I'd have nothing to gain by losing the chance to get my own story in my own newspaper. I mean, that is my profession."

"We figured as much," Truman said.

"We also considered that you might have a motive in killing the competition," Fletcher said, "but then we examined the story more closely." She picked up a folder from the table, opened it, and summarized what she saw. "Contrary to your assertions, Andrei Slovodakov was not a member of the Estonian Mafia. However, he was a member of the Chechen Mafia, and he *was* spying on the Russians." She paused to look at Nate, who was obviously flummoxed. "After he was outed by the CogInGear story, the Russians arrested him and provided him a complimentary trip back to Russia."

"No doubt with free room and board in a cozy room in one of their prisons," Truman said. "For the rest of his probably short life."

Nate opened his mouth, but remembered the *Lighthouse* lawyer's advice on police interrogations. "*Always answer truthfully, but never volunteer information.*" Nate definitely wasn't going to mention the fake story. On the other hand, maybe there was a second news story in all this, one about the entire affair? One that would not mention a fake story? Finally, he spoke.

"That's incredible."

"It seems the Chechens were not happy with having one of their own outed. Apparently, they tracked the hacker back, and...well, I doubt we'll be able to find the specific person who killed Spengler and his girlfriend."

Nate nodded, but the inner feedback had suddenly vaulted to a screech. *'Jesus! Spengler killed by a story?...my story.'* Nate had always taken pride in his profession, and not only because of his journalistic skills. His stories kept the world informed. But now...now they had gotten someone killed. But who? *'Someone who jeopardized my career...and the newspaper...and everyone else who worked there. For that matter, every other legitimate news journal. Hell, he was a thief, just a leech. Screw him!'* Then he recalled Eddie's talk about a red-tabbed file. *'My God! Lucky for Eddie he didn't run the story.'* Nate decided he would definitely not pursue any second story.

"It gets worse than that,"Fletcher said.

While she paused, Nate tried to read her face. What was it? Sadness?

Finally, she continued. "You weren't hacked. Those memory sticks came from your computer." She waited while Nate absorbed her words. "We found your wife's prints throughout his house. They were in our database from when she applied for a position with the DMV several years ago."

"But why...she wouldn't...I don't understand."

"Your wife was having an affair with Spengler," Fletcher said. "He promised to marry her and whisk her off to somewhere or other once his so-called news company was bought out by a big tech firm for a big-buck jackpot."

"The rainbow dream of every hacker and app-maker," Truman added. "And all that time, Rickards was his actual girlfriend."

"I'm sorry," Fletcher said. "He played your wife, and your wife played you."

Nate took a breath. Actually, several breaths. He was desperately trying to reduce the dozen voices in his head vying for attention. Finally, he asked, "Is she under arrest? I mean, is she going to be charged?"

"We're definitely considering charging her with aiding and abetting communication theft," Truman said. "But we need your testimony that you did not give her those memory sticks."

"Nor give her permission to use them," Fletcher added.

The voices in Nate's head slowed. *'How much is my fault?...Then again, how much hers?...but I love her...betrayed me...been neglecting her...betrayal...love her...too wrapped up in work...'* Finally the thoughts coasted to a stop. *'Caroline in prison...horrible.'*

"Agents Truman and Fletcher. Let's be clear on one thing. Under no circumstances will I testify against her."

The two agents looked at him for several seconds. "After she cheated on you?" Fletcher asked.

"Yes. Even after she cheated on me. I love her, and we'll work it out, no matter what it takes."

The room went silent.

"Well, then, that's that," Truman finally said. "We can't force you. We'll have someone drive you back to the paper."

As Nate rode back, he figured he'd have time to talk to Blount within the hour it would take them to process her release. Blount would be relieved to know the hacking problem was behind them. *"And when he finds out we were both victims, he'll think of me more as an ally. I can get back in his good graces – at least until his next panic attack.'*

This time he knocked on Blount's door before entering. He explained everything.

"Jesus! Your wife was the source of the leak all along?"

"I know Hank. I was even more shocked. I mean, how would you feel if you found out your wife was cheating on you?"

His look was direct and hard. "I got divorced, is what I did." He shook his head. "Cheating on you? Nate, she was also trying to torpedo your career. That's a double-whammy!"

Nate nodded silently, his head drooping.

"What do you plan to do?"

"I'm not sure. We'll have to find some way to work it out."

"We? Which we?"

"Catherine and I."

Blount's eyebrows dropped lower than Nate had ever seen them before. "Work it out? Nate, she cheated on you and your job. What's there to work out?"

"The truth is, I've been wrapped up in my work and gone from home too much. I've been neglectful. She has a crap job and needed some attention, something to make her feel good about her life, and I haven't been giving her either of those. Frankly, at night I've mostly ignored her. It's partly my fault."

There were several seconds of silence, and when Nate looked up, Blount's expression was scary.

"What kind of a man are you? Your wife cheats, and you feel guilty? What kind of a reporter are you? Your wife gives your stories to another news source?"

Nate opened his mouth, but nothing came out.

"I tell you, I'm going to have the answer to both of those questions. You either ditch your cheating wife, or you ditch your relationship with your profession. Because if this story gets out, no one in journalism will want you even buying their newspaper. You get out of this building right now, spend the night thinking about it, and give me your answer in the morning."

Nate zombie-walked out to his car. As he drove back to the FBI facility, he wondered how he had been so wrong in surmising Blount's response. He really loved his wife. Perhaps Blount didn't understand real love. *'Perhaps he's incapable – maybe the reason he's been twice-divorced and then single for so many years. Was he always that way? Or does the business change a man? Is this the reason I've been neglecting our relationship? Is Blount what I'll be like in 20 years?'* He shuddered at the thought, repulsed, sickened.

He announced himself and his purpose to the receptionist. As Catherine walked out, slump-shouldered and eyes on the floor, he felt sorry for her. He wanted to comfort her, to protect her. He opened the car door for her, something he normally never did.

It was a silent 40-minute drive home, but thoughts kept flowing through his head, constant, like rainfall slowly cutting it's own channel to form a new river. He parked in the driveway and turned off the engine.

"I'm sorry," she said, then dropped her head and began to cry.

"I don't care," he replied. "Our marriage is done. And it's all your fault."

Epidemic

My heart was pounding. A rat reading my mind? But the results were clear. As long as I looked at the maze, the rats raced to the food in a third of the time; if I looked away, their ability was normal. And more astonishing, when I peered at a differently configured maze, they failed to complete their own. After I had returned the last rat to her cage, I sat down and considered the implications.

The kicker was that I couldn't write a paper on it, couldn't even report it. I had breached protocol, concocting the drug without authorization. If I were discovered, I'd certainly lose my job, perhaps my career.

My phone buzzed. No surprise. It was Francine. Irritated that I was late, also no surprise.

"Working on a Saturday? Joe, did you forget about our date?"

"Not at all. I thought I'd be finished here sooner."

"Are we going or not?" she asked with a serrated edge to her voice.

"I'm sorry, but it took longer than I'd expected. I think I've made a breakthrough. I'm just finishing. See you in a half-hour." I quickly put everything away and left for Francine's.

"So what's the big breakthrough?" she asked.

"False alarm," I lied. No, she wouldn't report me to the lab, or even blab to one of her friends.. I just didn't want her to suspect my sanity. I managed to keep up my end of the dinner conversation, which, as usual for her, dwelled excessively on current events. Frankly, it took all my discipline to keep my mind off the experiment and its implications. Who wants to think about rats over dinner;

or worse, during sex? However I could during the movie, when my distracted thoughts could hide within the theater's darkness and the film's dialogue. It was sufficient. By the end of the movie, I had decided.

The next morning, Francine was incredulous. "You're going in today – a Sunday?"

"In my rush to leave, I forgot to put some of the equipment away. I just remembered. Besides, I have some personal things I need to take care of today."

"Let me guess. Another art piece?"

"No, no. Just some personal errands." She was referring to the art repros in my condo – prints and small sculptures. It was one of my interests she didn't share. Her idea of interior decorating was a set of Maxfield Parrish prints. Don't misunderstand. I like Parrish too – just not the sentimental works she chose. And hanging multiple prints of the same size and the same distance apart and all in a level row…let's just say they proclaimed her engineer's mind, rather than an esthetic one. She did have one esthetic knack: personal appearance. She consistently bought outfits that displayed her figure well. Even in an off-the-rack pantsuit, people might have mistaken her for a professional model.

Back at the Keller Cognitive lab, I mixed the components of the new drug: Mescaline and ligase-6 heated to 160-degrees. I'd decided to call it *psymes* for its psychic effect. Too bad I had to keep it a secret. When I look back on my decision, I wonder at my recklessness. Perhaps I was irritated over the fact that a mere rat could read my mind – my theoretically more highly evolved human mind. Or did I hope a proportional improvement would mean I'd become the most psychically advanced person in history? I now grasp the extent of risk, though I knew even then that as a scientist, I should have first studied the long-term effects on the rats. What if the drug had proved carcinogenic or damaged organs?

***

The rats had imbibed psymes three days before my experiments, so I assumed I wouldn't be reading minds until Tuesday at the earliest. I was correct about the timing, but not the outcome. I wasn't reading anyone's mind. By noon my vision had become blurred. Everyone around me appeared to have hazy edges. I went to the animal cages. They too had a blur around their bodies. *'Infrared from body heat? Or some other energy field?'*

On the drive home, every pedestrian and bike rider had a blurred outline. Even dogs. My web searches finally directed me to the correct terminology: Auras. *'Auras? What the...'* I finally understood: the effect of psymes on humans was not the same as on rats. I couldn't read minds; only see auras. I was extremely disappointed, but I continued to explore on the web. I learned that different states of mind created different aura colors. But the 'experts' had a variety of opinions. By experts, I mean a lot of flaky people promising to read your pie-in-the-sky spiritual aura for a down-to-earth price. *'Can I pay in spiritual dollars?'* I mused. One claimed that the color of spirituality was violet; another assured me it was pink. Red was the color of anger; another said it was the color of love; still another identified it with good health.

Again, the scientist in me chose the logical course: Empirical research, which meant going out for dinner. *Bergers*, a local café, was a natural choice. It's always busy, even on weeknights. I figured, *'Go for the food, stay for the auras.'* And afterward, I dropped by *Pisces*, a slightly upscale bar. The colors I observed were only slightly varied – mostly light brown, with a few yellows and a smattering of greens. No violets or pinks in sight.

'*Perhaps Bergers should add vegan to their menu,*' I thought. At *Pisces, a* couple began bickering. When I'd walked in, I noticed their auras were a deeper brown than everyone else's; they quickly darkened. '*So, the darker the brown, the greater the anger?*' I speculated.

And so it went for the next week, me observing auras and comparing their colors with their owners' apparent dispositions. My lab colleagues had a preponderance of yellow, which I finally deciphered as an analytical state of mind. Ray, the director, shifted between yellow and turquoise, a transformation that mystified me. However, one afternoon, he asked me into his office.

"Joe, I want to compliment you for some really great work." His aura lit up in a solid turquoise.

"Thanks, Ray. Very nice to know one is appreciated."

"More than appreciated. I sent the compliment upstairs. I wanted them to know."

"Ah! Much obliged."

"Actually, it was part of a request for a raise. I know last year's was meager, but I wanted to get you a larger package this year."

'*He's going to tell me there's no raise this year,*' I realized.

"Unfortunately, they turned me down."

"I see."

"Keller Cognitive's parent company lost money in some of their other divisions, so we're all having to tighten our belts. None of the other associates will be getting one either."

"I see. So, tell me Ray: Did they give you an increase?" In truth, I wasn't interested in his answer. I had already surmised it. Nor was I slinging arrows of sarcasm. I was merely being a good scientist: I was testing his aura's reaction, which moved firmly into the brown before changing into a bright turquoise. _'Hmm, appears to be a flash of...anger, followed immediately by...what?'_

"I'm not allowed to discuss compensation issues of any associate with another."

'Ah! So, turquoise is politics.' But then I reconsidered. _'Or maybe_ diplomacy _would be a kinder term.'_ Politics had earned an ugly connotation, and Ray wasn't a bad guy. He was just the messenger. And that was the reason I refrained from pointing out that he had already discussed the "compensation issues" of other associates. Besides, he had repaid me in furthering my private project, which was interpreting the many colors of auras I was now able to perceive. _'So brown reveals anger; turquoise shows diplomatic mode.'_ Even more important, I had seen a gray cloud around Ray's mouth during his moment of deception. Over the previous few weeks, I had seen it off and on around others' mouths. _'Lies,'_ I realized. We all tell them – the little, innocuous fabrications we give and receive to maintain the social fabric. His was unmistakable. I decided it was time for me to go turquoise on him.

"You're right, Ray, and I apologize for asking. It's just a little disappointing."

"For me too," he said, without any gray mouth. "Your work certainly deserves a raise, but I'm constrained by a budget set by others."

The ten minutes I spent in his office were the most rewarding in my life – not counting my birth, of course. It took a while for me to recognize the gift that far exceeded any raise he could have offered. I'm not talking about knowledge – merely recognizing when various people fibbed. Though I valued knowledge for its own sake, that consideration was myopic. The larger perspective rose in my mind a couple of weeks later when the auras began to fade. *'The effect isn't permanent,'* I discovered. Psymes only lasted about a month. It was only when threatened by the loss of my new perceptual ability that I realized how much I'd been wasting it. I reinjected myself the following Saturday, and, purely as an experiment, took a one-day trip to Vegas.

The only game that interested me was live poker. Crap tables and roulette wheels have no auras, but poker players do. I played conservatively for several hands, folding on the second card. I noticed that the auras of players with good cards shifted to red when they first looked at them; that of players holding garbage turned blue. And bluffers showed an unmistakable smudge of gray around the mouth. Once my data had been gathered, I played for real, and after winning a couple of hundred dollars, moved to a higher stakes table. After a couple of hours, I was another $5000 ahead.

But then I noticed a lot of strange auras beyond the table. A lot of yellow surrounded several observers. *'Yellow – analytical. Ah! Employees. Security.'* I was attracting attention. *'Time to go'.*

On the flight back, I realized I could easily clean up ten grand in one day, but I had to be discreet. *'Not just moving from table to table, but from casino to casino.'* It again occurred to me that I was thinking small. *'In fact, city to city: Reno, Sparks – hell, there are a lot of small towns in Nevada with live poker.'* By the time I had landed, the possibilities had widened to the whole country. *'Indian – that is, Native American…oh, hell! – Indian casinos have live poker. I can move state to state, play every weekend, and never attract unwanted attention.'* I had also done a mental calculation of my potential winnings over a weekend, minus airfare, hotel room and meals, and…well, I have to say that I needed to restrain my excitement. When I reached home, I immediately searched the web for IRS taxes related to gambling. It turned out that casinos only reported winnings to the IRS for poker tournaments and large machine payouts. That meant I would be able to keep all of my gains. Still, I realized winning too big at a single sitting would put me on the casinos' radar screens and get me permanently uninvited. I revised Gordon Gecko's famous dictum – '*Greed is bad; careful greed is good.*' Yes, I now admit I had become inspired by bad examples.

Over the next several months, I spent a lot of weekends traveling around the country. The tricky part was taking Francine on a "fun trip". While she was delighted, I had to hide the size of my winnings even from her. What if she were called as a witness in an IRS trial? She preferred slots, anyway, and so never observed me raking in some large pots – which I had to cash in frequently, in case she got bored and came over to watch. My insistence in switching tables and even casinos annoyed her, but she was having a good enough time. It was on the fourth return flight that the conversation became strained.

"You know, Joe, I think you need to back off the gambling."

"What do you mean, 'back off'?"

"I think you may have a problem."

"I don't have a problem. I just enjoy poker. That's all."

"Then why not pick a lower-stakes table? I mean, it's the same game."

"The better players sit at the higher-stakes table. It's more of a challenge."

"But you end up losing so often. How can you afford it?"

My lie had caught up to me. "I win some. Actually, my net losses are small. I'm getting really good at it."

"I'm just concerned…and also, I'm getting tired of it. Maybe just one weekend every couple of months, from now on? Can't we get back to just normal dating? You know, like we used to do before you became obsessed with cards?"

A good question. Could I?

I wanted to make it work. At first we tried dating in the middle of the week, but both of us were too tired the next morning. Friday nights didn't work for me – I always took an early flight on Saturdays. I finally had to face the fact: '*Francine or money?*' Even today, I have to admit to some guilt feelings over my decision, but it wasn't like we were married. Besides, our differing interests tended to weaken the gravitational tie between us. As I mentioned before, there was her fixation on current events and her lack of interest in art. Half our dinner conversations involved her talking about politics or economics or the latest armed conflict in some country I couldn't locate on a map.

"I don't suppose you'd want to go to a demonstration with me next weekend?"

"Which demonstration is that?"

"It's to protest starvation in America," she said, while lifting another shu mai with her chopsticks.

"Not my thing, as you know. Besides, it's the museum's opening of the Knutson exhibit. He'll be there for a personal meet and greet."

"And that's more important than starvation?"

I ignored the sarcasm. "Probably not, but I know Knutson personally – well, not like an old friend, but I've met him personally, and once joined him for lunch in Denver. Besides, starvation is like poverty or war. It's depressing. Sorry. I prefer art. I know how it makes me feel. Hell, I have more than enough trouble keeping my own life afloat without trying to save others."

"I wouldn't call it depressing," she said. "I'd call it 'angrifying', like all the other crap going on. Like scrapping the water quality bill. Or military procurement, with all the pork hanging from it like an over-decorated Christmas tree. What a waste. While people starve."

Her manner of speaking had become intense, and her aura increasingly darker shades of brown. I just looked at her.

"Sorry," she said quietly. "Sometimes I do feel it's futile. There's been a few times I've even tried avoiding the news and the talk shows, but honestly, it's like a horrible accident. I just can't not look."

"Well, I can. I'm not out to save the world. Anyway, I'm kept busy enough with work and art. And frankly, I'd rather not let the rest of the world get me down."

And so, our relationship frayed and finally ripped, though without acrimony. One day, she calmly told me it was over, that she'd met some guy named Ron at a demonstration, and yada, yada… In a way I was relieved. I would be able to travel almost every weekend to different casinos without making excuses or cashing in chips every half-hour. The only other problem was one that would make most people jealous: I had to hide my winnings from the IRS.

About a year after our split, I ran into Francine at the mall. It was a friendly conversation. She and Ron What's-His-Face had parted ways, so I suggested lunch, then invited her to my place for coffee and some catching up. I could see her aura had turned to a darker brown since I'd last seen her. Of course, I never mentioned auras or poker tables.

"So you got a new car," she observed. "And a BMW, at that."

"No, not new. A couple of years old. I got a good deal on it."

"Same art pieces?" she noticed. "I'd have thought you'd have added to the collection".

"No. The car swallowed a large chunk of change." Of course, I avoided mentioning that the statuettes and paintings she was looking at were not the old reproductions. I had gradually replaced those with originals. I also didn't mention the fireproof safe I'd recently installed in my bedroom closet. Her life, on the other hand hadn't changed, a fact that saddens me still. She had continued with her protest groups and other activities to "wake people up" to this or that threat, or the suffering of one group or another. The conversation was pleasant, but the door to our previous relationship had become walled over.

At a casino one Sunday, I was cleaning up pretty good. The guy opposite me had a deep blue aura, even during the shuffle. He lost his entire buy-in. The next morning, on my drive to work, I heard on the radio that someone staying in the same casino hotel had broken the window in his eighth-floor room and jumped. I stopped breathing. I just knew. I pulled over, and after a few minutes, called in sick to work. I returned home and went on the web. What I saw made me sicker. I went to _Pisces_. And for the first time, I began to look around at people. I mean really look at them _as_ people. So many blue and brown auras! And the browns were darker than when I had begun my 'casino tour' two years earlier. And I had never paid attention.

Over the following week, I was more observant. My coworkers' auras were still yellow, but a darker shade, more like Dijon mustard. And then it hit me. It was brown mixed into yellow. But they didn't seem seem angry.

And finally it hit me. They – and a whole lot of other people were angry and depressed without even realizing it. While I had been wrapped up in science for science's sake and art for art's sake and – most self-centered of all – money for money's sake, society around me had been falling apart. The celebrated "we the people" had become angrier. And I had gotten someone killed. Perhaps he would have taken his life anyway, but I had sped him to his death. I finally recognized the extent of my selfishness in totally ignoring them. I felt ashamed; and more important, lonely. Even my practice of science had been self-serving. I'd never even considered sharing the secret of psymes. At first, I wondered if I should have joined Francine in at least one of her quests. But then I remembered she had embarked on so many of them. She must have demonstrated or worked for 20 causes during the two years we had dated – like trying to empty the sea with a teacup.

I realized I needed guidance. It had been a long time since I'd attended church. I searched on the web and found the St. Andrew's Lutheran Church nearby. I called and made an appointment for the next evening.

Pastor Raymond Mendes was a stocky man with dark brown hair and a handsome full beard. His sports shoes and gabardine pants proclaimed an informality at odds with his black shirt and jacket, not to mention the clerical collar. "Before I hear your confession, Joe, I'd like to ask if you've been baptized."

"I was, as a child, though I haven't attended church in years. However, I now find myself at a crisis in my life."

"Tell me about it."

I explained everything. Everything, except the auras. After all, I needed sober advice, and even pastors aren't likely to take seriously a stranger jabbering about auras. So, I just mentioned that I had become an expert at poker, entirely self-absorbed and thoughtless about helping the rest of humanity; and that one of the losers had killed himself. I told him how that death had awakened me to the terrible condition of society, and that I now felt a need to help others.

"Well, the church can always use financial support. We're involved in several social projects that aid the poor and feed the hungry."

I had anticipated the suggestion of donations, which I welcomed; but I had something further in mind. Again, I avoided mentioning auras. "Pastor Mendes, most people I encounter are neither hungry, homeless, nor impoverished. Yet they are not happy. Perhaps they aren't suicidal, but they are angry and aggressive. I want to help them internalize a feeling of peace in place of anger. And I want to compensate for the life that I've lived – all the years of self-absorption. Perhaps you could think of some way I could get through to these people, make them recognize their own inner feelings, the tension within them that they camouflage behind their comforts and busyness and narrow self-interests."

"Wow," he replied. "You are quite eloquent, Joe. If you don't mind, I'd like to include some of what you just said into next Sunday's sermon."

"I'd be honored. Thank you." However, I noticed he hadn't answered my question. "So, any suggestions?"

"It's an odd question. My task, my function in the community, is to bring people to God; to expose them to His love. However, what you are seeking is entirely different. You want people to see their own sins – no not sins. Sins are acts that offend God or injure others. But you are talking about people who have internalized a hellish state. I almost feel like advising you to ask a psychiatrist, but they only treat people who come to them – individuals who already recognize their inner suffering."

"Most people don't," I said. "Their anger and angst are too deep. And their way of life is like a cocoon; they are too snug within it to see that they need to escape from it."

He nodded. "Exactly. So frankly, here's all I can do." At this point he stood, put his hand on my head, and prayed for me, asking God to bring me peace, and to help me find a pathway for my endeavor. Then he said, "The fact that you recognize your selfishness, and particularly how much loneliness it brings you, means you've already moved closer to God; and that you've taken the initial step to change your life. As for changing others, you'll have to make them recognize their own anxiety. I see two possibilities: First, by spreading your story, bearing witness to this lesson in your own life, you can make others more receptive to examining theirs. This is similar to what we do in our church. The other means would be to network with others – perhaps an online seminar. Those who recognize their need will reply. It would be more like a psychiatrist's approach."

I was happy to make a generous donation, for I did feel better after our conversation. However, it took a few days before I could distill his advice down to a specific idea. Perhaps changing other's auras would change the inner feelings that created them – sort of a reverse feedback. Except, it wasn't a solution. Obviously, I could change someone's aura momentarily by impacting their emotions, but how could I have a lasting effect? And also, how could I affect the auras of large numbers of people, short of creating some kind of worldwide miracle? My first thought, of course, was a new drug, but I had no clue where to begin. Psymes had been the result of a string of lucky accidents.

As usual, I continued on this new quest via the web, but soon found myself mired in a swamp of starry-eyed opinionators trumpeting a hodgepodge of ideas. Besides, they all talked about reading auras, not helping others change theirs. However, eventually I came across a blog site that mentioned a school named Manusyata. Another search brought me to the school's website, which specifically mentioned, "Change your aura; change your life." This was exactly what I was seeking. *'If I observe and copy their methods, perhaps I can apply them to others; maybe even scale it up to a movement.'* What I began to understand was that I had become more like Francine. I wanted to save people – not from tyrants or corporations or guns, but from the creeping darkness that was permeating society. Once that was done, they would spontaneously work to solve social problems like poverty and starvation.

Manusyata was located in Greeley. *'Heck, that's within easy driving distance.'* I jotted down the phone number and called the next day and made an appointment to join them for their next weekend open house.

On a Saturday, I presented myself to the desk and was shown into a room with a dozen or so people. They ranged in age from about 20 to 50 years. All were dressed casually, in varying degrees of new-ageyness – some with sandals, one with yoga pants, one with a steampunk skirt – all with pullover shirts emblazoned with various mandalas. Except me. I was the only one with a buttoned shirt, though its nature-like grassy pattern probably helped me fit in. What struck me were their auras: Only a few browns. Most of them ranged from green to yellow.

After a few minutes a man in an ornate robe entered. His aura glowed with an intense violet, the only person I'd ever seen with this color. Our guide announced, "Everyone, I'd like to introduce you to Dasan Sarah. He is the teacher and founder of Manusyata."

Sarah smiled and nodded to everyone and shook hands with all the guests. When he reached me, he eyed me intensely. His sustained stare made me wonder if he could see that I could see. I became nervous. But then he smiled and moved on. I never did learn why he paused with me so long. After a few more greetings, he conducted us all on a guided tour.

"Manusyata," he informed us, "is about helping to heal the world, a few students at a time. The world is in turmoil. People are plagued with unhappiness and tainted by angst. A week on retreat here will heal your spiritual wounds. You will return to the world not only healed, but able to heal those around you."

My heavens! It was almost as if he had read my mind. Manusyata was exactly what I was looking for. Before I left, I signed up for a retreat, paid the hefty fee, and on the following Monday, scheduled vacation time from Keller.

***

I could not deny the power of the retreat. As I sat in the meditation circle, I could clearly see that everyone's aura glowed with a bright pink, even those whose colors had been brown the first day. And in casual conversations, they all told me how their previous classes at Manusyata had changed their lives. They had become renewed – less angry, more peaceful, closer to the universal spirit. Relationships were enriched and health had improved. Each day, I very carefully memorized all the procedures and exercises in the expectation of recalling and assembling them later into some kind of project for healing others.

At the end of the week, Sarah led us in prayer. And as he conferred a blessing on us all I observed most of the people held their arms with palms upward, as if to receive the spirit his blessing was calling down from above.

At the end of the retreat, some of the acolytes needed rides home, and I volunteered. I drove off with three passengers.

"So what do you think?" Henry said.

"I'm very impressed," I replied.

"Has it changed you – I mean internally?" Peter asked.

"Absolutely. I feel so much more at peace inside." It was true. I had found an answer to my question: How to heal the masses, even if only a few people at a time. I now could fulfill my quest.

"Wow," Henry remarked. Then turning to the others, "And this is just his first time."

"Really?" Christine said. "And you already feel a difference?"

"Uh, yes. Of course."

Henry was impressed. "Man, I went here every other month for two years before I could feel a change."

"Twelve times?" I said. "Really?"

"He took longer than most," Peter explained. "It took me only five times."

"But I think my internal changes went deeper," Henry said.

"How many classes did you take, Christine?" I asked.

"I guess this makes it eight. But I noticed changes after the third class."

"What do you mean, 'deeper'?" Peter asked Henry.

"Just that. They went down to my core."

"Actually, I think that's true of everyone," Peter said. Then turning toward Christine, he asked, "Wouldn't you say yours affected your core?"

"Of course they did. I…"

Henry interrupted, asking Christine, "Then why do you have to come back so often? I come every other month, but you're back here every couple of weeks."

"I have a high-pressure job," she said. "I don't just sit around computing numbers all day."

"Not numbers, Christine. Programs. I write programs. And what makes you think there isn't pressure to produce? I'm always struggling to maintain schedule."

"Whatever," Christine shot back. "You're only responsible for the program. I have a staff to supervise."

"How big's your staff?" I asked.

"Six people," she said, "and all with their own personalities and egos."

"So, you have six people to help you do your job?" Peter suggested.

"Good one!" Henry said to Peter.

"What is this? The guys ganging up on the women?" she asked.

"So now you're going to make this about gender?" Henry said.

"Not gender; sexism. Not that I'd expect you to know the difference."

"Obviously, the retreat hasn't made you less arrogant," Peter said.

"Arrogant? Why? Because I enjoy returning for a retreat more often than you?"

"No. It's the put down," Peter said. "Henry wouldn't know the difference? That definitely disparaged Henry."

And as the road continued downward from the mountain, so did the conversation. And as they conversed – to use the most generous characterization – I noticed their auras gradually shifting from pink to orange to brown. By the time I dropped them off, their auras were all dark brown. Their relapses had taken less than two hours. As I drove back, I thought, *'And I'm going to change the world?'* I had to smile and shake my head at my grandiose naiveté. Little me was going to change the world. What self-conceit!

***

I still work at Keller Cognitive, and still keep up the psymes injections – it's always good to know when someone's lying. I no longer go to casinos, but during those two years, I accumulated a small fortune, which is now doing some good in the world. At the first Joe Pyramides Art Competition, the winner received a full scholarship for a course at the City Art Institute. Among our volunteer assistants was a lovely gal named Colpura, an artist from India. She has a part-time job sufficient for her worldly needs; one which allows her enough free time to paint. She has her priorities right. She also has beautiful eyes. We've dated for several months now. And in all our conversations, neither of us has ever brought up the question of solving mankind's problems.

Whiteout

French president Gerard Cassan looked around the table for several seconds. "Ladies and gntlemen, France is under attack. You know of the recent hacker attacks against our military, and the one against a nuclear generating plant. Then there was the break-in and theft of advanced technology at one of Soute Tech's laboratories. And now we have the death of immigrant Sergei Zhukov on French soil. We know these were all perpetrated by Russia. I've called you here for advice on our response.

Justice Minister Charlotte Mateau was the first to respond. "Mr. President, we have precedent for preventive detention, but we do not know the specific identities of the perpetrators. Moreover, hackers can operate from beyond our borders, and are therefore beyond our reach. In short, Mr. President, the justice ministry is helpless."

Cassan nodded. "Mr. Fabre?"

Economic minister Richard Fabre pursed his lips. "If successful, some of the attacks could have had grave economic effects. Future hack attacks might cripple our economy. And the theft of technology will have long term negative consequences."

"Mr. Desseuse?"

Interior Minister Laurent Desseuse leaned forward. "Mr. President, I think it is vital to consider not just what has happened, but the potential for future vulnerabilities."

"Of course. The security concerns of the Interior Ministry are preventative, as are those of the Defense Ministry."

"Not necessarily," Defense Minister Baer replied.

Cassan raised his eyebrows.

Baer continued. "I think you should know that Mr. Desseuse and I have had informal conversations, from which we have reached certain points of agreement."

"In that case," Cassan said, "please proceed. We need answers."

"I'm afraid the answers will create a measure of discomfort for all around this table. However, facts cannot be avoided."

"Agreed," replied Cassan with a brusqueness that testified to his reputation for impatience.

"We call the recent attacks on our nation, *gray warfare*," Desseuse began. "Gray warfare consists of small injuries, small intrusions – too small to warrant a full military response, but great enough to cause harm to our nation, or to prepare for some possible future conventional attack." Desseuse then launched into a disquisition on the options for a response. He quickly dismissed diplomacy as ineffective, and sanctions as useless for Russia – already under sanctions for other acts.

"The third possibility is a series of in-kind responses. They poison someone on French soil; we poison someone on theirs. They hack our generating station, we hack one of theirs. We have the good fortune to be a richer and more developed country, which, paradoxically, would make us the loser in this kind of tit-for-tat."

"Excuse me, Mr. Desseuse," Mrs. Mateau interrupted. Why would that be so?"

"An understandable question, Justice Minister. More advanced societies are more complex. That complexity makes them more efficient, but also more vulnerable. As an extreme example, a country like Mali has minimal internet. Their electrical utilities consist of entirely separate generating plants. Hence, they have no electrical grid that could be attacked by an online hack."

Mateau nodded. "Thank you, Mr. Desseuse."

"Our fourth possible response is to use the gray attacks as a *casus belli*. We rejected this because it would not have public support; and, more important, would risk uncontrolled escalation."

At this point, Baer summed up. "We have concluded that option five is the only viable response. That is to respond to gray attacks with white attacks. Those are attacks that do not appear to be foreign in origin; and more important, do not appear to be retaliations."

Foreign Minister Yvonne Sagnier asked, "In that case, Mr. Baer, how does that discourage Russia from more gray attacks?"

Desseuse answered for them both. "Mr. Baer and I are responsible for security – he regarding foreign threats, and I with domestic ones. Unfortunately, such artificial demarcations lack relevance for these new kinds of attacks. The internet, international finance, even migrant labor all make modern borders little more than abstractions."

"Still," Cassan said, "Mrs. Sagnier's question remains. If these white attacks are not obvious punishment for their gray attacks, what would be their purpose?"

"Disruption," answered Baer. "If we cannot discourage through retaliation, we can weaken and distract them to reduce their capacity for such attacks."

"We should understand," added Desseuse, "our actions will reduce their gray attacks, but not totally eliminate them."

Mrs. Matteau asked the question on everybody's mind. "Could you give us an example of a white attack?"

Desseuse nodded. "Absolutely, Justice Minister. As one example, we could sow crime and violence among the populace. The effect would be to destabilize their society."

"Or," Baer added, "generate crime among members of government – graft, for instance – then expose the malfeasance, which would reduce public respect and support for the government."

For the first time during the meeting, Cassan smiled. "Excellent! Does anyone have any objections?"

There were none.

***

A month later, the Group of Five, as they had chosen to call themselves, met again. Cassan was in a foul mood. "I've received news just this morning of another hack of a nuclear power facility. Could either the Defense Minister or Interior Minister explain how much longer we will have to wait for our white attacks to begin?"

Baer and Desseuse looked at each other. Finally, Baer spoke. "Mr. President, we thought you understood. White operations have already begun."

"Actually, some have been completed," Desseuse added.

Cassan wrinkled his brow.

"The killings at the Volgograd police station?" Baer suggested.

"That was ours?"

"Yes, Mr. President."

"My God!" Mr. Fabre said. "We're responsible for all those deaths?"

"But how…?" the Foreign Minister asked.

"We peddled increasingly addictive drugs to several of their citizens. Later we included some paranoia-inducing chemicals in the mix. Oh, and we also gave them guns and ammunition. They did the rest themselves." Desseuse's offhand manner did nothing to soothe the others.

Mrs. Mateau spoke for everyone. "But the choice of targets. They included teenagers."

"Oh, we have no control over their targets." He smiled. "The shooters choose whatever targets happen to cross their mind on whatever day they happen to flip out. We just provide the drugs and guns."

Baer was more sensitive to the other ministers' reactions. "Look. This is war. Even in conventional war there's some collateral damage. Mr. Desseuse and I both find these tasks distasteful, but also necessary."

"Could you give us a general idea of some of our other white operations?" The president asked.

"You might have read of the two mafia bosses who were assassinated," Desseuse said. "We paid some Russian ex-military to do that. Since then, we have led the mafia to believe the killings were set up by specific government ministers, who we expect will soon be assassinated. Once that happens, state security will go to war with the mafia. It should be quite bloody. In another operation, we've distributed explosives among the punk rock crowd, which, as in any country, includes a lot of disaffected young men. Some of them are bound to blow up a few buildings."

***

And so, the white attacks on Russia continued. Military officers were subverted with money, drugs, and sex. Scandals filled the news. Bombs destroyed buildings, and public places became dangerous. People went out less often. Economic activity slowed and public disaffection rose.

Of course, eventually the Russian government realized their society was the target of a sustained program of attacks.

"So who is it?" President Latinsky demanded.

Boris Flenkhov, head of the Federal Security Service readily answered. "We haven't caught any of the actual agents, Mr. President, but it's fairly easy to figure out the source."

"The Americans?"

"Of course."

"Then we will hit back. We will deliver responses in kind." He turned toward Andrei Karkhov, head of the Foreign Intelligence Service. "Can you instigate these kinds of low-level attacks in America?"

"Of course. Whatever storm they visit upon us, we can inflict on them double."

"Make it so."

"With pleasure, Mr. President."

Six months later, President Murtaugh asked, "Where's all this coming from?"

FBI director Thomas Clearman said, "We're certain it's the Chinese, Mr. President. They've been inserting their people into this country for over a decade."

"Well, two can play the same game, right Roger?"

CIA director Roger Plinker pursed his lips and looked down. "Unfortunately, no."

Murtaugh knitted his brow. "Why not?"

"We would need agents who could blend in. That would mean Asian-looking, and able to speak Chinese well. Perhaps we have one or two in the entire CIA. And China is a heavily monitored society. Sneaking drugs into their country would be difficult. Arms and explosives? Almost impossible."

"How about farming it out?" suggested Clearman. "You've done that with Arabs, haven't you?"

"Hmm. Yeah, we have some contacts in Vietnam. And the northern Vietnamese have a historical dislike of the Chinese."

"In that case, I'd like you to make it a priority."

"With pleasure Mr. President."

A year later, the Chinese Politburo met to consider their crisis.

"Mr. President, if we can't restore order and safety, the people will lose faith in our ability to govern. Moreover, some – particularly the far western provinces – will feel encouraged toward rebellion; possibly even secession."

"Yes, Minister Ling, I understand the larger implicit threats of this situation," President Tung said. "However, the more important question is, do we know who is orchestrating these outbreaks of mayhem?"

"I suspect the Americans," Kao Wei said.

Tai Ling shook his head. "The Minister of State Security has stated my original suspicion. However, on consideration, I realized that the Americans are too incompetent to carry out these widespread disruptions successfully."

Wei nodded. "The defense minister has a point. I spoke too quickly." He smiled. "In some ways, I wish it had been the Americans. We couldn't have been safer."

At this everyone in the room broke into laughter. Even the ceremonial guard had trouble suppressing a smile.

"Then who?" President Tung insisted.

Party Secretary Zhang spoke with an air of authority. "The Indians. Remember, this all began a few months after the clash at the southern border."

Everyone paused, then slowly nodded.

"The Indians think they can do this to us without cost," Wei observed.

"Minister Wei is correct," declared Tung. "We shall disabuse them of their fantasy."

Eight months later, Indian prime minister Khagan stared at his Home Secretary. "Mr. Singh, explain why the Ministry of Home Affairs seems incapable of protecting our nation."

Singh was able to deliver his reply without seeming the least bit ruffled. After all, he'd anticipated the question and practiced his script a hundred times. "Mr. Prime Minister, our staff have worked tirelessly and relentlessly to investigate and analyze the attacks of the last several months. Our conclusions are consistent and irrefutable. The attacks are coming from outside our country. The source is foreign, outside our area of authority."

"Mr. Roy?" the prime minister asked.

"It is my responsibility to defend our nation against armed attacks. I am certain the Minister of Home Affairs has noticed that no enemy soldiers have invaded our country. I am equally certain he has noticed that no missiles or artillery shells or aircraft have breached our country's defenses. The party or parties who have instigated these subversive acts within our country have in all probability entered this country through either our ports or airports. As Mr. Singh certainly recognizes, these are areas whose security fall entirely within the purview of his ministry. In addition, border security is also part of the Home Ministry, except in cases wherein a large invading military force…"

"Yes, yes, Mr. Roy," Khagan said. He gave a hard look to both of them. "We get the picture. And might I congratulate you both on your finger-pointing skills? Mr. Arundhatti, has the Foreign Ministry received any communications concerning these events?"

"We have received condolences from several nations, especially after the train derailment and the bombing of the marketplace. It has gained us much sympathy from the rest of the world."

"I should point out," Khagan replied testily, "that these disasters have also gained us uproar and dissension across the country. Every single city has seen at least one riot. The people are demanding action, not condolences."

Everyone around the table nodded in agreement.

"And what is the source of these acts of terrorism?"

"Pakistan," Singh replied.

"Pakistan," Roy said.

"Undoubtedly Pakistan," Arundhatti agreed.

Khagan nodded. "As I suspected. Minister Singh and Minister Roy, I am charging you both to work together to reply in kind to our enemy." Singh and Roy nodded silently. "Understand," Khagen continued, "no overt cross-border attacks. You will subvert their people and cause disruptions throughout their country without revealing the source of the operations. It is imperative they do not know of our actions. Otherwise, we could find ourselves in a nuclear war."

"Understood, Mr. Prime Minister," Singh replied, as everyone else nodded.

Seven months later, Pakistani Prime Minister Wasim Khan called a meeting to order. Defense Minister Abdul Borphu spoke first. "Excuse me, Mr. Prime Minister, but where are the rest of the ministers?"

"Mr. Borphu, you and I have already discussed the issue that forms the purpose of this meeting. Naturally, you understand the need to keep it as restricted as possible."

"You mean we're finally going to do something?" Borphu's tone bordered on rude, though not because he disliked Khan. They got along well. A military man from the top of his head down to his soles, Borphu's nature skirted the kind of finesse most government ministers practiced out of habit.

"Yes," Khan replied.

"Excuse me," interrupted Foreign Minister Javed Kazmi, "but apparently you two have chosen to leave me in the dark. Just what *is* the 'issue that forms the purpose of this meeting?'"

Finance Minister Tariq Fawad, a man whose unassuming personality embodied his accounting background, chimed in. "I have the same question."

Khan turned toward Kazmi and Fawad. "You both are aware of the terrible terrorist attacks we have experienced in the last half-year. Civil society is on the verge of collapse. Hundreds of deaths, including at police and military facilities have undermined the public's faith in our ability to maintain order. Mr. Borphu and I have had discussions on how to solve this existential problem."

"Do we know who is responsible, Mr. Prime Minister?" Kazmi asked.

"The defense minister and I believe we know the perpetrators."

"Believe?" asked Fawad. "Shouldn't we have the Intelligence Services Director here? Surely he could shed some light on the terrorists' identities."

Borphu chuckled. Khan merely smiled.

Fawad's face reddened. "Excuse me, Mr. Defense Minister, I fail to see what you find so amusing."

"The ISI is part of the problem," Khan explained with obvious patience. "Remember how they did not happen to notice that Bin Laden was living in the middle of the most secure area of our nation? If the Intelligence Services Director were here, he would likely leak our intentions to the enemy."

Kazmi asked, "But who is the enemy? Do we know who the terrorists are?"

"We do. They are the Taliban and their allies in the northwest. Previously they restricted most of their attacks to areas near the Afghan border, but now they are attempting to cripple the entire country."

Kazmi wrinkled his brow. "But what do you propose for a solution?"

"The defense minister and I have decided on a series of nuclear strikes."

Kazmi and Fawad gasped.

Khan said, "Unfortunately, this has become the only alternative. We've lost soldiers and policemen to their terrorist attacks. We've sent special forces into the region on several occasions, with high casualties. The area is mountainous and difficult. Moreover, during the operations, the enemy just blends in with the civilian population."

Fawad spoke quietly. "But surely this will kill innocent civilians. Including women and children. How in the name of Allah can you justify this?"

"How many innocent people died in the train explosion last week? Or the movie theater a few days earlier? As prime minister, I have an obligation to stop these killings. Otherwise, our ability to govern will disintegrate, chaos will ensue, and some provinces will break into open rebellion."

Borphu, until now uncharacteristically silent, said, "We've put up with these outlaws long enough. What? Are we to be bullied by some ragtag scumbags?"

Kazmi looked down at the table. "Given that you've already made the decision, why have you bothered conferring with us?"

"From you," Khan replied, "I need to know the probable response of foreign governments."

"They will condemn it, of course. Most severely. Likely recall ambassadors. Break off diplomatic relations."

"And probably impose economic sanctions," added Fawad. "They may unilaterally cancel trade agreements. We will lose America's aid. They will likely forbid exports to us of vital goods, particularly goods that could have military and technological uses."

Khan nodded. "In that case, your tasks, are to prepare responses to these possibilities. We'll need to blunt the effects of foreign reactions – both political and economic. Consider the aftermath and the best measures we will need to adjust to it. And keep in mind – not a word to the ISI."

"Or even your wives, Borphu said. You know how women are. They'll talk to other wives, and on and on."

Four days later, two dozen nuclear bombs were exploded in the northwest tribal areas of Pakistan, effectively rendering them devoid of human habitation.

As expected, an emergency session of the United Nations was convened two days later. Kazmi was proven partially correct, in that there were swift and strident reactions from foreign governments. However, they were not condemnations. To the contrary, the ambassadors from France, Russia, America, China and India took turns with effusive praise for Pakistan, "taking decisive steps against the perpetrators of terrorism and disorder," and "standing up to intimidation," and "taking resolute action against murder and destruction."

And Fawad's predictions were also partially correct. Foreign nations did respond economically, though not with sanctions. The American government increased its aid to Pakistan to help finance, "their half of our reawakened partnership in this ongoing war on terror." The Chinese offered to give Pakistan enough enriched uranium to replace the warheads used in the, "unfortunate, but necessary operation that has restored order to their nation and to the world."

Russian ambassador Boris Yackoff suggested his country could offer bio-weapons as a more efficient method for future operations in Pakistan's war on terror. "Your nation will find it a cheaper method, one that leaves no radiation behind." He was recalled an hour later and his replacement, Alexander Yucksei assured the world that

Yackoff had misspoken. "Russia has no bio-weapons, nor has it had any since we signed the international accord renouncing them."

Of course, Yackoff was never heard from again.

And, equally predictable, no one believed Yucksei. The following day, French president Gerard Cassan convened a meeting of the Group of Five for the purpose of devising a response to the threat of Russia's bio-weapons.

Interior Decorating

Entering the waiting room of the Life Potential Center, the first thing he noticed was a woman of about 40 years sitting in one of the padded chairs. She smiled at him with an intent gaze. "Hi, I'm Rita."

"Nice to meet you, Rita. I'm Paul. I suppose you also have an appointment with Mahasubani?"

She inclined her head. "I do."

Paul lowered himself slowly into a chair. "I'm a little early. I get off work at 4:30, and didn't see much point in going home and coming back."

"And what kind of work do you do?"

"I'm a chemical engineer at Rhombus PlastiCity."

"Sounds very technical. Do you find it interesting?"

"It is. And what do you do?"

"I'm a psychotherapist. Here's my card."

"*Gorsch Better Living Group*," he read aloud, then looked up at her. "Perhaps I should have gone to you instead of Mahasubani."

"What are your goals?"

"I want to improve my people skills. Psychotherapists help clients with that, don't they?"

"But I'm sure Mahasubani will get you there a lot faster. Anyway, if you're disappointed, you have my card."

He nodded, then pulled out his cell phone and scanned the card. "I'll keep you in mind. Always good to have a plan B."

Rita nodded. "I've been wondering. Maybe you could tell me. What is the name of the god in that picture?" She pointed to a print on the wall, disproportionately large for the 10- by 15-foot waiting room.

"Oh that...the elephant god. What *is* his name? I can't remember, but he's the god of beginnings and success."

"Let's hope he brings us both luck." She noted the rather gaudy gold-painted frame. "He's running late. My appointment was for 10 minutes ago. I'm sorry, but it appears you'll likely have a long wait."

"Won't be wasted time," he said. "Brought my tablet. Lot's to read."

Five minutes later, the inner door opened. They saw a young woman with pink hair and tattoos on both arms – '*And who knows where else?*' Rita thought – emerge from the inner room. She smiled at the two of them and proceeded briskly toward the outer door.

A few minutes later, a dark-complected man entered from the inner room. "Rita Caraco?"

She rose and walked toward the bearded stranger, whose purple turban was decorated with gold threads. The man smiled as he directed her inside. The room was about 25-feet square, hung with purple and blue curtains from ceiling to floor. The red lighting behind the curtains reflected off the ceiling sufficiently for her to see the two rows of chairs just in front of the stage. As the man directed, she sat down in the front row and waited.

After a few minutes, Swami Mahasubani entered from the back of the stage, wearing a white outfit with purple embroidered edging. At the front of his turban was a red decoration, which seemed flower-like, though the light was too dim for her to see it clearly. His long hair shaded his face, making his features difficult to discern, but it seemed to be square, well fleshed, with a mouth whose semblance of gravitas impressed her. He sat down cross-legged on a tall cushion.

"You are Rita Caraco?"

"Yes. You must be Mahasubani. I'm honored to meet you."

He half bowed his head with closed eyes. "The honor is mine." Raising his head, he looked at her in silence.

His stare made her uneasy. Was he reading her? What did he see? What should she say? Or should she wait until he spoke?

After about 30 seconds, just when she was about to break the silence, he said, "How may I help you?"

"Well, I've come for the mystical paint, of course."

"Of course. But I mean to ask, what ability are you seeking?"

"I want the power of prophecy. I'd like to be able to see the future of society and the world. I'm a psychotherapist, and I believe it would allow me to help my patients adjust better."

Mahasubani nodded. "Yes. Yes. This is possible. You have a healthy enough aura, but first, we must assess your neuro-cerebral vibrations. You have already met my disciple, Rahul Kumar. He will help you put on the monitor and instruct you."

Those words were barely out of Mahasubani's mouth when Rahul appeared through a side curtain pushing a wheeled cabinet. He positioned the cabinet behind Rita's chair, and handed her a large and complex headgear. "Allow me to assist you in putting this on." After a bit of wrestling with the gear, Rita had it firmly on her head, and was staring into the darkness of two seemingly opaque lenses.

"Just stare at the red dot in the center," Rahul said. "Hold your eye as still a possible. Don't be alarmed by the flashes. They are there to measure the brain and optical response. The analysis will take about three minutes, so kindly relax and enjoy the experience."

Rita was a bit more at ease than she would have been without the verbal preview. The flashes of straight lines and webs were unexpected, but not alarming. The test seemed to go on for at least six or seven minutes before the image went blank.

"There. You did very well." Rahul's voice was confident and soothing. He removed the apparatus from her head, and returned it to the cabinet, which he wheeled away.

Mahasubani was still seated in front of her.

"What happens now?" she asked.

"Now we will use the readings to precisely set the color of your paint to match your neuro-cerebral vibrations. I will personally add the unique compounds that will convey the power of prophecy. Finally, I will meditate on the completed mixture and speak an incantation prayer over it. Only then will the lid be place on the cans. Rahul will call you when the cans are ready."

"How long can I keep the cans before I have to paint my bedroom?"

"You can keep them a long time, but once you open them, you have to use them before the next new moon. Otherwise, their potency dissipates."

"Anything else I'll have to do?"

"No, my child – except, of course, you'll have to sleep in the painted room. And also, you must have faith in the power of the paint. Our method is successful for 94 percent of our followers."

"No problem. How long does it take before the power develops?"

"It will grow over time. Some of our followers notice their power in a few days; others require a few months. No one knows for certain. You must be patient, my dear."

"Yeah. My parents always told me that. But at $200 a gallon, I'm naturally in a hurry."

At this, Mahasubani raised one hand toward her, drew a figure eight in the air, and mumbled some indecipherable words. Then he brought his palms together at his chest, fingers pointing upward, and with eyes closed, rocked forward and back for a quarter-minute. At the end of this ritual, he said, "Thank you letting me help you, Rita."

At this point, Rahul appeared and escorted her to the door. As she passed through the waiting room, she smiled at Paul. "No need to be nervous. You'll enjoy it."

Rahul disappeared for several minutes, then opened the inner door. "Paul Harris?"

"Here." He rose and marched to the door.

"I'm Rahul, assistant to Swami Mahasubani. Be pleased to follow me."

An almost identical process occurred with Paul as for Rita.

"I am curious," Mahasubani said. "You say, 'improved people skills.' What does this mean?"

"I mean an improved ability to read people. I've become aware that people often mean more than what they say. My wife believes that my lack of understanding in this area has held me back in my career. I think she's right."

"On your application, you gave your work as a chemical engineer. How might you advance?"

"After a decade at my workplace, I should have reached at least the supervisory level. However, people with better – shall we say, political – skills have passed me by. I need to raise…no, to get in the game. I have finally realized that life is not all about physics and chemistry."

Mahasubani nodded. "Yes. Yes. You have made a very wise observation, my son. And I can see that you have a healthy enough aura. To begin, we must assess your neuro-cerebral vibrations. You have already met my disciple, Rahul Kumar. He will help with the monitor and instruct you."

Once again, Rahul performed the same steps as he had with Rita. And once again, Mahasubani fielded the same questions with the same answers, after which he performed the same blessings.

*****

A half-hour later, Karen Harris heard the front door close. "That you Paul?" As he walked into the kitchen, she said, "How did it go? Did he cast any magic spells on you?"

Paul was accustomed to her skepticism. He would have seen Mahasubani eight months earlier if it wasn't for her criticism and ridicule. He recalled her look of disbelief. "For heavens sake, Paul," she had said, "you're a scientist. What is this? A midlife crisis?" She never let go of that idea, but also the thought, *'Then again, better than some floozy fling.'* After all, despite his 45 years, he was still trim and tall. His almost full head of hair had prolonged his good looks, and the beginnings of gray at the sides made him look distinguished. He wasn't the straying type, but if he were…

And so, eventually she had agreed to let him repaint the bedroom – even offered to help him – as much from fear of him spinning out of their mutual orbit, as from simple resignation.

Two weeks after his session with Mahasubani, Paul picked up the paint, and within another couple of weeks the two of them had finished painting and putting the bed and furniture to their original places.

She appraised the final result. "Actually, it's kind of pretty." She nodded, uncertain of her own reaction. *'Unusual,'* she thought, *' but nice. Definitely not as I feared. Not gaudy.'*

Paul's reaction was more confident. "It even looks spiritual. The hue is…undefinable. Subtle. I get a good feeling from it already."

Karen looked at her husband, but said nothing.

Over the next few weeks, Paul did not notice any change. But Mahasubani had said the effect could take several months. After a month, doubts began to nibble at the edges of his faith. However, the following week, as he left a project-planning meeting, his manager asked what he thought of the proposal the group had discussed, Paul was surprised by his own answer.

"You know, Dan, I was impressed at all the ideas we were able to generate. It was a very productive meeting. More so than usual."

Daniel Yeager hesitated. He too was surprised at Paul's response. Dan had come to rely on Paul to be the one person who could spot the fly in the ointment – even when there was no fly.

Over the next few months, Paul found himself paying more attention to the emotional states of his co-workers. Of course, it also created negative effects. For instance, he noticed that some of the men in the office were spending more time talking with Cindy Warner than he had realized. She was the structural engineer, a very competent one. He watched the interchanges intently, and realized that despite her smiles, she did not like the attention. In fact, he realized she felt a certain contempt for them. *'If only they knew…'* That was when he realized Mahasubani's paint was working.

***

"Really? You want to go to the party? It's only going to be teachers and admin staff."

Paul raised a quizzical eyebrow. "So? You embarrassed to be seen with your husband?"

"But you never like parties. Even with your gang at Rhombus."

"I just think it's about time I met the rest of *your* gang. I've only met the principal and Sue Ann. It'll be good to make them all feel we're a part of their family. It might help with your promotion."

"My *hope* for a promotion," she corrected.

"You should be more optimistic. After all, you're one of a few teachers with a masters degree."

"Not actually a requirement. Janet Wooster made assistant principal at Thurgand Elementary, and she just has a bachelors."

"Like I said, Karen, be optimistic. People pick up on negative feelings." He checked in the mirror, and shifted his shirt slightly. "I'm going to leave the suit jacket behind. The black leather will look more casual."

As they began the drive to the Principal's house, she thought, *'He never cared much about sartorial issues before. Maybe that Maha-Whats-His-Face paint is for real.'*

After a while, she said, "I've been wondering. Why doesn't the Swami paint affect me? I can see the changes in your…sensitivities. But I haven't noticed any change in myself."

"Oh, he tunes the paint to the individual's brain. How did he say…the 'neuro-cerebral vibrations' of each person." Paul explained the process in detail. He had never done so before, mostly because of her skepticism.

However, this time she seemed more receptive. "The thing is, if I wanted some ability, we'd have to repaint the room. Then what would happen to your personal changes?"

He turned his toward her. "Interesting speculation. I've never thought of that." Her question gave him pause. She had come to accept the paint's effect. "What power would you want?"

"Oh, I don't know. I was just toying with the idea. It's just that…well, I'm very impressed with how much progress you've made."

The party was already underway at principal Brian Knowles house, with about a dozen people gathered in the backyard. Paul soon discovered that other than Lucy Knowles and himself, everyone was a member of the school staff. Still, they were friendly and he easily mixed with them.

"So you're the mysterious husband Karen has mentioned," Lucy said.

"Hopefully she's put me in a good light."

"Absolutely. I was hoping she'd bring you to our gathering."

"Actually, I was hoping to meet some of the staff. She's had such good things to say about them."

"Well, let me start you around the group."

As he made the rounds, he glad-handed everyone successfully. About halfway through the introductions he was passed on to a pretty woman of about 35 with a reddish-brown long bob.

"Hi. I'm Victoria Klimt."

"Nice to meet you Victoria. I'm Paul."

"Have we met before? Or are you from county admin?" Her smile was modest, but displayed teeth as perfect as her complexion.

"No, no. I'm Karen Harris' husband."

She paused. That plus her nod and tight smile rang an alarm. He intuited something – some unidentifiable shadow of expression that flashed across her face. And he saw her posture change slightly. He could feel the defensiveness. Before Mahasubani, he had never payed attention to body language, and certainly had never read anything about it, but there he was, reading it with clear fluency. The conversation instantly became a cliché, covering the thumbnail sketches of occupations and birthplaces and colleges. Paul had figured out how to jump over these barriers with other people, but none of his attempts succeeded with Victoria. She wanted to skim over the tops of the waves. And there was something else that bothered him, some inner whisper behind the party noise. It took another half hour for him to decipher it.

On the drive home, Karen said. "It was a nice party. Did you enjoy yourself?"

"Sure."

"I'm glad."

After a few minutes, he said, "Honey, I've been thinking for a couple of hours how to tell you, but there's no way to put a bow on it."

She just looked at him.

"You're not going to get the promotion."

"Why? What did you hear?"

"Not what I heard. What I saw. And what I felt."

She didn't respond, but stared at him.

"Brian's going to promote Victoria Klimt."

"Victoria Klimt? She's been in the district just three years. And she only has a bachelor's with a teaching certificate. What makes you think he'd pick her?"

He tilted his head toward her and only half-turned his head. The sideways glance answered for him.

"What? You think Brian and Victoria…you think they're involved?" And after a few seconds of dead air, "Well, say something." She realized her voice had risen in both decibels and pitch.

"I could feel something when I talked with her. And I noticed that she and Brian remained pretty much on opposite side of the crowd all evening."

She wrinkled her face. "What does that prove?"

"Everyone eventually wound their way throughout the group – except them. They were the only two who rotated opposite each other. And his eyes kept flicking in her direction."

She looked forward in silence, playing mental ping pong, between doubting her husband's assessment – the possibility his newfound sensitivities had thrown him off balance – and feeling wounded that she had lost the promotion and the $15,000 salary increase that went with it, and for all the wrong reasons, and despite her qualifications, despite…

When they got home, Paul said, "Let's have some brandy."

They never drank brandy alone. It was for guests on special occasions. She retrieved the bottle and two glasses. "Okay. We can sit in the kitchen."

"No, the living room."

They both slouched as they settled in. He, looked at his glass as he began. "I know you're even more upset than I am. But we have to take a bigger view." He turned toward her as he continued. "I don't want you to make a decision for at least a day. Will you promise me that?"

"Decision? What decision?"

"You do have options, you know."

"Like what?"

"You could keep your present position and do nothing. Is that what you want?"

She just looked at him, knowing he knew the answer.

"Or you could go try for a similar position at another school."

"I considered multiple applications, but Laztec Middle School is a close drive. And the neighborhood is better, which means the students are better behaved."

He nodded. "Then there's the third choice, the only one left."

She raised her eyebrows and lowered her head. She was not going to ask.

He smiled at her refusal to follow his script. Her independent nature was one of the qualities he had always admired. "Get Brian to offer you the position at Laztec."

"I remember you saying I wasn't going to get it."

"Yeah. I misspoke. I should have said that Brian did not intend to offer it to you. But you can change his mind." He let the words sink in as he nodded.

"Okay, I'm listening."

"His affair with Victoria is her high card, but it's also his weak point."

"You want me to threaten to expose him? That's extortion. In the end, it could weaken me more than her. And even if it got me the position, he could make my days difficult. Remember, he also controls the reviews."

"Of course," he replied. "Instead, you go to him as a friend – or even better, a counselor. Tell him you've heard rumors about him having an affair. That alone will make him nervous about giving the slot to her. You won't even have to mention Victoria's name. As a friend of many years to both him and Lucy, you want to plead with him not to destroy his marriage, not to hurt Lucy, how he's a better husband than that, yada, yada."

"Jesus! You *have* changed, Paul. This is scary."

"Scary? How?"

"I'd never imagined you could be so…so Machiavellian."

"This is nothing. You should see the kind of shit that goes on at Rhombus. As soon as I became supervisor, people who had trouble remembering my name suddenly became my good buddies. And my previous friends changed too. Some grovel, which I hate; and others, like Sam, want to toss banana peels in my path. He thought he'd get the promotion. I can see his jealousy, but he pretends he's my brother. The thing is, now I can read all these people like an eye chart a yard away."

As he said this, Karen opened her mouth, but said nothing. Finally, "I had no idea it was causing you stress. I thought your ability to read people was a wonderful gift."

"Yeah. That's what I thought it would be. It did get me the promotion, but it's not a gift. The price tag is still hanging from it. I have to keep paying for it every day."

She spoke slowly, thinking aloud. "You see into their lives too deeply."

"Exactly. Like Cindy Warner. Nice gal. Good worker. More important, good mother. When I asked how her daughter was doing, she said, 'Fine.' But it isn't fine. I wasn't sure why, but I could read the doubt and pain all over her face. Later, when Rick was talking about druggies, I caught a glimpse of her face. So now I know – her daughter's doing drugs, which explains the small signs of stress I see on her every Monday morning, when most everyone else comes back refreshed. I feel bad for her. Worse, I feel what she feels. See what I mean?"

"Yeah. Susan Malek's husband is a psychiatrist. She told me he needs periodic therapy. It seems that listening to troubled people all day can cause emotional stress. That's kind of what's happening to you." Karen took hold of his hand. "I had no idea. Let's strip off the paint this weekend."

Paul's brow wrinkled as he pursed his lips. "I thought of that. I called the Life Potential Center. They proudly state that their process produces a permanent rewiring of the mind."

"Then, what are you going to do?"

"Right now, I'm going to bed." He rose from the bed. "Be sure to remember what I said about handling Brian. I know it will work. I read him too."

The next day, on the drive to work, Paul recalled a piece of the evening's conversation – the part about Susan Malek. When he got to work, he looked up the number. "Hi, I need to see Dr. Caraco…The earliest opening you have…The 17th? Yes, that works fine for me…Paul Harris…No, I'd rather not discuss it for now. I'll explain the problem when I see her."

***

Rita recognized him instantly. "I didn't recollect the name. How have you been?"

"Well, I'm here, so obviously not too well."

"Before I begin the background survey, I'd like to know – how did Mahasubani's paint work for you?"

"That's what I'm here about." He was about to go on, but was surprised by her reaction, which he easily deciphered. "You've had a problem too?"

She looked down, and when she raised her head, the professional mask was gone, dissolved in some sort of pain he well understood. She nodded. "You received the power you asked for, and it's brought you suffering. Right?"

He leaned back in the chair. "Yeah. Pretty much, that's it There's a saying – be careful what you pray for."

"It's an old saying, and one I've been repeating over and over again to myself. What was it you asked for?"

"The ability to read people. And you?"

"The power of prophecy. What happened with you?"

He explained the stress his new-found ability was causing. "And let me guess. You've seen the future, and it isn't pretty."

"No, it isn't. It's uglier than you can imagine, but that's not the only source of pain. My family, my friends, none of them believe me. They think I'm losing it."

"Ah! A Cassandra. Didn't she go insane?"

"I've done some reading about her, lately, for obvious reasons. The answer is no, she wasn't driven insane, but was considered so. I don't worry about insanity, but the isolation this power produces is emotionally painful. My daughter thinks I'm a carping pessimist. I told her not to move to Indiana to take a new job. I didn't dare tell her the true reason. And my cousin probably thinks I'm losing it. She was the only one who I told about the Swami and my ability to see the future. I'll never do that again."

Paul tried to lighten the mood. "Did she recommend a good shrink?"

"All I can do now is wait for my daughter's job to fall apart, perhaps her career. But there's something else."

Paul waited while she fidgeted.

Her look flashed with a greater intensity. "I can see the times that are coming. They are awful. Both here and around the rest of the planet. Paul, our grandchildren will live to see a horrible world."

He furrowed his brow. "Is it any worse than our grandparents' world? I mean, they survived the Great Depression and the Second World War, plus the cold war, which threatened a nuclear holocaust. Matter of fact, they saw the Holocaust, for heaven's sake. What's worse than that?"

"Perhaps you're right. But they didn't see it every single day. I do. And they had hope. They knew that if they could get through this or that struggle, life would return to the better times. That's not going to happen. I see it every day, no matter where I am or where I look. I can see the scene a hundred years on. It's causing constant stress, and it's wearing me down."

He could clearly see her suffering, but he felt helpless. "I'm curious. Why prophecy?"

"Two reasons. I'm a news junkie. I thought, 'Why not just skip all the news and the yakkity-yak?' And then there was the chance to help my patients. If I could see their future, I could guide them toward a better pathway. But I've found my patients resist advice when I can't give them a full explanation of the reasons. Of course, if I did, they'd think I was a whack job."

"I suppose you called to try to erase the ability?"

"Yep," she said in a snappy manner. "I'd guess you did too. But it seems that once you've bitten the apple, you get kicked out of Eden for good."

"I'm thinking you need someone to talk to, someone to confide in."

She chuckled. "I'd lose my board certification. Any shrink would be duty-bound to report me as delusional, and therefore unfit."

"What about a priest? Their conversations are protected."

She looked at him for several seconds. "You're serious? Any man of the cloth is going to assume I'm possessed by the devil. Catholic, Protestant – all of them. I'd be lucky if they regarded me as merely delusional."

He nodded, and they remained silent for several seconds. He quickly raised his head. "What about Mahasubani?"

At first, she appeared confused, but then her face brightened. She smiled and said, "Why didn't I think of that? He's definitely not going to report me. Yes. Why don't we both go? We're both troubled. Maybe he could offer us a path toward solace."

"If you don't mind, why don't you call him right now for an appointment? My schedule's more flexible."

Rita went to her computer, pulled up her schedule, and called the Life Potential Center. As she arranged the meeting, Paul noted she had shifted gears. She was more animated, and an expression of cheer suffused her expression. She again had hope, and so did he.

A week later, Paul took time off work to meet Rita at the center. He hadn't told Karen about the meeting. *'What if the Swami can't help? Besides, she has her own problems. Not a good time to add distractions.'*

Mahasubani was already seated on his cushion when Rahul led them into the inner room.

"On the phone, you told Rahul you needed counsel. Please to tell me what kind of help you require."

Rita spoke for both of them. "We would like to get rid of our powers. Both of us have phoned this center, and we were told that it's not possible. Perhaps you have some method of reducing it?"

Mahasubani swayed forward and back for several seconds before replying. "I see. I'm afraid not. For you see, the brain has become rewired, and in these procedures, the soul wraps around the new wiring, becoming thoroughly enmeshed with it."

She persisted. "Then can you at least tell us how to live with these powers? How to adjust to them? They are making day-to-day living difficult."

"I can give you only one piece of advice. It's simple, yet very hard. You need to live with it by ignoring it as much as possible. And I very strongly suggest you both immediately begin a course in meditiation. You must commit to it thoroughly if you are to gain a measure of peace."

"Can you recommend someone?" Paul asked.

"Yes. Rahul will give you contact information with one of the best teachers in the area. I cannot praise him to excess."

"Thank you Swami, for your time," Paul said.

"Yes. Many thanks," agreed Rita.

Mahasubani brought his palms together at his chest, and bowed his head. "I'm honored to be able to serve you."

Several minutes later Raul Suarez, alias Rahul Kumar entered the room backstage. His father, Jorge, alias Mahasubani was removing his wig. "Let's get lunch."

"Okay." Raul removed his beard. "We have one more for this afternoon."

"Yeah. Some days are slower than normal. KFC sound good to you?"

"I actually feel like a burger."

"Okay, Nancy's Burgers it is."

Twenty minutes later, as he dipped the end of a french fry in ketchup, Raul said, "Do you think she can actually see the future?"

"I doubt it. Usually, it's all just a matter of suggestion. Like with the Harris fellow. He always had the ability to read people. I'm sure of it. He just never paid attention. We just bring out of people what was always there. But that Rita...I think she's a head case."

"But what if she's not? Remember Aunt Cecilia? Man, she had a few dreams that foretold things."

"Maybe so, but then, why can't she see the scam? Or that the meditation teacher is your uncle Cesar?"

Raul nodded as he drew a noisy sip through the straw. "Yeah. Didn't think of that."

At that moment, across town, Rita and Paul were enjoying a Thai cuisine lunch, when she suddenly looked up and said, "Oh my God!"

Message To The Reader:

If you enjoyed this collection, let others know. Share your opinion by reviewing this book on Amazon, Kobo, and Google Play Books.

Thanks for reading,

Fred Melden